ABOUT THE AUTHOR

Stephen Timmins has spent a significant portion of his adult life working in television, although his wife, Elaine, maintains that "working" is too strong a word and he, himself, declines to call it a career. Born and brought up in Surrey he now lives in a village near Bristol. He has been a fan of John Buchan's Richard Hannay stories since childhood and often wondered what would have happened to Hannay's descendants. This book and its two sequels tell their story.

Published in Great Britain in 2021
By Diamond Crime

ISBN 978-1-8384026-4-8

Diamond Crime is an imprint of Diamond Books Ltd.

Thanks to Roger and Jeff and Phil and Paul.

Book cover design:
jacksonbone.co.uk

To Elaine

THE FORTIETH STEP

VOLUME ONE

LEGACY

STEPHEN TIMMINS

CHAPTER ONE

The Mark VI .455 revolver made in 1916 by Webley and Scott is a heavy gun. You have to pull back the trigger – cocking, it's called – to fire the first bullet. If you're using it indoors it helps to wear earplugs as there's an eardrum–shattering crack when the trigger is squeezed. I had forgotten about the ear plugs. I had forgotten about the recoil…

The recoil that had knocked my arm up high enough for my second shot to miss the silhouette in the doorway altogether. The silhouette now with a jagged, one inch hole just below the hair line on the right side of his neck. The silhouette, now executing a slow–motion, unsteady, inebriated dance. The silhouette, now with a sluggish, bright red torrent pulsing from his carotid artery. The silhouette, whose empty, dying eyes held only half–frozen irritation, a pistol half–gripped in his half–raised hand, still coughing out slow bullets into the Persian rug. His legs buckled – finally. I was over him – through the door before the second man had even begun to react. I grappled with the third, tearing at his coat, then I was past him too.

Only then did the adrenalin rush drain away and the world speed back up and I was left with just the breathless ache in the base of my spine from the fight–or–flight chemical that had pumped through my nervous

system. And at that point reality bit. I had killed a man. I was a murderer. So I did what any sensible murderer should do. I ran.

* * *

And yet... this had been a day that had started normally enough – by my standards that is: twisting and turning in the bed sheets, dripping sweat, panting, puling and, finally, curled up, shaking on the floor in the corner of the bedroom. Just that early morning horror of the worst of my nightmares. The one about the awful pain; the one about the day of my eighth birthday just before the end of the school term, although no one had sent me a present or even phoned; a privileged childhood you understand, sent away to boarding school from the age of seven.

Over my childhood years I had stored up enough material for quite a collection of these nightmares, most of which dated from the time of the awful pain – oh, and a limp too, a limp I'd tried to disguise to this day – the day when I thought they had come to kill me – twenty–seven years, five months and fourteen days later.

* * *

The house phone had rung once. I'd watched it. I'd watched it because I'd assumed a phone call this early was just going to be one more threat from my habitual threatening caller. But it wasn't. The phone had bleeped. It rang again. It bleeped then bleeped again. It rang once.

2

Now I know Morse code. My father had thought my learning it might be useful for some reason. He would play a game with me at breakfast, tapping out Morse requests to pass the toast or the tea – even the marmalade (that one didn't really work though – I was too slow). I'd loved that game. It was one of the few things I can remember doing with my father before he was killed.

I had grabbed the house phone, dialled 1471 and listened. A mobile phone had made that call. I entered its number into my own mobile and walked to the window tapping out the Morse code message with my thumbnail against my bottom teeth.

G E T O U T. Why?

Then the house phone had rung once more and, once more, I had watched it. Three, four, five rings: back to normal. I'd waited for my voicemail message to end and listened to the now familiar, soft voice with a hint of the brogue. I had sighed.

"Ah, your outmoded answer machine is back on again. Do you still think I am just a crank caller, John? Is that it? Is that why you stopped speaking to me?"

It was true. I had spoken to him once – at the beginning. And I had thought then that he was a crank caller. Mind you that was before he had revealed how much he knew about me, how much he knew about my family and my family's friends and it was before he had mentioned what he called 'the information'. I'd been puzzled at first, then angry, and now? Well, what do you think?

Get Out.

"Have I not told you that ignoring me just makes things worse for you, John? Have I not told you what I will do to all your family friends if you do not co–operate?"

Get Out.

"It has been a long time, John – far *too* long in fact. For many years I had no need of the information, but now I do."

I heard him draw in a breath, and for reasons which only now have I begun to understand… I stayed.

"Very well. We're coming to see you. It is time for an ending."

An ending so soon and I've only just begun.

* * *

Such is the contrariness of my black, depressive nature that the thought of probable and immediate death cheered me no end. I remember I walked through into the drawing room with the suspicion of a spring in my step and opened my grandfather's safe behind the Rex Whistler portrait of the great man himself. I pocketed my passport and the small bag of personal papers. The surprisingly large sum of cash I had withdrawn over the last six months went into my pouch and then I stared at the final object in the safe – my grandfather's Webley revolver. Eventually I picked it up, broke open the head and slotted the cartridges into the holes. I hauled an armchair in front of the window and closed the heavy wooden shutters, allowing just the narrowest shaft of light to hit the back of the chair.

4

And then I waited, crouched in the darkness, for a man I didn't think I knew, who wanted some information I didn't know I had, clutching a World War One gun I had never tried to use.

Seconds passed.

I heard a click, which I guessed to be the front door, a creak that was probably the boards in the corridor and then silence and I blinked and missed the drawing room door opening and the figure that had ghosted in and tripped over the edge of the Persian rug by the hearth. He spoke from the floor through what sounded like gritted teeth. "Turn a bloody light on, will you!"

The voice was that of an irritated, upper class Englishman. He didn't sound quite so frighteningly professional as I had expected, but still I stayed where I was, crouched on the floor at the far end of the sofa in the dark. The figure clambered to his feet, muttering. Finally, he found the windows, pushed the shutters right back into the walls and turned to look for me. I raised the revolver and cocked the hammer. He jumped, shied back for an instant, looked at me more closely, cleared his throat and spoke.

"Um, could you put that down… Aah, carefully, please."

It was most definitely not the voice of my crank caller. The man scrutinised me. I returned the compliment. He was tall, wide shouldered, very handsome in an haut monde kind of way, with that hint of a sneer permanently visible – you know the look. You know the type too – cut back shirt collar, old school tie (Rugby, I believed), Anderson and Sheppard suit, glossy, 'dirty' blonde hair, expensively cut, brushed back, (gelled probably) and a little too long – a cad I imagine my grandfather would have said. I asked the obvious question. "Was it you who sent me the Morse code message?"

"Well, not me as such, but…"

We both heard the front door latch click at the same time. Something that looked distinctly like panic came into his eyes for a second then he grabbed me clumsily by the shoulder and pushed me hard behind the sofa and hurried towards the door, calling out as he walked. "That you, John? Where have you been? Your front door was open so I…"

His voice tailed off. He teetered on the balls of his feet as he saw who was there. I peered round the edge of the sofa, but could see only silhouettes in the doorway beyond him.

"Hang on, you're not John! Have I made a giant cock of it all again? This is John Hannay's flat, isn't it? I haven't gone and gatecrashed the wrong bloody place, have I?

A soft voice – *the* soft voice with that hint of the brogue – answered him.

"I too am a friend of Sir John's. He's expecting me."

"Well, thank God for that. He's probably gone out to get some milk. For tea, you know. His door was open. Always was the most disorganised bugger when it came to milk. I'll see if he left the kettle on."

"Wait."

"Wait for what, old boy? Hang on, that sounds like someone outside. Must be him coming back. John? John? Is that you?"

He disappeared into the hall. I crouched behind the sofa once again as I heard him walking towards the front door, the walking turn to running and he then he was out and sprinting for the stairs. My supposed rescuer had abandoned his supposed rescuee. The soft voice spoke again. "Don't bother with him. Look for the target. He may still be here."

So, there were two of them at least, and I was a target – *the* target. One of the silhouettes appeared in the doorway, pistol raised in front of him, I didn't think any more…

* * *

The Mark VI .455 revolver made in 1916 by Webley and Scott is a heavy gun. You have to pull back the trigger – cocking, it's called – to fire the first bullet. If you're using it indoors it helps to wear earplugs as there's an eardrum–shattering crack when the trigger is squeezed. I had forgotten about the ear plugs. I had forgotten about the recoil…

CHAPTER TWO

I sprinted away from Piccadilly, across Shepherd Street, into Curzon Street, up Queen Street – three hundred yards now and my lungs were burning – right into Charles Street where there are always taxis outside the Chesterfield Hotel – my thigh muscles were cramping. I'd had it. There were two taxis. I staggered into the front one.

"Where to, guv?"

I panted, found my voice and let the words tumble out. "Paddington station. Can you make it in fifteen minutes? I've got to catch the Swansea train."

"Fifteen minutes? Well, I wouldn't want to say that it's never been done, but what with the traffic being snarled up back round Victoria all the way up to Marble Arch…"

There are three basic types of cab driver: morose, chatty, and offensively garrulous. You may guess into which category this one fell, but for once it was OK by me. I swallowed bile, nodded at him in the mirror and said yes at the appropriate times. He dropped me on Praed Street and I ran down the ramp into Paddington station to make it look as though I really did need to catch a train, paused, turned left, strolled up past the statue of Paddington Bear and out at the top of Platform One.

It took me an aimless half hour to wander across Hyde Park on that pleasantly warm May morning, but by time I'd reached the bridge over the Serpentine I found I could walk no further. The shock had hit. I sank to my knees, shivering. I was going to be sick. Just so long as I didn't throw up on the ducks swimming towards me. They were probably royal ducks and murder was more than enough crime against me for one day – for one life. I swallowed bile and carried on shivering.

My grandfather, Sir Richard Hannay, the First World War hero, may have been good at this. I wasn't. I was just a City trader turned restaurateur, turned nothing at all. I was neither a man of action nor a killer. Except I was – a killer, I mean. I closed my eyes and there was that silhouette again and that obscene, leaking red hole in his head – a new, adult addition to my childhood collection of nightmares. I opened my eyes, pushing back the nausea for a third time. A Parks Police car slowed on the road above where I knelt. I lifted my phone to my ear and pretended to talk in to it, laughing as I did. The car drove on. I paused, looked up across the water towards the Princess Diana memorial and started to do something I should have done an hour ago. I thought. It wasn't coherent or logical, but it was thought.

The man who had just failed to make an ending of me knew of my childhood guardians, of my father and my grandfather. If he knew that much, who else would he know – my grandfather's friends? Even if he did, who were they? And could they, would they, help?

Lord James Artinswell! Now there was a name I knew. Why? I also knew his family name was Bullivant. Why did I know that too? I didn't know him. I didn't know any member of his family. I had never met the man. I struggled on with the incoherent, illogical thinking. Someone at some early stage of my childhood must have told me that my grandfather had been a close friend of his grandfather. That must be it and I'd even checked his address once and I still didn't know why, but I was pretty sure my surname would get me in the Artinswell/Bullivant front door. I got to my feet and forced myself to stroll slowly to the tube station in Knightsbridge.

Queen Anne's Gate was quiet. I tried to summon up the courage to cross the road and take the short walk to the Artinswell front door, but in my paranoid head every van held a watcher, every loiterer a gun, every bike an aggressor. An elderly cab turned the corner. I stepped forward, hailed it, opened the door and before I could turn to take my seat, the 'rescuer' who had run away from my flat was climbing in behind me and pulling the door shut. He sat down on the jump seat and got out his mobile, watching me all the time. The cabbie glanced over his shoulder. "If we're all in, Guv, where to?"

He turned on the seat. "The In and Out, driver."

As we turned up into St James Street his phone rang. He looked at the caller ID and answered it. He looked at me. I was being discussed. "Yes. Yes. Thirty minutes."

He rang off and spoke into the mic. "Driver, change of plan. Lothbury."

Then I remembered. I shrugged out of my suit jacket and peered at the shoulder. There was something like a heavy pin stuck in the seam. I looked at him. "You grabbed me by the shoulder in the flat, didn't you?"

He gave me a slow handclap of applause. I turned the pin in my fingers. "Transmitter?"

"Something like that, Johnny, boy – something like that."

I flicked it out of the half open window before he could stop me and went to put the jacket on again, noticing a heavy weight in my left coat pocket. I put my hand in to move whatever it was. It was the revolver. He smiled at me mockingly.

"They ruin the cut of a suit you know. My tailor thoroughly disapproves of keys in a jacket pocket let alone a mobile phone, so God alone knows what he would say about one of those."

He was enjoying himself.

"Why did you run away?"

That amused him even more. "Because, my dear Johnny, I didn't want to get hurt. Bloody silly question, unless you're a masochist. You're not, are you?"

I ignored the question. "Why are we going to the City?"

"Because it's not the West End."

I felt the nausea rising for a fourth time and sat forwards with my head hanging down. He pressed the button to lower the window and pushed me towards the fresh air. I looked at him as the nausea receded once more. Another question seemed to be in order. "What do you know about me?"

"You? Nada, Johnny boy. You keep the lowest profile – digital or otherwise – of anyone I've ever come across. No friends of yours that I could track down; no one who could say: 'my best chum, John Hannay, yes I know what's he's been up to'."

No 'best chum'. He was right about that! I'd succeeded in being off everyone's radar for the last two years – everyone's, that is, except the voice on the phone – wherever I had hidden that voice had found me. Eventually the taxi slowed to a stop beside the Bank of England. My new (possibly) friend paid and led the way, nodding at the doorman at the discreet entrance of the Threadneedles Hotel. We went through into the converted banking hall, leaving me to gaze at the domed glass atrium while he whispered what I presumed to be sweet nothings into the ear of the receptionist. She didn't object.

I walked to the back of the circular hall and seated myself in a leather armchair near to the toilets and the staff exit – I could always hide in one or escape through the other. A young woman walked towards me and sat down. I waited for a cue. She was young–ish, thin – no, slender – pale, hair so blonde as to be almost white, wide set eyes which slanted upwards at their edges and high, wide–set cheekbones. My companion from the cab seated himself beside her and effected introductions. "Anna Haraldsen, Johnny Hannay – Johnny Hannay, Anna Haraldsen."

Anna Haraldsen nodded at him. "Thank you, Harry."

So now he had a name. Anna Haraldsen turned to me. "Years ago, my family swore to help your grandfather's descendants and… look, John, you won't be able to hide out here in this hotel."

"Why?"

"Why which?"

"Why did your family swear to help me? And what do you know about my family – or me for that matter?"

I raised my hands at her in an interrogative manner. "As a for instance, how old am I?"

She shrugged. "You're 36, Sir John Richard Hannay. You were born at Fosse Manor in Oxfordshire; your grandfather was General Sir Richard Hannay, made KCB after the First War and then created the first Baronet Hannay of Sherborne in 1940 for unspecified services to His Majesty. You came into the baronetcy at the age of seven following the unexplained death of your father, Sir Peter John Hannay. Your mother died a year later, possibly by suicide due to a broken heart, but more probably of something else. Shall I go on?"

I hoped she wouldn't. Harry applauded.

She turned her head to look at him, the curtain of white blonde hair swinging in front of her eyes. I realised that she was looking at him with affection. That didn't surprise me. He was irritatingly pretty. She turned back. "Harry," she informed me, "is full of shit."

"Can't argue with that," said Harry.

I stared at her. "You're Swedish?"

Harry applauded again. "Don't mean to say she's not extremely posh though. Owns half of Norrland, does our Anna."

She ignored him and watched me for a moment. "We need to leave here now. Harry?" She nodded in my direction.

Harry steered me towards the lifts. From the top floor we descended two floors on a service staircase. He paused front of a fire exit, pressed the bar down and sighed with relief when there was silence. "Wasn't sure if La Haraldsen really had sorted the door. Clever lady, mind."

We went down the fire escape, past over–full rubbish bins, into a narrow yard full of kitchen waste where a pair of East European kitchen workers were sharing a cigarette. One of them passed a comment in Russian. "будьте грубы" said Harry. They stared at him sullenly. Harry answered my unasked question.

"Told em not to be rude. Know lots of languages. Learn 'em easily. Gift of God, really."

I played along. "Do you believe in God, Harry?"

"Ah, my name – a breakthrough. As a reward, I shall stop calling you Johnny. No. Matter of fact I don't. Not through any deep thought, you understand, just that when you come from a family like mine and then you see the kind of things a soldier sees, you don't tend to see the point in God. And since we're now chatting so happily to each other, John, old boy, what about you?

"No."

"Just no? Funny, I saw you as a true Tory type – spinsters cycling to village churches, bells tolling, harvest home." He paused. "Did you know that an oriental gentleman has been following us for the last hundred yards? Do not look round. It's considered terribly bad form to do so when being followed."

I walked on rigid necked. "Do you want to give me the address of where you are supposed to be taking me, Harry, as I assume you will follow your previous practice of running at the first opportunity?"

Harry turned, his face attempting to reveal hurt and reproach. His eyes flickered past me for a second and back. "Yes, definitely following us. This way! Briskly now, Sir John, briskly."

He yanked me by the arm and ran me down the nearest alley – Post Office Court. I panted out a sentence. "Tell me where we're going!"

"Cannon Street."

I pointed towards Abchurch Yard: strange to think that these tiny, cigarette–strewn alleys were once City thoroughfares. We sprinted down the narrow paths until Harry held up his hand and we paused, leaning against the wall ignoring the curious looks and waving away the cigarette smoke. He walked back to the corner, resting his weight on his hands on the top of his knees, his breathing slowing – he was in better shape than me. I raised my hand. "Why would a Chinese – or Japanese? – man be following us, Harry?"

He shrugged. "Not us, dear boy, you. And I have no idea. He was Chinese, by the way."

He held me back, glanced left and right, led me across the road between two of Mayor Johnson's disastrous double decker red buses and into a small tower block next to Cannon Street Station. We emerged from the lift on the fifth floor and walked through into a reception area beside a trading floor. I glanced at it with little interest. I had worked on floors three times this size. This one looked like a retail outfit. Thirty or so boys in cheap suits, flashy gold watches and tasteless socks would be pressurising little old ladies into putting their money into worthless stocks which they would then go short on for a while before abandoning – a Boiler Room in all but name. Harry half dragged me across the floor to make an introduction.

"Keith, this is Alex Bruce from Australia. Trader with BTD in Sydney – looking for a week or two's work to pick up some cash before heading off to Argentina – Alex meet Keith Morgan, senior trader with Continental Atlantic."

Keith held out a hand. Clearly a response was required from me. "G'day, mate."

Harry glared at me over Keith's shoulder.

"Alright, Alex. Harry's told me about you. I won't stick you on the floor with these cowboys." He indicated the multi–coloured socks brigade on the trading floor. "But as Harry here knows, I've just bought a list of Aussie clients who'd definitely like to hear a familiar voice. Could be decent dosh. Normal terms – two per cent bonus. I'll get Robbi to give you a contract. Office over there – OK?"

He pointed at a glass walled box by the window.

"Fine, thanks."

He peered round the office, scratched his head then yelled. "Robbi? Robbi? Robbi!"

A young woman wearing a white cotton blouse and a short black, pleated skirt appeared from behind a desk divider pushing yellow strands of hair back behind one neat little ear. The other ear was pressed to a phone. She mouthed 'shhhhh' at Keith, finished her conversation with a musical laugh and looked straight at me with a cool, assessing gaze. She was… unexpected I suppose; quite astonishingly beautiful – a twenty first century, golden Nefertiti. And there was something else – another quality – something… innocence: that was it – the quality of innocence. What an interesting juxtaposition. I gazed back at her, my murderous morning for the moment quite forgotten.

"Robbi, meet Alex. Do us a favour, please, Robbi. If you could just spare a minute to set Alex up with a phone and an email address, I'll get the files on the punters. Harry says you know the score, Alex."

I nodded. Harry was also smiling at her, well not so much smiling as leering. She looked directly at me once more before smiling back at him. I walked into the glass box of an office. Harry followed me in and shut the door. "John, can I emphasise that you need to blend in here for a few days and become invisible."

"Streuth, mate."

"Oh for f...! Unless I am much mistaken, you killed a man earlier. You may not have noticed, but we came to your help."

I shrugged. "And I live where?"

"Here."

I looked round. The glass walled room contained a desk, an office chair (with arms), an office chair (without arms), a four–drawer filing cabinet, and a coat stand.

"Here?"

"Here. You just look as though you're first in and last out. You've got the perfect excuse if you're calling Australia: time zone difference. There's a shower through there."

He indicated a door behind the back office.

"Gee, thanks, mate."

"John, you do realise you're in serious trouble, don't you?"

I stared at him in amazement. Did he really think I was that stupid? "It had crossed my mind, yes. Especially as the police will have my complete description as soon as someone finds the body."

"I doubt that will happen."

I raised an eyebrow.

"Let's just say your intruders have, er… things to hide. Now, I'll bring in a mobile phone tomorrow."

He glanced sideways and raised his voice. "So you could do well here…"

Keith re–entered with some files. "Here you go, Alex. Harry, can I have a word?"

I nodded at him. They left. I sat down and shivered – that jagged red hole above his hairline. I shivered until the young woman whom Keith had called Robbi entered. Immediately the world looked brighter.

"You all right, Alex?"

The image of the dying gunman faded. "Yeah, it's just I'm not good with the jet lag, Robbi. Robbi – is that short for Roberta?"

"That's right. Your friend's rather gorgeous, isn't he?"

Why did I have to have met someone as interesting as her in the company of such a handsome bastard *and* on the very day I had committed my first – and last, I hoped – murder? "Not my type, Roberta."

She smiled mischievously and I studied her openly: beauty, innocence and mischief. Fascinating. I blundered on. "Your mum and dad liked late sixties soul music by any chance?"

The mischievous smile broadened. "Ah, the name. Yes."

"The First Time Ever I saw Your Face – Roberta Flack?"

"Clever boy."

She clapped her hands patronisingly then took pity on me. "My dad was there when I was born and they hadn't thought of a name and he saw me popping out into the world, so…"

The phone rang. She picked it up. "Hallo, Alex Bruce's phone. Yep. Yep. Works fine. Thanks Louise."

She put the phone down – and to me. "It's Robbi, not Roberta."

"Robbi," I said aloud, half to myself.

She swayed out leaving me looking at two perfect, long legs beneath the short, black, pleated skirt: a sexual thought – committing murder must be stimulating. I picked up a file and swivelled round to look out over the roofs towards the River Thames. Nothing much to see. Roofs are roofs.

CHAPTER THREE

By four thirty I felt I was as close to being Alex Bruce as I could desire. If you had offered me roast venison 'Pierre Koffmann', chou à la crème, accompanied by an '81 Lafitte I swear I would have rejected it in favour of a tinnie of the amber nectar and a barbie – well perhaps just the barbie. At five thirty Robbi peeped round the door.

"Meeting your friend later, Alex?"

"Me, nah, got to get on top of this crap, Roberta. In any case I don't think Harry's the right kind of bloke to get to know."

"What do you mean?"

Why had I started this conversation? I was not – never had been – a conversationalist. I tried again. "I don't think he's good to women. You know. And... um well er, he's a bit of a bad 'un."

"Aaaah. You're worried about me. How sweet." And she smiled that mischievous smile, swung on her heel and left. I put the desk light on and thought about beauty and how little it had always had to do with me.

"Penny for 'em, Alex?"

"Oh hi, Keith, mate. Nah, nothing of any importance, except how does anyone get any work done when Roberta walks past?"

Keith laughed. "Robbi? Yeah, she's a star. Not just drop dead gorgeous, but good at her job and sweet."

"Sweet?"

"Yeah."

He laughed again and I found myself smiling too.

"We took her on 'cos her brother asked us to. He runs the document shredding company we use. She's worth her weight in platinum. Started as a trainee and now she's the general manager – runs the whole shebang. She could do my job – don't tell her that for God's sake. Clients love her 'cos she remembers all their voices on the phone. She's super-efficient. Everyone fancies her, but her brother is ex SAS and built like two and a half brick shit houses so no one tries it on. Coming for a swift one?"

"Nah, thanks mate. I had a purple patch up until about five, but not had any luck since then. It's a bit of a superstition with me not to leave the office until I break a bad run. 'Sides which I got to call some contacts back in Oz."

He looked at me quizzically. "How much business you done today, then?"

"Er, ninety, a hundred, a hundred and twenty-four k. That all right?"

His draw dropped. "All right? You Aussie genius. If you can keep that up tomorrow, we'll have hit our monthly target by the tenth."

"No worries."

"Genius."

I won't bore you with the sordid details of my days and nights at Continental Atlantic: well, maybe just a bit. How I realised too late that I had no food for the first evening; how I found a packet of old biscuits in the little canteen;

how I slept on the floor wrapped in two coats left by other staff members; how I played out a Feydeau farce with the unwitting cleaners, creeping from room to room in front of them as they gossiped in Bengali; how I got a reputation for greed by ordering double bacon butties off the breakfast run as well as sandwiches from the lunch delivery; how Robbi had concluded that I was a social inadequate who needed to be mocked at regular intervals.

It was early on the fourth day. Robbi came in with one of the cups she claimed was coffee. She hesitated, tidied the edge of my desk, adjusted the coat rack…

"Robbi, what?"

She sniffed. "Your friend Harry. You were right."

"Aah. What did he do?"

The sniff turned into a snivel. "I feel such a prat. I always walk into these situations." The tears had filled her eyes now. "He called me just as I was leaving last night. Said, did I want to go over to his place? And before I could even begin to think of an excuse he said, by the way who was the brunette on reception and why didn't I get her to come over as well and we could have a nice little threesome? The shit."

I agreed and passed her a handkerchief. The phone rang. I picked it up. It was Louise, the receptionist and potential third member of the proposed threesome.

"Call for Robbi, Alex."

I was still staring at her as she sniffed into my handkerchief. I took the call to give her time to blow her nose.

"Good morning. Continental Atlantic, Alex Bruce speaking. How may I help you?"

"Is Sir John Hannay there, please?"

I froze. That voice, that soft, persuasive voice with the Irish inflection: I found myself wanting to tell him it was me, to tell him I would meet him, that I would... At that moment Robbi blew her nose. The spell was broken.

"I don't know any one of that name here, sir, but I shall ask the general manager. If you are calling about a stock, I would be very happy to help you."

"No. Thank you. Let me speak to the general manager."

"Certainly, sir. One moment."

I pressed the mute button. "Robbi."

She stopped sniffing and looked at me. "This call sounds odd. Like a copper or your FCA or something – asked for a Sir John someone or other. Is he the chairman?"

She shook her head. "No, the chairman lives in Switzerland. Tax exile."

She reached for the phone. I held my hand up warningly. "Robbi, be careful."

She nodded.

"Good morning, sir, Roberta Lord speaking. How may I help you? Sir John who, sir? No, sir, there's no one of that name here. I don't think I understand, sir. Why wouldn't he be using his own name? Sorry, he looks like what, sir?"

Robbi went still. Her eyes widened. She stared at me, looking slowly from my hair down to where the desk hid my lower body. I groaned inwardly.

"No, sir. I can't say there's anyone like that here. The traders are all younger than that. I don't think I quite understand why you are asking these questions, sir. May I put you through to the senior trader? Hello? Hello?"

She put the phone down. "That man described you, Alex."

"Robbi, it's complicated."

The phone rang again. I saw it was a client. "Can I speak to you at lunch time?"

She hesitated then nodded. I picked up the phone.

* * *

I struggled on with my phone calls until a sandwich landed on my desk. Robbi stood there watching me warily.

"You forgot the sandwich run."

She sat down and bit into an eight–inch long tuna baguette. How she kept her perfect figure I don't know. "Talk to me, Alex or Sir John or whoever you really are."

I cleared my throat. How to explain? How to sound? My Etonian drawl might scare her off for good and anyway who on earth would want to help a fully paid up member of the one–per–cent?

"Robbi." I sighed. "Look, I owe someone a deal of money."

"How much?"

"About four hundred k including interest."

She wasn't fazed by the amount. Everyone in the City is used to hearing talk of millions. "Who is the someone?"

"You don't want to know."

She did want to know. "That man on the phone. Was he one of them?"

24

"He's their enforcer."

You could see the thoughts ticking round beneath the golden hair. "Who is Sir John Hannay?"

"He's no one. I made him up."

She chewed some more and studied me. I realised she was trying to work out if I was yet another Harry.

"I looked him up in Who's Who. He's real. The point is… who are you?"

"Robbi, if I tell you anything more, you'll be at risk – and I mean really at risk."

She chewed her baguette and stared at me. God, why did I have to explain anything to anybody? I know you're beautiful and intelligent and fun, but seriously, just leave me alone. I tried blatant flattery. She kept chewing her baguette and staring at me. It was an unnerving stare. I put my head in my hands, which helped until I looked up and she was still chewing and staring. I looked down once more and as a desperate last measure tried thinking again – and the penny dropped. They had traced me through Harry. Harry had called Robbi for a date and they must be monitoring Harry's calls. The last sighting of me had been in the City, but they didn't necessarily know I was here. I smiled.

"What's to smile about?"

I repeated my thought process. She stared at me some more. "That still doesn't explain who you are. Anyway, where are you staying?"

"Here."

"What?"

I unlocked the bottom drawer of my desk revealing my used socks, shirts and boxers. I shrugged.

"So that's why you never come out for a drink. You couldn't get back in. And there was I thinking it was because you must be gay."

I think I may have blushed.

She carried on regardless. "But how are you going to get out of here? They may have the place watched."

"They most certainly will. This must be one of their very few links to me. Wait a minute. Keith said your brother ran the document shredding company that services this place. When are they next due?"

"Why were you talking to Keith about my brother?"

"I er, because I was, um, thinking about security."

She smiled the mischievous smile, back in charge of the conversation once more – where she liked to be. "You were asking him about me, weren't you?"

Bloody woman – time to go on the offensive. "As you have long since stopped snivelling and appear to have taken up grinning like a Cheshire cat, I would be grateful for the return of my handkerchief."

"Sounded very English then, Alex forward–slash Sir John. I don't think Aussies say handkerchiefs. I think they call them snot rags. So what about my brother?"

"When's his company next due in?"

She was still watching me dubiously, still assessing me in some strange female manner that I couldn't begin to fathom.

"Tomorrow night. Why?"

"Well, if they were to bring in a spare set of overalls, I should be able to smuggle myself out in their van if that's what they use."

26

She looked at me, considering her response. "OK. I'll speak to him. But Alex, I wouldn't mess my brother around. He's a bit of a hard case."

So far as I could see that was the least of my current problems. I held out my hand.

"What?"

"Snot rag."

She shook her head and left. I kept my back to the trading floor and hit the phones again thanking God I have the gift of concentration. Eventually I looked up. The floor was empty and I was alone. Normally I preferred to be alone – I had been alone for pretty much the last twenty–eight years of my life, but not here, not tonight. The blackness stooped over me and when at last I slept I had my usual nightmare and the one about the child psychiatrist who hit me when I wouldn't speak and touched me when we were alone. It wasn't one of my good nights. By four a.m., half an hour before the alarm was due to go off, I knew I had to get out whatever the risk.

Daytime was even worse. My sales count plummeted. I didn't get the chance to ask Robbi if she had spoken to her brother either, but when I came back from the lavatory just after eleven, my handkerchief was there on my desk, washed and ironed. I looked across the office to where I could see her seated at her desk, gazing at me expressionlessly, her chin resting on the back of linked fingers. I stood up, slipped the smart phone into my pocket, slung the pouch holding my gun and my money over my shoulder and walked out. As the lift doors opened, I heard her quick steps and turned to see her, toes pointed outwards, chin up, hands behind her back like a soldier at ease. Without thinking I spoke to her in my normal voice. "Robbi, the truth is someone's trying to kill me. And I don't want you to be…"

The doors closed. Five days ago, I had stopped in Hyde Park to think, but this time I didn't allow myself time for any reflection – straight through the lobby, down the four steps, arm up high to hail a cab in Cannon Street. "Tottenham Court Road."

At least this gave me half an hour to consider my future – longer, the traffic was gridlocked round St Paul's – but as it began to move again along High Holborn, I swivelled round to watch the road behind – buses, vans, cabs and, of course, motorbikes… Three motorbikes being driven in a phalanx behind my cab and the trouble with motorbikes is they could use all the same bus lanes and short cuts that cab drivers use. I tried to picture the street grid. It was no good. If they were following me, I would have to go underground and head out – west maybe – to an anonymous suburb. I flicked the speaker switch and gave the driver instructions.

The motorbikes stayed behind my cab. They were still there after my diversion and still there as we crawled into the chaos beneath Centrepoint where Oxford Street runs out of energy at the top of Charing Cross Road. I leaned forward and slipped two twenty-pound notes into the unresisting hand of the driver. He drove straight on to Oxford Street as the traffic lights turned to green and slammed his brakes on outside the entrance to Tottenham Court Road tube station. I leapt out, pushing through the crowds outside the station entrance, down the steps, slapping my oyster card onto the sensor and running for the escalator.

I heard a shout behind me and half–turned as the moving staircase took me downwards to see a man in black leathers and a motorcycle helmet vault the barrier and run for the escalator, flicking up his visor as he reached the top. I froze for a second, regained control, turned, and hurtled down the long, steep flight of stairs two steps at a time, trying desperately not to fall: *Jack be nimble, Jack be quick, Jack jump over the candlestick.*

I skidded on *candlestick* – went down on one knee like a clumsy sprinter on the blocks and was away down the crowded corridor, dodging between travellers – a crash behind me, a shrill squeal of rage – I risked a glance back. The bike rider was trying to shake his left leg out of a folded baby buggy while fending off an outraged, young mother. I slowed.

* * *

I surfaced at Lancaster Gate skulked across the edge of Bayswater to the Edgware Road, found a cheap chain hotel and paid for five nights in advance in cash. I liked the simple anonymity of the bedroom. It played the trick well that all hotels try – this room is clean and no one has slept or had sex with himself or herself or anyone else on this double bed before. It is your room, created just for you alone. I showered in the tiny bathroom, hung the do–not–disturb sign on the door knob, drew the heavy blackout curtains, turned on the TV, curled up in the middle of the bed and slept… and slept.

CHAPTER FOUR

There was a muttering in the background: laughter, applause. I wrenched myself out of sleep to face this new threat and found myself shaking, dripping with sweat, curled up on the floor while a chat show of some sort filled the TV screen on the wall at the foot of the bed. I pushed the blackness away, peered at my watch, wiped the sweat from my eyes, uncurled, went into the bathroom and showered again. I had slept for seventeen hours. I sat back down on the bed, stared dully at the TV and fought to keep my eyes open – delayed shock, I knew. I slept again, haunted by pictures of a man collapsing in front of me with blood gushing from a red hole in the side of his neck, tormented by visions of a mocking, golden haired Egyptian queen who walked round and round me trying to see inside my brain.

By mid-morning on Tuesday, I'd had enough – even the delights of Daytime TV had begun to pall. I put on the dark glasses I had sneaked out to buy yesterday, turned the collar of the newly bought coat up, tilted the absurd Trilby forward. The effect was dreadful and entirely unlike the suave, conservative, elegantly turned-out John Hannay – apart from the fact that I was still six foot two with dark brown hair and the slight limp that was the result of my childhood trauma.

I sank back underground and headed towards Queen Anne's Gate. This time I simply crossed the road and knocked on the front door of the Artinswell house. A pretty, no more than pretty – sexy – Filipina maid in a tight grey uniform, opened it. I smiled at her in the friendliest way that I could. I was now very, very Etonian.

"Sorry to disturb, but is James in?"

She shook her head. I tried to look appealing. "Damn."

She smiled and held the front door open. "If you tell me who you are, sir, I can call him for you."

I strolled in and glanced at a small bust on the big mantelshelf and then at the art displayed on the walls. Whatever James, Lord Artinswell did for a living, he certainly wasn't mired in wretched poverty.

"The name's Hannay, John Hannay."

"Would you wait here, please sir. I shall check to see when he is coming back."

I nodded and waved a hand dismissively. She wiggled her bottom across the hall and climbed the stairs, smiling back down at me – she had dimples. I dug out my mobile. I had made a practice in my four days at Continental Atlantic of acquiring as many of the mobile phone numbers of the traders as I could – it had passed the time in the long, long evenings. I dialled Darren's number. He answered immediately. "Darren, mate, it's Alex here. I got a problem phoning into the office. I need a word with Robbi and yours was the only number I had."

"Hang on, mate."

I heard him shout – a rustle – a woman's voice – and then she was there.

"Where are you?"

I didn't bother with the Oz accent. "Robbi, I'm sorry."

"What do you want?"

"I think I need your brother's help if he'd be willing to give it."

"He'll do what I ask. Where are you?"

No mischief, no mockery. I told her. There was a long pause and some distant murmuring. Hurry up, hurry up, the maid would be back any second.

"John?

"Yes."

"Be outside in exactly two minutes. A motorcycle courier will pick you up. And John, the point about life is that you don't run away however bad it gets!"

The phone went dead. I looked at the second hand on my watch: twenty-one, twenty-two, twenty-three, twenty-four. But should I stay here or...? The maid was back holding out a portable phone. I groaned.

"Hello?"

"Is that really a Hannay in my house?"

"Lord Artinswell, look I'm really sorry to gate crash. Totally wrong of me, but I just wanted to ask something about my grandfather."

Sixty-one, sixty-two, sixty-three. The fruity voice changed. He was laughing at me.

"Of course you do, John. You and everyone else. Stay there and I'll be straight back."

"No, I really don't want to trouble you. Perhaps I can make an appointment. It was just that..."

"Stay there. We need to see you."

That was a warning. This was not what I had expected. I had been right to call Robbi.

"Very well. Thank you."

I gave the phone back to the maid, raised her hands to my lips and bowed, still watching the second hand on my watch. I wandered round the hallway – one hundred and nine, one hundred and ten, one hundred and eleven... I strolled towards the front door, staring at a painting high on the wall above me. One hundred and eighteen, one hundred and nineteen, one hundred and twenty.

I whipped open the door and stepped out into the street as the courier roared up to the kerb holding out a helmet. Thankfully he was small. I perched on the pillion seat, clinging on with my knees, tightening the helmet strap beneath my chin. I glanced back and caught a glimpse of another motorbike pulling into the street behind us. A second bike joined the pursuer at the corner. I leaned forward and shouted a warning into my driver's ear. He nodded and, breathtakingly, while crashing a red light, took one hand off the handlebar and spoke into his microphone. He then yelled the two most unnecessary words of our brief relationship. "Hang on."

I grabbed his waist. He patted my hand reassuringly, swung into Victoria Street heading towards Hyde Park Corner, weaving, braking, accelerating up to what, peeking over the top of his shoulder, appeared to be seventy-eight miles per hour. I squinted into the wing mirror. The pursuit was way back. He spoke into his mic again and laughed. He bloody laughed. I had heard the stories about coke–snorting courier lunatics – well here was the proof. He gave the finger to a bus, slipped inside a taxi on Bird Cage Walk, made the lights on the corner of Westminster Square as they went from Amber to Red, leaned low enough to catch a spark from the foot pedal as he swung right in front of the Houses of Parliament and pulled up in front of a policeman. The constable stepped forward, alert to potential trouble as the courier took off his helmet and… shook out her long, wavy brown hair. She looked up the officer of the law and laughed again, her pretty, snub nose wrinkling as she did so.

"Has he fainted, constable?"

She jerked her thumb at me over her shoulder as I just about managed to swing my leg over the bike and rocked on wobbly legs. The policeman laughed and waved her away. "Come on, move along now."

She looked back at the traffic lights. The two riders had been joined by their third partner, but here, in front of the best protected building in the country, in front of hundreds of witnesses, one of them being Police Constable P874, there was absolutely nothing they could do. They rode past. My angel of mercy waved at them and pointed them out to the policeman.

"Tried to run me off the road, they did. Bastards."

The officer stepped out to look after them as they roared off down the embankment. A white Transit van pulled into the kerb. She pointed at me.

"There's your lift. Bye."

She reached out, took the helmet off me, pulled her own helmet back on and weaved out into the traffic. I smiled at the policeman who was shaking his head in admiration and walked towards the van. The door was opened and I climbed in – in to the giant's lair. He was huge. Even hunched over the wheel he seemed to fill the cab.

"In the back."

"The motorcycle courier, does she work for you?"

He studied me without interest and raised one finger to his lip. I decided, off my own bat you understand, not to talk any further and climbed over the seat into the empty shell of the van where I stretched out on my back. I could just see the sky and the tops of buildings through the front windscreen over the seat headrests. We were heading into the City again. I closed my eyes. Eventually he stopped, reversed, stopped again, turned off the engine and turned to me, jerking his head. I undid the rear door, stepped out into a dimly lit basement and waited while he pressed a button to lower the metal roller door.

Now as I have mentioned I am six foot two, but Robbi's brother Dave towered over me. That was the thing about him you never forgot – his sheer size. He filled every room he was in, dominated it by his sheer massiveness. You missed the fact that there wasn't an ounce of fat on him, that his eyes were amber like his sister's and strangely gentle, almost dreamy. You missed the wide mouth, which rarely showed more humour than a sardonic half–smile and the calm self–containment of his every move. You missed it because David Lord, I was to discover, used his size not just as a lethal weapon, but as an emotional disguise of considerable subtlety.

"Dave?"

He nodded. "My sister isn't going to get into any trouble because of you is she? I wouldn't be happy about that."

"No. After I get out of here, she need never see me again."

"Hmmm. You see the trouble with Robbi is that she likes to take care of birds with broken wings."

"I don't have broken wings, Dave."

"Not yet you don't… What do you want?"

I didn't know. My shoulders slumped. He studied me impassively.

"She said she thought you were a fighter."

I took a breath and then another. After all that's what life's about – one breath after another, however little you feel like taking the next one.

He looked over my shoulder. "You sure, love?"

And she was there.

She nodded. Dave glanced at his watch. "Right. I'll go and see Keith."

He left and she walked round me slowly. She spoke. "I took yesterday off, you know. I left instructions for Louise to give you my mobile number if you called. Do you know where I went?"

I shook my head.

"I went to Eton College."

I stopped breathing.

"Do you want to know why?"

I nodded uncertainly and breathed again – once.

"Your tutor, Henry Maslin. I went to see him."

Why on earth would she…?

"I phoned the school secretary and said I'd been researching a book on your family and I understood that you and your father had both gone there. She was very helpful."

36

"But…"

"Your tutor remembered you very well. Said you were very academic, exceptionally clever, but the most withdrawn boy he had ever taught."

She paused and studied me curiously. "The teachers knew you had nightmares. Did you realise that?"

I shook my head slowly. All I had ever wanted was for no one to notice me, let alone know that I had ever dreamed of anything.

"He said he only found out by accident because someone set off a fire alarm and when he went to wake up the boys, he found you still asleep, curled up on the floor in a corner of your room, drenched with sweat, shaking with what he thought must have been terror, with a handkerchief stuffed in your mouth so nobody would hear if you screamed."

I shook my head again in protest and tried to speak, to tell her to stop, to tell her that no one knew about me, that no one could ever have known, that I didn't want to remember, that I couldn't remember, that all I thought I knew was that when I was a child, I had let my parents down so badly.

"He wished you had stayed in contact. He said he felt he had failed you. He said to say sorry to you."

The mischievous smile was back suddenly. "He also said that every female within ten miles of the school wanted to…"

"Robbi." I paused, not sure whether to continue the bizarre sentence that had formed in my head.

"John?"

"I shot a man. I killed him."

"What, as in: 'I shot a man in Reno just to watch him die'?"

I stared at her blankly.

She rolled her eyes in exasperation. "It's a Johnny Cash song. Oh, for God's sake. Look, John, I come from an army family. People get shot in the army – if not all the time, then quite often. Sometimes it comes very close to home." She grimaced. "Too close. So, either you did it for fun – in which case you're a psycho and I am out of here – or you had a reason. Did you have a reason, John?"

I returned to silence. She waved her hand in front of my eyes. "Hellooo?"

"He and two others had broken into my flat. They had guns. I'd had… threats."

She smiled patronisingly. "There, see? You're not a psycho. I knew it!"

I had no idea what to say next. I had just told someone I scarcely knew that I was a murderer and it didn't appear to have worried her. The lift door opened. Robbi stepped back, turned to her brother questioningly.

Dave sighed. "You!"

That meant me.

"Get back upstairs and go back to work as before. I have friends who will watch this place to see if there are any other watchers. And Alex or John or whatever?"

"Yes, Dave?"

"This time you stay here."

"Yes, Dave.

CHAPTER FIVE

The next three days were just like the first four only completely different. Did I sleep any better? No. Did I feel any more secure? No. And then it was Friday.

It being Friday, by four o'clock business had slowed. I put on the headphones, opened YouTube on my desktop and typed in Miles Davis' In A Silent Way. An hour later I was agreeing with Sonny Rollins that I didn't know what love was when the door opened. I stood up and shook Dave's hand. He looked at me quizzically.

"You still sure, Robs?"

That wasn't a vote of approval. Robbi just nodded. Dave sighed and passed me a set of overalls and a company branded baseball cap. He turned to his sister. "Go on then, I'll meet you where we agreed."

I opened my bottom drawer, wrapped the dirty shirts round my waist and dropped the rest of the underclothes down the leggings with my pouch. The Australian flag on the desk went into a pocket. I zipped up the uniform and rammed the baseball cap over my ears. I was now an overweight, middle–aged, working man. I slouched. Dave nodded approval. "Take those bags over there with the shredded paper in and carry them into the lobby. Then come back for more."

I did as I was told and ten minutes later the lobby was half full and the service lift was on its first journey down filled with rustling bags. The lift went to the basement. "Stay there."

I nodded. I was more than happy to let Dave do the thinking. I heard the van being backed up to the exit, then Dave's voice. "Open up, mate. I ain't got all bleeding night."

I started slinging bags into the van. He glanced around. "Stay in the back of the van. I'll get the next load down."

He shut and locked the doors and I sat down on a bag. The paper rustled loudly. I attempted immobility. The paper still rustled. I heard a step outside – a light tap near the back doors – the handle turned slowly – the lock resisted it – a scraping in the lock. Should I move? Was there a weapon anywhere to hand? Then a voice, a big voice!

"Good evening. Nice to meet you. That your van, is it? No, it's not. Know why? 'Cos it's mine."

A muffled shuffle, a thud and then the handle was turned. Dave looked in. "We've got company. They'll be more of them. Get this lot in while I take a look."

A body was slumped by the back of the van. I tried to ignore it while I slung bag after bag into the interior. I heard a step. It was Dave. He looked at the bags. "You know I'd offer you a job if you always worked that fast."

"Anyone out there?"

"Yeah – couple of dodgy looking blokes in a car on the corner. Looks like they're Chinese too."

"Chinese?"

"Mmm. This one had a knife too."

He tossed it onto the seat beside me. I stared at it. More Chinese? What had I done to upset the People's

Republic? Dave picked up his phone, dialled and spoke. I looked at him. This was a new Dave, heavy Cockney, more teddy, less grizzly. "That Keef? 'Allo Keef, Dave 'ere, mate. You've got a security problem. Just caught a geezer trying to break into my van with all the shredded stuff in it. You got that FCA up your arse again?"

He paused and listened. "No, no one in the office when I left. What Australian? No. No one. I'll wait. S'what you pay me for."

I looked at him. "What happens now?"

"That's up to Keith and whether or not they've been at it again. If they have, then the security firm comes round to help out. If they're on the level, it'll be Old Bill."

He sensed my concern. "Don't worry. If they're not up to something... well there's always a first time."

His phone rang. "OK, Keef, you're the boss." He gave me his half smile. "Told you. Security firm will be here in two minutes."

"So, this isn't the first time this has happened."

"No. Won't be the last either."

"So, this is nothing to do with me, then?"

Dave just looked at me. His phone rang again. "'Allo Declan. You outside already? Anyone there? Little car, eh? Well let's make sure they ain't going to be able to follow anyone, shall we?"

I heard the distant noise of a van outside. Dave swung the unconscious body of the Chinese man on to his shoulder with minimal effort, walked to the door and pressed the green buzzer. The strips of sheet metal rattled noisily back up on their ungreased roller. A security van was parked just down the alley, blocking a

Citroen Berlingo from getting out. Dave carried the inert body across to them while I belted up and pulled the peak of my baseball cap down. What looked like an interesting conversation began.

Dave drove carefully through the City, continually checking his wing mirrors. At one point in Gresham Street, he did a sudden U turn to the fury of a taxi driver who clearly regarded it as his sole right to perform such manoeuvres, but we were clean – no motorbikes, no followers of any kind. His phone rang.

"Hallo, love. No, all well. Yes, he's with me. I'm still not sure about this, Robbs. He... OK, all right, all right."

He turned into Clerkenwell Green and pulled up behind a silver Nissan Micra.

"There she is." He put a heavy hand on my arm. "If anything happens to her."

"It won't, Dave. I wouldn't do anything to hurt her."

He watched me. "It's not you I'm worried about."

I got out of the van and climbed into the car beside her. She was smiling her sunny, happy smile. My spirits lifted.

"Where to?"

"Somewhere safe."

"I have a little brother as well as a big brother. He's in the army. His house is empty."

"Where is it?"

"Newbury. It's nothing special. Friday night it'll take an hour or more. We can buy some grub on the way."

I looked across at her. She still had her work outfit on.

"I'll buy something to wear too. You can spend some of the humungous bonus on me that Keith has been going on and on about this week."

42

"Harry's got that. I'm going to have to speak to him at some stage."

"Not this weekend you won't. By the way, I love the outfit."

I looked down at my messy, grey, zippy, tubby uniform. "Oh, yes."

I reached into the pocket and pulled out the Australian flag. I unzipped the front of the overalls and started to pull out my collection of dirty shirts, socks and boxer shorts.

"What's in the pouch?"

"Just money and stuff."

"What stuff?"

"I'll show you later."

We joined the grey ribbon of traffic crawling out towards weekends in Maidenhead, Windsor, Reading and all points west. The rain started at Slough.

I told her as little of my story as I could while we sat in a series of traffic jams on a rain soaked M4 motorway until an hour later we reached the A34 turn off and headed south onto the roundabout strewn ring road that is Newbury and found a Sainsbury's. I hadn't realised you could buy clothes at Sainsbury's. To be honest I had never been inside one before. It may have been this confession that encouraged Robbi to inform the world of my ignorance of supermarkets, or it may have been some kind of cold dish revenge for walking out last week. What did I know of the female mind?

She left me at the wine aisle where I swallowed my snobbishness and bought some overpriced Bordeaux, some even more overpriced Marlborough Sauvignon

Blanc and was considering an Albariño when I was interrupted by a nudge to the ribs.

"Shift over."

Robbi had bought clothes. I had already realised that being incognito with her around was going to prove difficult. People noticed Robbi especially when she held up clothes against her body and asked if they would look good on her. Men drooled and even women smiled. I understood why Keith thought she was worth her weight in precious metals.

"Robbi, do you think you could possibly be a little less noticeable."

She bridled. "What do you mean, noticeable?" Then she smiled – that mischievous smile. "Whatever you say, Sir John." And dropped me what passed for a deferential curtsy. I decided to quit while I was still (possibly) ahead and bought food. We paid what seemed to be an enormous bill with some of the cash in my pouch.

It was nearly eight by the time we arrived at her brother Dean's house. She had been there a couple of times, but as I was still in paranoid mode I ducked down in the front seat, while she showed off the remote garage door opener and carefully reversed in.

I carried the bags in to the tiny kitchen, laid out our goodies and hunted for a knife. She stared at me. "Don't tell me you can cook."

"All right, I won't. I don't know where the glasses are, but I've put the white in the freezer so it's either red or…"

"G&T."

She disappeared into the lounge and came back with two glasses half full of G and what appeared to be a non–

existent amount of T. I gulped, chopped garlic, simmered pasta, grated Parmesan, fried pancetta, whisked eggs and generally showed off. After the meal I was pushed out of the kitchen and into the tiny lounge where a fake wood burner was burning fake wood in a fake fireplace. I sat down on the overstuffed sofa and listened to the domestic noises coming from the kitchen.

CHAPTER SIX

I awoke to a cold room. Robbi had thrown a duvet over me, taken off my shoes and pushed a cushion behind my head. I yawned. Her head appeared in my vision.

"About time."

"About what time?

"One o'clock on Saturday afternoon."

"What? I am so sorry."

I was chivvied into the bathroom. I heard her yell something while I was under the shower, but it was only when I got out that I saw a pair of what I assumed to be her brother Dean's jodhpurs on the floor by the door. Horse riding? I dressed. A Barbour was pushed in my face and I made my paranoid way into the front seat of the Nissan chewing the proffered bacon sandwich. I straightened up in the seat as we hit the bypass. "You know that bacon is supposed to be cooked, don't you? Where are we going?"

"It's bread and it's meat. Count yourself lucky. Lambourn Downs. Dean knows a trainer up there who lets me hack whenever I'm around."

I slipped the sandwich out of the window when she wasn't looking. I hadn't ridden for nearly three years, but the thought of being up on a horse's back on a sun filled May day nearly drove all the events of the last weeks out of my head. Robbi was a good rider – not in my class, but then that's one of the advantages of a country upbringing. I slowed my hunter so I could watch her in the saddle as she cantered ahead.

"If you're looking at my bum, I'll belt you one."

"You would if you could catch me." I leaned forward with my knees bent, gripping hard, raising my backside and whispering into the horse's ear. He moved into a gallop with a stutter and switch of hooves and we leapt forward and away up on to the high grassy downs. I felt alive again.

The sun was dropping towards the horizon over Marlborough as we drove back, following the old A4 back into Newbury. She yawned then poked me in the arm.

"You can cook again."

"Thank you."

Cooking had always been therapeutic. I was over an hour in the kitchen. Robbi disappeared to the bathroom after pouring two huge glasses of the Bordeaux. I had told her to let it breathe, but that had led merely to a gargling exercise and a giggling fit. The Fois Gras was acceptable and I had made Couscous to go with my Lamb Tagine. The conversation was mainly finding common ground – not much; sharing childhood family losses – more memorable. But I do remember her bloody mobile ringing. I shrugged. It would go away. It did. I poured another glass of wine. The mobile rang again.

"Just a sec, Dave is the only person who has that number. "She ran to her bag. "Dave? Yes. We're at Dean's. No. Yes. I'll put him on."

She pressed the speaker button and held the phone out.

"Yes Dave."

"Just had a call from Keith at Atlantic."

"And?"

"Someone's broken into the office. Among lots of other things your desk had been tampered with and so had Robbi's. Did you have anything in yours?"

"No. You saw me empty it when you were there."

"Robbs?"

I looked at her.

"No, Dave. Nothing."

I added a question.

"No address book with Dean's number or this address in it?"

"No. It's all in this phone."

Dave butted in.

"You better be sure girl, or you'd better get out of there."

I made up my mind. "We'll go, Dave."

"Good."

"Dave, can you get a pay–as–you–go mobile and only phone me on this number?" I gave him the number of one of the phones I had bought in Sainsbury's yesterday.

I had just finished tidying the bedroom when Robbi came in. "There was one thing."

"What?"

"Two weeks ago, I had Dean's sheets and duvet cover dry–cleaned in Newbury. I left the receipt in my desk drawer to remind me to ask him for the money when I next saw him."

If they had burgled Continental Atlantic last night, they would have had been able to get to Newbury when the shops opened and would have had the rest of the day to make the connection to Dean's house. I sighed. "The trouble, Roberta Lord, is you."

"Me?"

"Was it a man who served you?"

She nodded.

"Then he'll remember you."

The sudden, mischievous smile curved her lips. "I can't help being gorgeous. You wouldn't fancy me if I was a total munter."

"Who said I fancied you? You're not even my type – and total what?"

"Munter – dog – minger. Yeah, I imagine you're into dim, upper class, Sloaney birds."

She walked out, smirking impudently. I wiped surfaces that we had touched, left one light on upstairs and we loaded the Micra in the half–dark.

"Stay here. I'll be two minutes."

Revolver in hand, I crawled out of the back door and snuck through the untidy patch of garden to the side alley. A TV blared in the distance to the right and from the left came the sound of a dinner party breaking up. In the orange sodium light, there wasn't a villain in sight… apart from, maybe, inside the car parked beyond the house from where the dinner party noise was now echoing across the street. One of the guests drove away, honking goodbye, headlights playing over the parked vehicle. A shadow of a head ducked down in the driver's seat. Heedless of noise now, I ran back in. "Quick – into the car. I'll open the garage door from the inside."

I pressed the zapper of which Robbi had been so proud yesterday evening to raise the garage door.

Thankfully, unlike Continental Atlantic's roller door, it was quiet. I peered out into the street trying to gauge the right time to make our move. "Lights off. Wait... Now!"

We scooted out into the road as the headlights from another dinner party leaver lit up the windows of the parked car. Whoever was in it must still have been keeping their head down as I saw no movement.

As Dean's garage door rolled back down, Robbi slipped the Nissan in behind a car with a couple in who were calling out of the window to their hosts – thank God for noisy, selfish bastards I thought – still no sign of the watcher in the parked car.

"Go, go!"

She went. Headlights on full she overtook the car in front and whizzed on to the Bath Road.

"Where to?"

"Lambourn Downs."

At the point where we turned on to the A338 just before Hungerford I thought I saw a single headlight in my wing mirror. I told myself it was nothing, but as we went round the roundabout under the M4 it was still there.

"Turn left."

We turned onto the B4000, the ancient Roman road, Ermin Street. The motorbike, if such it were, couldn't hide up here on the Berkshire downs, but then neither could we.

"Right."

Robbi spun the wheel and the car rocked as we turned up a lane leading to the village of East Garston. The bike turned too, about four hundred yards behind us

– a bend to the left and it was out of sight. "Stop! By the gate. Turn round. Quick! Leave the headlights on full. Give me a few seconds and then drive at the bike!"

I pulled the Webley from my pouch as she spun the wheel, and as the car started to bucket back to face the way we had come I had the door open and was out on the ground before she could say anything. I heard the squeal of motorbike's tyres as the rider braked hard. Hidden in the shadows of the ditch I ran, nearly stumbling, back to where he sat irresolute, revving his engine. I was as near as I could get to him. I heard Robbi gun her engine as I raised the Webley. Two blinding crashes – I'd allowed for the kick this time – and she hit the brakes. The first bullet went through his front forks and the second exploded the petrol tank as he tried to turn. The blast knocked him off the bike and I was beside him in an instant pulling at his helmet ready to strike at the first sign of life. But he was limp, his breathing shallow. Robbi got out of the car and ran towards the still burning bike.

"Have you got a fire extinguisher?" I pointed at the blaze. By now I had his helmet off – Chinese… again! He had a mobile phone, some cash, a pistol and nothing else that a quick search would reveal. I dragged him towards the ditch and rolled him in.

I looked at her. She was shivering in the cool of the night.

"Come on. I'll drive."

She climbed in the passenger side without saying a word. I turned the heater on. We drove in the direction of Swindon.

"Where are we going now?"

"I don't know."

"Haven't you got a country mansion somewhere?"

"It's a manor and it's been rented out for years. Anyway, they're sure to have it covered."

"We'll be alright, John."

"You think?"

She didn't reply. I glanced across as her head slumped forward, snapped back up and dropped again. She was asleep.

It was after midnight when I turned on to the A419 and headed in towards the pleasantly scruffy old Cotswold town of Stroud. I got lost on the one–way system, but after two attempts I found a Tesco car park and tucked the Micra into the far side, away from the road and any nosy security guards. Before I closed my eyes, I spent ten minutes on the mobile looking for a suitable hotel for tomorrow.

* * *

A Blackbird's alarm call startled me awake. I peered at my watch. Six fifteen. Robbi was curled up in her seat, still dead to the world. I climbed cautiously out of the car and walked off the stiffness in my limbs. I found the station, noted the number of the 01 Taxi Company, checked train times and fifteen minutes later was back peering in at Robbi. She opened her eyes, drew a picture of a smiley face in the condensation on the side window and jumped out doing knee bends and arm swings to restore her circulation.

"I need to pee."

"There's the hedge."

She looked round, ordered me back into the car and joined me two minutes later looking smug.

"Anything you can do I can…"

"You drive."

We swapped sides.

"Where to?"

"Station."

"Why?"

"I have a plan… of sorts. Left here."

I dialled a number.

"01 Taxis? Hello, I'm arriving from London on the train – supposed to be there at eight twenty-two. Have you got a car that can take me to the Cotswold Way Hotel at Ullenwood? You have? Excellent. There are two of us – one bag. We'll be outside the station."

She looked at me.

"Hurry up. The train's due in 10 minutes. Left here."

I dialled again. "Cotswold Way hotel? Would it be possible to have breakfast for two at 9.00am? Yes? Jolly good. My name? Smith. Thank you."

Robbi shook her head at me pityingly. "Smith? Is that the best you can do?"

I pointed at the parking ticket machine. We headed into another inconspicuous corner and paid for a day.

"Two minutes before the train comes in. Come on."

We waited and then walked out with the stragglers and found the old, dirty and somewhat malodorous taxi. The hotel was even older, not in any way dirty and far from malodourous. Robbi peered at it through the side window. "Is this going to be expensive?"

I shrugged, paid off the driver and walked her up the steps pulling her beanie off her head as I did so. She understood immediately and entered the reception area shaking out her beautiful golden hair and looking around with her beautiful golden smile. I came in behind her, ignored by one and all. At the desk the young receptionist managed to take her envious eyes off Robbi long enough to acknowledge my existence.

"Smith. I called earlier to see about breakfast. The train was on time for once so I'm afraid we're early." I yawned.

"Have you been travelling long, sir?"

"Just a tad. Kiev, Tallinn, Berlin in three days. The damn flight was held up at Brussels for six hours and then, as we were British, we had to spend another two hours at customs. I do not remember when we last slept."

I turned to Robbi who was still wowing the natives, paused and walked back to the reception desk. I spoke quietly. "I don't suppose you have any rooms available, do you? We were heading north for a wedding, but thanks to the flights cock up we missed it. Happy to pay for last night and tonight if we can get some kip now."

"We've only got a suite sir at..." she lowered her voice in case I was going to be embarrassed... "four hundred and twenty-five pounds."

I showed no embarrassment.

"And breakfast, sir, is an extra twenty-five pounds each, sir."

I snorted with amusement – the ever–welcoming English hotel. I paid, walked over to where Robbi was waiting and led the way into the dining room where we ate an enormous breakfast amid that depressingly genteel silence that goes with the English middle classes at public meal times.

In our overly twee suite, I ran a huge bath, pushed Robbi into the bathroom, sat on the bed to think again and made a decision. I dialled the number Harry had given me in London. It rang once and a woman's voice answered.

"John? John Hannay? Is that you?"

"Hello, Anna Haraldsen. Should we meet?"

"They've got Harry."

Shit. "When? Is this phone safe?"

"For the moment, yes. It's safe for this call at any rate. I've turned off Location Services. Where are you?"

"Out of harm's way. But what about Harry?"

"I know where he is."

"Don't tell me. I'll text you a number. Call it from a different phone."

I sent her the number of another of the Sainsbury's phones. It rang. "So, what happened, Anna?"

"They got him in Town. He was leaving the flat of the receptionist at that broker's."

Of course, Louise, the brunette for the threesome... "Bloody idiot."

"Harry doesn't know, but I have a microchip on him so I know exactly where he is."

"And where's that?"

"In a car on the M40."

That wasn't so far away. "I can join you wherever you want this afternoon."

"You have transport?"

"Yes. Listen, Anna. I have a companion."

"The beauteous Roberta. Yes, I know."

"How?"

"Harry isn't as stupid as you think."

"He's put her life in danger and both her brothers."

"He knows that."

I nodded to myself. Yes, he would know. Whether it would bother him or not was a different matter. "OK. Give me a new number and I'll call you at two. I'm getting rid of this Sim card and you should do the same. Harry will talk."

She agreed. I called Stroud Cars on my other phone and arranged to be met at the gates in 15 minutes. I tapped on the bathroom door. "Robbi, I'm going to get the car. We have to leave this afternoon so get some more sleep. I'll be back within the hour."

CHAPTER SEVEN

I let her sleep until one o'clock at which time I showered, shaved, packed and tidied the room. By one thirty we had left. I had to stop Robbi from removing the fluffy white bathrobes and emptying the mini bar.

"But at the price they charge, these should be freebies," she kept saying.

We drove north and then west towards Tewkesbury. I glanced at my watch and turned on the new mobile. At two I called Anna. "We're heading into Worcestershire, Anna."

"Good. Soon as you can get to a place called Lower Apperley."

"I'll call you back."

I looked it up on Robbi's out of date road map, checked my smart phone and called Anna again. "Farmer's Arms – two o'clock."

"We won't make it by then."

"We'll wait."

I disconnected and then thought: 'we'? Did she mean 'we'?

We headed down off the Cotswold escarpment onto the flood plain of the River Severn, across the M5 and with the gothic bulk of Tewkesbury Abbey looming over our right shoulders followed the small cross–country road past hedges full of the sprays of May blossom and fields full of the violent yellow and pungent aroma of Rape. We nearly missed the Farmer's Arms and Robbi had to brake hard at the last second. She basked at a table in the sun in the empty garden while I went to order both liquid and solid sustenance. She talked about Continental Atlantic. "The whole trading floor was in awe of you."

"Why?"

"Because of the business you did. Keith was raving about you. First two days he thought was a lucky streak, but by the end of day three he was saying you were an f–ing genius."

"I am."

"F–ing modest too."

A car braked hard on the road and turned sharply into the car park. "We", I murmured gazing at the wiry young man beside Anna who pushed his black rimmed glasses up on to his Roman nose and studied us through the passenger window. Robbi sat up. "The man with her. He looks nasty. Who is he?"

"I have no idea."

They came within introduction range. "Good afternoon. May I introduce you to Roberta Lord? Robbi this is Anna Haraldsen and er…"

"Palmer, just Palmer. No point in saying that you shouldn't be here is there, Roberta?"

"No."

Anna Haraldsen stepped in. "Stop it, Palmer. Roberta it's nice to meet you. May I say immediately that I do think you should get away from here and have nothing more to do with John until we have sorted out his problems."

She looked at me. I shrugged. "This isn't safe, Robbi. You know that."

'Just Palmer's' shoulder bag beeped. He opened it and pulled out a laptop. "It's reading the data pusher on Harry's microchip."

"Meaning?"

"Meaning he's about 400 yards away give or take."

I raised my eyebrows, but Just Palmer was not inclined to elucidate. "Could they see us?"

"Not unless they can see through two fields and a wood. Anyhow where's my drink? Get us a beer, Anna, will you."

Anna stood up. "Come on, Roberta. Palmer can't help being a prick."

They walked away.

"And a Cheese Ploughman's." called Palmer.

I watched them go and heard Anna's voice – almost resigned. "Well, I have to say that you are even more beautiful than Harry said – and that's saying something."

Robbi laughed. "I can't help it and I'm Robbi, please."

That bit was OK then. I looked at Just Palmer. "Who are you?"

"I'm Harry's guardian angel."

I shrugged – asshole! We looked at the beep. Anna came back first.

"Palmer is right, John."

"I know. But I promised her brother I would take care of her."

"Well fucking well do so then."

"To use your own vernacular, Palmer – fuck off."

"Stop it, you two. Palmer, for God's sake has no one ever told you that confrontation is rarely the best way to get what you want? John, it's your call, but you know what we think."

I watched Robbi walk back towards us. "For now she stays. She's safer with us than on her own in London. They've already kidnapped one of us. Had you considered what a perfect hostage she would make?"

Palmer looked at me and deflated. "No, I hadn't."

Robbi sat down looking from one to the other. Palmer spoke first. "Roberta, I started out wrong with you. I'm sorry."

She looked up at him, searched his face and pointed at herself. "Me Robbi."

Palmer's cheeks reddened. Anna laughed.

Time to move on. "So, what's the plan, Palmer?"

"They're over by the River Severn somewhere. We'll have to do a recce, but whatever happens we have to move fast. Our guess is that he's being held by a couple of minders while they wait for orders."

I raised a finger. "I've only met Harry once, but I got the impression he wasn't over–fond of pain."

Palmer smiled for the first time. "Harry has a one-way relationship with pain – he likes inflicting it. Look, his data pusher's been static for at least two hours now so if we're going to do anything we should do it quick, before anyone else comes."

Leaving Robbi and Anna to move the cars, Palmer and I crossed the garden, stepped over the stile and turned right onto a footpath beside a low wall of green, gently waving barley. We walked in silence for three minutes with nothing to hear besides the muted buzzing of a few solitary bees braving the pesticides. I could see the Severn now. The great grey–green, greasy Limpopo of a river meandered south and west. Pieces of flotsam, mementos from the April floods, were washed up on the muddy bank – a wooden door, a car tyre, half a tree with torn newspaper pages held in its branches, the ubiquitous black plastic bin liners. Palmer put a hand on my shoulder and I crouched as he crawled to the edge of the wood. He raised his head, lowered it and beckoned me. "Look, twenty metres downstream."

I peered through the long grass. A fly landed on my forehead. It was an old caravan. The door was open. The ragged curtains over the back window did a slow-motion wave in the slight breeze. The fly took off, changed its mind and landed on my eyelid. I blinked it off, turned my head and looked at the river. Above the bend upstream a small dinghy was moored. I slid back down. "How about using the boat?"

Palmer nodded. "Stay here."

He offered me his Glock. I shook my head and showed him the handgun I had appropriated from the Chinese motorbike rider. He smiled. "You'll do, Sir John."

Well weren't we getting along just fine and dandy now? I moved to where I could watch both him and the caravan. Three minutes and he was finished. He crept back towards me, pulling the painter. Behind him, on the river, I could see what looked like a half–sunken dinghy drifting towards the bank. It bumped near the caravan. No reaction. Palmer reached into his bag again and pulled out what I took to be a silencer, which he screwed on to the end of his pistol. He saw my glance. "Muzzle suppressor. You any good with one of these?"

I shook my head.

"I've put an old block of Semtex in the boat. Get ready to run to the far end of the caravan, beyond the door."

He rested the gun on his left forearm and closed one eye. The cough sounded incredibly loud to my ears, but there was no hint of movement in the caravan. Whatever Palmer had been aiming at in the boat, he had missed. He spoke over his shoulder. "I won't miss it with this shot."

I took him at his word and was running as he squeezed the trigger. The explosion nearly knocked me off my feet and I ignored Palmer's instruction. I went straight through the open door in a rolling dive, squeezing the trigger of my gun. I saw a shocked Chinese face whip round in my direction while the second was still staring out at the burning boat.

"Drop it!" Harry yelled in Mandarin and I thanked the God Harry and I didn't believe in for Harry's God given gift of languages. The gun was dropped. Palmer appeared in the door. One of the Chinese was on the floor with my bullet in him; the other began to move. He may have been going to scratch his nose, but Palmer's bullet caught him in the shoulder and he went back over the chair. Harry glared round wildly. "Stop dozing about and get me out of here. And where the hell did you come from, Palmer?"

Palmer ignored him and passed me a knife. I cut the plastic ties. "Harry, tell them to stay on the floor."

He kicked the nearest man on his wounded shoulder to emphasise his point. They sat. I tied them up while Palmer watched the door. When they were secure, he frisked them, pocketing phones and weapons. We left immediately, hurrying up the path with Palmer's shoulder bag rattling from his newly acquired toys. I paused, suddenly uncertain, as the others walked on. "Wait. Let's go back a different way."

"Why, for fuck's sake?" said Harry.

"I don't know. It's just that…"

Palmer looked at me thoughtfully. His phone rang. "Anna? What? Where are you? OK we'll see you at the bridge. Oh, Anna. Slash their tyres if you can."

He turned to me. "Well done. Some people have just arrived and are coming down the footpath. Robbi and Anna had already moved the cars and were watching the pub. Come on."

We ran, with me realising yet again, how unfit my months of self–isolation had left me. Back in our cars and heading towards the M5, I had just managed to downgrade from panting to heavy breathing when a phone rang. Robbi passed it across. "Anna gave it to me. Answer it."

"Anna? Yes. OK. We need to dump this car somewhere. Someone's bound to have seen it, but I can't hire anything without using my driving licence, which would almost certainly compromise us. In any event they have tracking devices in Hire Cars."

I sat and thought. A month ago, I could have hired a car. A month ago, I hadn't fired a handgun. A month ago, I wasn't a murderer. Robbi nudged me with her left elbow. A month ago, I hadn't met her.

"Instructions?"

"Follow that car."

We changed motorways onto the M50 and were heading towards Wales – through Ross on Wye – up to the Heads of the Valleys Road when Robbi yawned for the second time. I called Anna. "We need a pee break. Where? OK."

I played with my smart phone and texted Anna to propose the Bus Station car park at Abergavenny. We were getting good at leaving the car in remote corners of car parks, but just to add to any confusion there might be in our pursuers' minds, I went into the booking office and ordered two single bus tickets to Chepstow. We piled into the hire car.

"Where are we going?"

"Llangrannog", said Anna.

"Oh."

Palmer drove us on through Wales. The last half–mile I didn't think we'd make – up a steep, slippery, single–track lane, grass in the middle where tyres had not touched, hedges sprouting their sprays of May blossom and banks washed with fading bluebells. A small mid-Victorian cottage was tucked into the hill on the left with a stream beside it hurrying down a moss lined, open drain into the slate gutter by the road.

Anna opened the front door. The cottage smelt damp as she led the way in, opening windows. I walked back to the car with Palmer and picked up a box that chinked. He offered me his twisted smile. "I am told that man cannot live by bread alone."

Back in the house, Anna and Robbi were already making beds and Harry was adding wood to the open fire. It started to crackle and spit. I went through to the tiny kitchen. I was getting used to tiny kitchens. Good God, it was only 24 hours ago that I had cooked a meal in Berkshire. I found an ancient corkscrew, opened bottles and turned to the food.

After we had eaten and cleared the table, we moved the chairs closer to the blaze to talk. I leaned forward and placed a log on the fire. It blazed up, under–lighting our faces and making Harry's sardonic smile look quite diabolic. I looked round. "Anna?"

"No, after you. Your story's got to be the cornerstone."

I settled back and began as near to the beginning as I could. I had long ago come to the conclusion that my father had felt that he was very much in his father's shadow and to be honest I knew more about my grandfather than my father. He didn't marry until he was nearly sixty, which meant we were never likely to be close. I only vaguely remembered him as gentle and withdrawn, scarcely leaving the Manor with its wildlife and seasons that he loved so much. He was killed in a motor accident when I was seven, very close to home, on a road he knew well, on a clear morning. After that I was pretty sure that my mother was terrified of going anywhere. She let the Manor out and she and I moved into the family apartment just off Piccadilly.

"I was sent away to prep school."

This was getting to the bit I really didn't want to share. I steeled myself. The blackness lurked above me, deep and threatening.

"I didn't hear anything from my mother after the first week. There'd been no arrangement made at the end of term for picking me up for the Christmas holidays so I sneaked out of school, walked the five miles to the nearest railway station, caught a train to Paddington and walked to Mayfair. I let myself in and it smelt bad, like there was something rotting. I ran in though, calling for my mother and that's when I found her. She had been dead for most of the term, I think. She was… messy."

Robbi had twisted round to stare at me. "How old did you say you were?"

"Er, eight by then. I wasn't old enough to absorb it all really. The funny thing is – well not funny – that I think some people came. I think someone spoke to me. I think someone did something to me. Someone hurt me – very badly."

Once again, I struggled with the black fog that enveloped me when I tried to remember this dreadful time. "I… I… I… "

I closed my eyes, opened them and started again. "I can't remember anything about it. All I do know is that I went into the kitchen and had a drink of water and found a tin of baked beans. The police arrived an hour later. The school had called them and said I had disappeared. The coroner's verdict on my mother was suicide whilst of unsound mind."

Anna cleared her throat. I stopped her. "It was almost thirty years ago, Anna. I'm just telling my story. Look at Harry here. How old were you when you were sent away to school, Harry?"

"Seven."

"Did you want to go?"

"Well, it made a change from being beaten at home to being sexually assaulted at school."

Palmer shook his head. I remembered something and reached into my pocket and tossed an iPhone onto the coffee table. "I took this from one of the people who broke into my flat."

Palmer's eyes gleamed. "At last – something to work with. Have you tried it at all?"

"No, I turned it off immediately. You may have noticed there's no signal here on EE or Vodafone."

"Or 02," said Harry.

Palmer smiled greedily. "I had indeed, boyos. So, we can see what he has on here without being tracked. Well, my beauty, let's have a look at you."

I watched him start to play with the phone for a second or two then looked away. "Anna?"

Anna straightened in her chair. "It was something my grandfather said just before he died. I had gone back to the island in Norrland the family owned to see him when my father said it was close. The day before he died, he became much more lucid. I actually thought he was going to get better, but he didn't of course. Anyway, he opened his eyes, saw me and smiled. He asked how I was and sniffed the air from the open window saying the weather was going to turn bad and we talked about the family for a bit and then out of the blue he sat up straight and seemed to stare through me. He pointed a finger at the corner of the room and said very loudly: 'they will come again. I know they will. When they come you have to find Hannay. Find Hannay.'"

I jolted upright.

"And it was then that he told me about a strange pact with someone called Sir Richard Hannay and how he had let Sir Richard down, but I mustn't. I must find Hannay and protect him. That's all. He rambled a bit for the next two hours and the next day when I went in to see him in the morning, he had died."

"So, fast forward two years and I was in London doing PR for an international Polo event and I met Harry. He was captain of one of the teams. By this time, I'd found that Sir Richard Hannay's grandson was called John and his address was Fosse Manor. It didn't take long to find out you weren't living there, but then I ran up against a brick wall. No one seemed to know anything about you or your whereabouts. So in an idle moment when Harry wasn't trying to chat up any female under eighty, I asked him if he knew someone called John Hannay."

"I didn't, but I said I knew a man who could find anyone." Harry pointed at Palmer.

I studied him. "What is it exactly that you do, Palmer?"

Palmer looked shifty. Mind you, that did appear to be his default setting. "By training I'm a mathematician."

Harry let out a bark of laughter. "I knew he'd say that. I knew it."

"Sod off, Harry. I have a PhD in developments in class field theory."

Harry was loving this. "Yes, dear boy, but when we met you were doing what in essence was some very sophisticated card counting for some very dodgy people."

Palmer looked at me, shaking his head. "Harry was in trouble. He had a nasty little gambling habit and was in debt. I actually felt sorry for him although, in my defence, that was because I didn't know him very well then. I made him enough money to pay off his debts and we've stayed in touch as he had a few friends who needed a bit of help once in a while."

He went back to his exploration of the iPhone. Anna took over again. "So, Palmer did some digging. We found that you had a London address and Palmer did a bit of surveillance and…"

"I found that your flat was the centre of a network of electronic eavesdropping."

Anna ignored the further interruption. "The more I thought about it the more I wondered if the eavesdroppers were the "they" that my grandfather had referred to. Then Palmer managed to access the line with your answer phone and we found that you really were under siege."

Palmer exclaimed. The light had come on in the iPhone display. He connected it to his laptop and started the file transfers. Robbi yawned. Anna looked at her watch. "God, it's One Thirty. Harry, we'll have to leave it to tomorrow morning to find out what you have learnt about them during your little escapade."

I noted an expression of more than marginal discomfiture slide across Harry's face as he reached across to lift the bottle beside him. It was Anna's turn to yawn. "Robbi and I decided who was sleeping where. Harry, Palmer, you have the two back rooms, I have the front bedroom and Robbi and John can sleep down here."

She stood up and stretched. "Night all."

Harry put the empty bottle down regretfully. Palmer simply stood up with his eyes still glued to the laptop.

Robbi removed dead bottles and glasses to the kitchen. I chucked another log on the fire, pushed a heavy armchair into a corner and resigned myself to a night of backache. There was the noise of water running in the main bathroom as I came back out of the downstairs lavatory wondering what Robbi and Anna were talking about upstairs. Out of the remotest corner of my eye I caught a glimpse of a wrist and a cufflink bearing what I thought was an old school crest. Then I was hit from behind. This wasn't a fade to black moment. It was a cut.

CHAPTER EIGHT

I was eight and in the kitchen of my mother's flat. Something dreadful was in another room. The man in front of me was telling me it was all right, but why couldn't I remember? Again and again, he asked why I couldn't remember? His eyes burned at me and got bigger and bigger and filled the world and then there was agony and I surfaced. I sat up, which was a mistake. A blinding light complemented the shooting pain. Hands pushed me back down and a voice spoke to me through the fog.

"John? John?"

I kept my eyes closed. It seemed the safer option – speaking was OK though. "I saw a cufflink. Does Palmer wear cufflinks?"

"It was Harry." Anna's voice.

I opened my eyes and looked round at the circle of eyes. "I'm going to try and sit up."

It hurt, but less than the last time. "We'd better get out of here before he alerts anyone. You tracking him, Palmer?"

Palmer shook his head. "No internet connection. But he didn't take the car."

"Why not?"

"I had the keys in my pocket and I don't suppose he fancied trying to lay two of us out."

I stood, rocked, blurred, rocked again, but stayed upright. "We have to leave."

I squinted round the room. The fire had died back, the remains of the log I had thrown on still glowing in the grate. Robbi held out some pills and a glass of water. I took them and swallowed. Ten minutes later we were back in the hire car in the lane.

"Got any idea as to where we can stay, Palmer?"

"I'll call someone when it gets light."

"OK. I'm sorry but I need to sleep now. I'll take over from you when we stop."

I leaned back against the headrest and looked out at the moonlit landscape, closed my eyes, forced them open, looked out again and was asleep before I could count to ten. The jolting of the car on to a rough surface woke me. It was sunrise over the Brecon Beacons. I got out to stretch in the cool Welsh morning and pee on the cool Welsh grass. Palmer turned his phone on and walked away from us to make a call. He listened for a moment and then turned in my direction making urgent writing gestures. I scrabbled in the glove compartment for paper and pencil.

"Grid reference NN238 NN469, normal. I owe you.""

He booted up his laptop, grabbed the paper from my hand and tapped. "'Normal' means count the letters five forward. The numbers are scrambled according to the day of the week we spoke and the time of day."

He connected to the Internet. "Dulverton. South Moor Cottage."

"On Exmoor," said Robbi.

I looked at her.

"I used to go sailing in Appledore and one year we stayed there. Nice place. Twee. Posh. You'll fit in."

We drove on. Abergavenny was an anti–climax: no one dangerous in sight, scarcely anyone around. Robbi and I transferred the luggage on to the Micra's roof rack, turned on to the Usk road and made our sedate way down the small side roads of South Glamorgan leaving the others to drive to Cardiff Airport. With my headache receding to a dull thump, I could even stomach, just, Radio 2. Robbi sang along – loudly.

"Robbi, my head hurts."

"Well, you shouldn't have got in the way of a cosh, should you?"

We collected Palmer and Anna from the airport and made an uneventful trip across the Prince of Wales Bridge, down through the Gordano valley, past Crook Peak and into Somerset. I was driving by the time we reached Exmoor with Palmer giving me directions from the sat–nav on his phone. We crossed cattle grids, passed freshly sheared sheep, gleaming white, with the nearly weaned lambs bleating and rushing to their mothers at the sight of the car, butting up underneath to suck out the remains of any milk. We turned down a small lane, through a five-bar gate by a copse on the edge of the moor, along a rough track to a clearing on a mound with a chocolate box cottage beside a clump of beech trees. We unloaded.

It was late morning by now so I cooked brunch and tried to exercise my brain. There was something about the way Artinswell had spoken to me on the phone when

I had gatecrashed his house in St Anne's Gate that had felt strange – as if he had been expecting the call. And what had he meant by: "everybody wants to know" about my grandfather. Who was everybody? It had seemed clever to me in my arrogant twenties to cut off contact with all and any of the childhood mentors, distant family members and well-meaning professional do-gooders who had tried to help me since the age of eight. Why would any of them want to help me now? I picked up one of the PAYG mobile phones we had bought at an Asda in Cardiff and called my solicitor on his private line.

"Sir John Hannay for Mr Wethers."

"Yes, Sir John."

She put me through.

"Young Hannay, how the devil are you, my boy."

"I'm well, sir."

"You know how much I love being sirred by a peer of the realm."

I smiled. Bizarre though it may seem and despite my having ignored them for ten years or more, my solicitor and his wife were the nearest thing to family I'd had since the age of eight. "I can't remember how many times I have told you that a baronet is not a peer, Uncle Marcus. How's Aunt Mary?"

"She's well, John. She's very well. Now I'm glad you did decide to call out of the blue as I had been wondering how to get in touch with you myself. Couple of pieces of news for you."

"Oh?"

"No, no, peers of the realm first."

I mock sighed. I heard him chuckle. He really did sound delighted to hear from me. An unaccustomed sense of guilt crept across my self–obsessed consciousness.

"Well, I was just thinking that it was about time I pulled myself together and moved back to the Manor so I wondered where we were with the current tenants?"

"Pull himself together? The top trader at BTD, Michelin star restaurateur by thirty-one and he needs to pull himself together?"

"Well, that was over four years ago, you know, and anyway how did you know all that?"

"How did I know all that, did he say? How did I…? Look, young John, you don't seriously think we haven't been keeping tabs on you. I even discovered a couple of days ago that you aren't in the flat any more, which frankly is a good thing – too many morbid associations. Right now, my news; the most recent tenants in the Manor have been an absolute pain in the backside. I have no idea how your land agent, Mallin, let them in. Your tenant farmer…"

"Jack Cartwright, from Home Farm?"

"That's the chappie. He actually called me a fortnight ago – I could hear his wife in the background prompting him."

I smiled. Jack Cartwright's wife, Joan, was a much-loved character from my childhood – fiercely protective of me and the only woman who'd been allowed to hug me in public despite the dreadful embarrassment. Marcus Wethers continued.

"Said he was hearing bad things. Heard they'd done some alterations without permission and tried to dig up the flagstones in the kitchen and they kept on asking damn fool questions of all the old folk in the village about when your grandfather lived there. I was going to turf them out at the end of their year anyway, but this gives me the perfect opportunity. I'll chuck 'em out before the next quarter day so you can have the place back pretty much whenever."

I felt a wave of pleasure build up from my stomach to my lungs and heart. Home! I had a home. I could go home! But his next words swept the wave away.

"The other thing was that I had a strange visit from a man who claimed to know you. He said he had been round to see you at your flat, that you had behaved very strangely, attacked him, robbed him of his phone and run off."

I started to pace.

"He wasn't willing to give me his name, so I read him the riot act and showed him the door. Next thing was I got a call from one my least favourite firms of Solicitors, Troth Law. Told me his client was willing to drop charges if you returned a phone you had stolen. I asked him if he regularly went around accusing baronets of robbery with violence and that I would sue whomever this man was for very serious damages if I heard another peep out of him and that I didn't appreciate calls from shady lawyers who represented nameless slanderers.

"I think that shocked him as he had been expecting some harmless old buffer who dealt in inheritances. He said that his client may have got his story wrong and that he would check it again with Mr Medina. He rang off damn quick after that."

I said nothing.

"John, are you in trouble?"

"When have I ever not been, Uncle Marcus?"

"Hmmm. Well, what can I do to help?"

"Nothing at the moment, thanks. I'm in hiding. I'm as safe as I can be."

"Do you want me to mention this to you know who, John?"

I had been wondering if he would ask that question. 'You know who' was the now retired head of MI5.

"I think you'd better, but only to keep a watching brief. It's been almost thirty years and I have to find an answer. I'd better go."

"You take care young man."

"Uncle Marcus…"

"Yes, John?"

"I'm sorry."

I disconnected and looked round to see three pairs of eyes watching me. "He's not my Uncle really. He's the family solicitor. That's his private line. Only three clients have that number. No one could trace it. He used to advise MI5. Look it's OK, really."

The doubt was still there.

"So what was that all about?" Palmer was not happy.

I explained why I had phoned him. "We have a name now, Palmer."

Palmer stopped looking suspicious. "Which is?"

"Medina."

He picked up his iPad and tapped at the screen.

"Yes, yes, yes. You little baronety beauty, you. What an idiot."

"Who, me?"

"No. Medina. The password is D E M A I N."

"No."

"Yes. Now piss off while I see what I've got here."

He sat down, totally absorbed in his work. I sat in the garden as the blackness hung over my head and thought about the train wreck of my childhood and whether I should just get up and walk out on all these people who seemed to want to help me... until a yell came from the house. Palmer was excited.

"Look."

We looked. On his screen was a 3D image slowly revolving. It appeared to be a green semi–translucent tablet of some sort with tiny writing on it. We huddled round the screen. I stared. One side was in hieroglyphs – classical Mandarin according to Anna – and on the other there was an inscription in what looked like Latin. I squinted at it. It was Latin. "Anna, what was your grandfather's name?"

"Valdemar Haraldsen, why?"

"Oh, OK. Must be just a coincidence then. It says; 'Marius Haraldsen, otirorus haec scripsit thesauro felciter invento.' God!"

Robbi glowered at me.

"Sorry – rough translation: 'Marius Haraldsen, being about to die and having fortunately', no, 'happily, found his treasure, has written this text.' The date is October 1919 or something. I can never work out Roman numerals."

They stared at me. They stared at the screen. Palmer spoke first. "You're kidding, right?"

Robbi peered at the writing. "Treasure?"

Anna, surprisingly kept her head. She was staring at the screen. I felt I had to say something. "Sorry, Anna, I just thought it might be a relation of yours."

"Marius Haraldsen was my great grandfather. He was a gold prospector in Africa and in China. I'd better translate the Mandarin."

CHAPTER NINE

The next four days were restorative. I walked alone on the high, windy moor and, with Robbi or Anna cycled on two rickety bikes down tiny, sunken lanes with primroses still in flower in the high hedgerows, sat on the edges of cornfields, stared at the sea. The sun shone. I turned my normal sallow olive colour and Robbi turned from golden to golden brown. Anna stayed inside or under hats. Apart the fact that I was in hiding from an obsessive killer who had stalked me for almost thirty years I had not a care in the world. The blackness lifted.

On the fifth day I detected tension. Palmer was snapping at the world in general. Anna had printed off a list of the hieroglyphs and was staring at them with an almost manic concentration. I was genuinely curious. "What are they?"

"Fucking numbers. They're just numbers. Look"

I'd never heard her swear before. She drew the appropriate number by each glyph and threw the pieces of paper across the table as Robbi walked back in. She glanced down.

"Oh, nice, a Fibonacci curve."

"What?" yelled Palmer and Anna together.

Robbi rolled her eyes. "The numbers beside your hieroglyphs – if you arrange them like so…" She moved the papers into a different order. "… they make a Fibonacci curve – 8, 13, 21, 34, 55…"

"You genius, Roberta Lord!" Palmer was all but dancing with excitement.

"I know. And I've uncorked the wine."

The tension was gone. I stared at the numbers. "So, Palmer, why the excitement?"

"Unless I am very mistaken, we have cracked the bastard's encryption. It probably works with his DEMAIN password."

I retired to the kitchen and cooked. Two hours later we were staring at Palmer's screen as the closed files opened themselves to our gaze. There were diagrams and what looked like maps and lists. Palmer sighed with contentment.

"Data."

His phone rang and he answered it, turning the speaker on. "Yes?"

"Hello, Mr Palmer. Do you know who this is?"

It was that soft voice with the Irish lilt. I felt my vision start to blur. Robbi gasped, grabbed Palmer's arm and shook her head frantically at him. Through the gathering haze, part of my consciousness recalled how Keith at Continental Atlantic had said the clients loved her because she knew all their voices. This was a voice she had heard before – in my little glass walled office in the City. Palmer stared at her, puzzled. "What? Who is this?"

The voice laughed. "Dear oh dear, Mr Palmer, don't consider a career on the stage will you? Is Hannay with you?"

"Listen, I don't know what this is about, but I don't like your tone of voice. Who are you and what do you want?"

"So many questions: so little time. You know what I want. Are you there, John?"

I had to speak to him. I had to stop myself speaking to him. The room was rocking and spinning. My mouth was dry. I tried to speak.

"John? John Hannay? John, acushla. Where are you, John?"

I was on my knees reaching towards the phone, sweat pouring down my face, dripping from the end of my nose. Then Palmer spoke.

"Medina."

There was a pause and then the voice, no longer soft. "So you have made progress, Mr Palmer. Now, I am calling at this time of evening for a reason. Turn on your TV."

"We don't have a TV."

"No matter. Listen." He must have held the phone towards his own radio as I heard the beeps of Radio 4 and the announcer's voice. The phone buzzed – he had moved it even closer to the TV's speaker. "The news headlines. A bomb blast rocked the Mayfair area of Central London at seven p.m. this evening, injuring thirty-one people. No deaths have been reported and no group has yet claimed responsibility. The blast which was close to the Saudi Arabian and Israeli embassies was…"

The radio was switched off. He spoke again. "Do you understand now the lengths we will go to, Mr Palmer? Is Sir John there?"

Robbi shook her head violently again. The voice on the phone sighed.

"John, you will be at the Duke of York's monument on Pall Mall one pm tomorrow. Do I need to say you must be alone? If you are not there, many people will die at exactly five minutes past one. Many. Goodbye."

"Wait."

Palmer was staring down at me shaking on the floor in front of him. "We're not on the mainland. We have a boat, but it will take us twenty-four hours just to get back and then another day to drive to London."

Nothing. Palmer leaned over the table. The connection was still there.

"Very well. You would not be so stupid as to risk the deaths of so many people. I have waited a long time for the information. I can wait another twenty–four hours. Tuesday – one pm. Please don't try and be clever."

The connection was terminated. Anna looked at Palmer. "Could they have traced the call?"

"If they did, they would have found we were in Hong Kong."

Robbi was on her knees beside me. "What was it, John?"

"The voice." I shook my head to clear it. Robbi grabbed my face with both hands and stared at me, willing me to concentrate.

"The voice. It… it…"

Without warning she slapped my face hard. The ring on her middle finger caught my cheek. The pain helped. Something came back.

"Someone hurt me… in the kitchen of my mother's flat. He said something. I can't hear that yet. He said something. He did something to me. He hurt me."

The beating of my heart began to slow, the hammering in my head to fade. I looked up at them. "That man on the phone – I think he and someone else knocked on the door of my mother's flat. I opened it and they took me into the kitchen. They hurt me. I – I can't remember."

"Acushla," murmured Anna. "Irish for darling."

I nodded. I looked at Robbi. "You hit me."

"So?"

"Well." Anna spoke. "As the man said, we have made progress."

CHAPTER TEN

We didn't bother to pack this time – just a change of clothes, the computers and what Palmer called the materiel. The Sunday evening traffic crawled into London over the elevated section of the M4.

"You haven't said where we're going, Palmer."

"No, I haven't. It isn't a twee cottage this time. It's in West Ealing."

Argyle Road is a half–and–half street – solid Victorian and Edwardian houses fetching a couple of million or more and their run-down brothers and sisters, the remnants of bedsitter land. The flat was in the remnants – two bedrooms, a kitchenette and an avocado-coloured bathroom suite.

"I've been thinking."

We all looked at Robbi. "We need help and I think we should bring my brother Dave in on this."

Palmer's hackles began to rise. "Why?"

I answered. "Because he's a regimental sergeant major in the SAS."

Palmer looked thoughtful. Robbi used the house phone. I did some shopping on Ealing Broadway. When I got back Dave was there. He looked at me – not in a very friendly way. "Right, Palmer here's filled me in on the situation. Your problem is you've got no battle plan."

I half smiled. *"He's a cheery old card, grunted Harry to Jack."*

"You're not the only one who's read war poetry, John. Do you know the place?"

"Of course. It's well selected. Long lines of sight and no cover."

He nodded. "You were in the Army?"

"Sandhurst and short-term commission – Queen's Royal Lancers."

"OK, they're going to have to take you. We know that. We can't risk this maniac blowing up half of Mayfair. So, we need to know where you'll be taken, so we have to have you followed."

Palmer raised a finger. "We have to assume that at the very least John will be given a polygraph and at the worst, tortured to find out what we know. It's going to be safest for him if we do the planning without him hearing."

I cooked. They talked. Dave phoned.

That evening saw people arrive and depart with instructions from Dave. A stick–on white board on the wall became a complex of arrows and numbers. Palmer was impressed. The next day, the pattern repeated itself and by the time the evening meal had been eaten, Dave was checking weaponry. He looked in my direction.

"OK, John. I'm going in a minute. We have a plan. That's all you need to know, but remember, they're going to treat you badly, very badly, so be prepared for everything. It's much less easy to frighten someone who is ready for it than someone who has no idea of what's going to happen next. They'll probably strip you and do a full body search and maybe a scan and then you'll get the sensory deprivation treatment. Robbi says you're pretty good at concentrating. Whatever happens, never lose that concentration. Show nothing on the outside apart from fear. On the inside remember us. Treat us as your sanity."

That night was even more difficult than the last. The little flat was airless. Television noise filtered through the thin walls. I slumped in an armchair staring at a party wall, fighting the blackness. In the morning Anna sat beside Robbi, holding her hand, silent. I was ready to go at ten thirty having barely spoken to anyone. Palmer gave me the iPhone I had taken from Medina in my flat. "He won't be able to tell if I got beyond his encryption so let's hope they don't ask you about that."

I nodded, put on the cheap tracksuit that Dave had left and looked at the three of them. Palmer and I shook hands. Anna hugged me and Robbi walked down the stairs ahead of me to the front door. She spoke slowly and stiffly. "John Hannay, take care of yourself. Please."

I tried to speak, to tell her that I wanted to care for her, that I couldn't care for her, that I didn't even know how to care for another person, that I had never even cared whether I lived or died. But I didn't. I turned away and walked down the road, past the shops on the Broadway to the tube station.

At twelve thirty-four I emerged from Piccadilly tube station, turned into the bus choked thoroughfare that is Lower Regent Street and made my way down towards the realm of institutes, societies and clubs. I knew I was early, but I didn't think it would matter. It started to drizzle and the annoying chatter of a group of Hong Kong tourists was halted momentarily as Big Ben started its chime for one o'clock. On the stroke of one, a van turned down Waterloo Place and drove towards me. I waited. The group of tourists walked in front of me still chattering in Mandarin until suddenly one of the women wrenched me towards the rear door of the van where, surrounded and shielded by cheap Union Jack umbrellas, I stumbled up the back step and was thrown roughly to the floor. The doors slammed.

As my eyes became accustomed to the gloom, I could see there was a metal chair bolted to the floor. There were three men standing round the chair – all Chinese. They watched me carefully, warily. The tallest of them stepped across the van, a knife appearing in his hand. He feinted with it. I didn't have to force myself to flinch. They laughed. I had been judged harmless. The blade ripped through my clothes. They were torn off me and I stood, naked. He pointed towards to the chair. I sat. A buzzing sound made me twitch, but my head was grabbed and held still. It was an electric razor. It sliced through my hair, tugging, tearing, cutting. Within a minute my head was shaved. My pubic hair followed. My mouth was forced open. A torch was shone into my nose and ears and finally and forcibly I was lifted out of the seat, bent forward, held down and given an anal probe.

The van had still not moved. A portable scanner ran over every inch of my body. The one who seemed to be in charge had found the iPhone. He turned it on and stared at it then leaned forward and knocked on the partition behind the cab. The van finally moved forward and as it did so a bag was stuffed over my head and earphones clamped over it: sensory deprivation, just as Dave had predicted. The bag smelt bad. My groin itched where they had shaved it.

I have no clear idea how long the drive went on for, but I would guess fifteen minutes. I was beginning to feel sick with the rocking unable, as I was, to anticipate any movement or brace myself against the chair. The van stopped with a jerk. The headphones were taken off. I was led out of the back, still naked, still with the bag over my head, stumbling and half falling. Out of a garage, up stairs, through two doors, more stairs, then carpet beneath my bare feet and finally floor boards, slippery, polished floorboards, and a crackle which I recognised as the sound of a wood fire, but with a different, half remembered scent – yes, peat smoke. The bag was tugged off. I stood, blinking in the firelight.

The room was a library. Books on panelled shelves up to a high ceiling, two wingback armchairs by the hearth, a table and other straight backed, single chairs in the background. Impressionist paintings on the wall and what looked like jade in a Georgian, breakfront glass bookcase. That was all I had time to take in before a door opened and closed and I heard the sound of steps on a wooden floor – a clicking of heels meant a woman, but other steps softer, blurred – two men? I was held still, facing the fire. Stay prepared. I waited, hoping I looked suitably cowed. He spoke.

"Turn him round."

That voice from the phone – I was turned. He stood directly in front of me.

"Well, Sir John?"

I said nothing.

"You remember me, John?"

I shook my head. The voice was all I remembered – the voice from the endless phone calls. Before he started talking again, I glanced round quickly. The woman was young, tall probably, and sallow skinned, sitting in the second armchair by the fire. The other man was further back in the semi–darkness of the panelled room by the bookcase. As I was looking in his direction, he crossed his legs at the ankles and I realised with an almost physical shock that it was Harry. It made me feel as though I had a friend in the room – strange when you think that the last time I had been with him he had knocked me out.

Medina started to speak again. "No, I suppose it would have been my father who had the most impact on you twenty-eight years ago in your parent's flat. I was only eighteen, just ten years older than you, but I remember it all so well. How my daddy had killed your daddy the year before and then how he had killed your mummy, what my daddy did to you. Do you remember the pain, John? Do you remember the pain?"

His eyes had grown wider and wider, filling my vision. His voice was haunting and melodic, tuning direct into my synapses, overriding my reason, destroying my self–belief. I forced myself to fall forward, hitting my head on the floor as I did. I could see the weave in the Persian rug under my head and hear the spit and hiss of the fire, but the voice… the voice was different now – the same harmonics, the same timbre, but the melody was gone. Now it grated against my ears, the hypnotic power diminished. I crawled to my feet.

Medina laughed. "It is so sad to see how genetic inheritance can result in abject failure in three generations. Your grandfather was a great man, you know."

Was I supposed to say anything? I nodded.

"You have information that I need. You know that, don't you?"

I nodded again. I was beginning to get into my role. He stared at me. Maybe more was required. "I do now."

"Good... So"

I stared at him. I knew he wanted me for this. I knew I had what he wanted, but I didn't know what it was: or whether to tell him or even how to tell him. The information was inside me somewhere, but... Medina watched me, still smiling. He pressed a buzzer beside the fireplace. Two more Chinese men entered pushing a trolley with medical apparatus on it. A third stood beside them holding a handgun. I struggled briefly, but within seconds I was strapped to a chair. Medina tapped a syringe and I felt the sharp prick and then I floated to the ceiling where I spun, humming like a top. A vast Medina loomed beneath me and strapped pads to my forehead and chest. I could hear myself babbling answers to his questions as one of the Chinese started to interpret the Polygraph. I must be spilling it all. My vision was blurring more and more and more... and then my world went white.

I came round with my head slumped forward on my chest, dribbling down my chin. I must have groaned as Medina looked up at me sharply. He spoke to the Chinese technician who was still studying the revelations of my polygraph. "Are you using old drugs?"

The technician shook his head. He unstrapped me and I staggered to my feet. "Well. Perhaps you are stronger than you look."

He stared at the polygraph results. "You appear to have no understanding of what I am after. How interesting."

He picked up the phone I had stolen at the end of my earlier life. "I understood your colleague to be a mathematician. He should have recognised a Fibonacci Curve when he saw one, but you have just told us that he didn't even crack my encryption code. Dear, oh dear."

He stared at me then turned to the woman and spoke in what I assumed was Mandarin. The young woman stood up and walked towards me, stopped inches away and stared at me expressionlessly. Medina spoke again. She moved nearer to me, her body all but touching my chest. I swayed back. She gave no indication of any emotion at all. Medina laughed. At another word from him she walked back across the floor and stood motionless in front of him. He looked at me. "Soon, you will be like this. Or like your friend, Harry. I know you have recognised him."

I found my voice. "He is not my friend."

That seemed to amuse Medina even more. He gestured towards the two Chinese. "Take him away. I will see him in two days' time." And to me. "I'm beginning to get impatient, John."

I saw the woman kneel in front of him as I was hustled to the door. I was taken up another two flights of stairs – this house was enormous – and pushed into a small attic room. The plastic ties round my wrists were cut. I was hurled to the floor and I heard the door close.

The room was bare apart from a washbasin in the corner. There was no window, only a sealed and blacked out skylight far too high to reach. I turned on the tap in the washbasin. No water. I sat down. I lay down. I slept. There was nothing else to do.

When I awoke I was still alone. I was grateful for this. If part of Medina's plan was to frighten me through solitude it was a waste of his time. I had been alone since the age of eight. I may have stayed there for two days, but it was hard to tell as I was pretty sure the lights went on and off at random times. I wasn't fed or watered. The room smelt. I smelt worse. By the end of what I believed to be the second day I was looking up into the blackness close above me. Eventually they came – the same two Chinese men. I was weak, hungry and tired and they had to drag me down the two flights of stairs to the library. The room was exactly the same. The same fire burned. The same players were ready to perform the same roles. Medina looked into my eyes again and spoke in that same half–remembered, haunting voice. I could feel that my defences were weaker. I was on my knees, sweat pouring off the stubble on my head when he stopped. "I can wait, Hannay. Can you?"

To the men. "Hold him still."

It was a repeat performance of the first day, the same needle, the same drug, the same spinning white blankness and, so far as I could tell, the same result. Only now I felt ill, not just weak, tired and hungry – ill. My heart had started beating too fast, pounding, missing, halting. Medina studied me dispassionately, and motioned for the Chinese to unstrap me from the chair. He stepped towards me and hit me backhanded. I fell to my side, blood dripping from my lip.

"Pick him up."

They pulled me to my feet. He stepped in front of me, still watching me. I tensed for the next blow, but he turned away and I breathed out just as his fist swung round and caught me in the throat. I collapsed, swinging by my arms between my two captors. The choking pain faded and I could look at him again. Somehow the pain he was inflicting diminished him, reduced his omnipotence. I didn't believe this was part of his plan. This was pleasure. I smiled at the thought forgetting how closely I was being watched.

"You think this is funny." He screamed at me, control completely gone as he rained punch after punch into my face, chest and abdomen. Well, that had worked. He was so angry now that the attack was entirely unscientific. None of these blows hurt anything like so much as the first two. The world was spinning faster, whiter. Soon I would be unconscious and that too would be good. I half heard his voice.

"Take him back."

I was dragged back upstairs to the filthy, empty room. One of the Chinese men threw a litre bottle of water at me when his colleague had turned away. I grabbed it and forced myself to drink slowly. I slept again. By now I had lost all sense of time and I knew I was beginning to lose my sense of self. This time the solitude hurt. The pain subsided to a dull throb, but whatever the drug they had used on me had been it had left its mark – strange hallucinations, sudden sweats, bouts of erratic, racing heart beats, empty retching, the disgusting remnants of diarrhoea from an empty bowel. I washed my legs with a trickle of water from the plastic bottle.

Perhaps another day or maybe even two days passed before they came for me again. I was very weak now, shaking with what felt like some kind of fever. The water had not lasted long and I had not eaten since the night before I came here. They carried me down the stairs this time. I must say I didn't envy them their task and I found myself apologising to them for my vile state. I was a stinking wreck with sores developing down the back of my thighs. They hosed me down in a bathroom.

The same library, the same people, the same voice: I was going to break this time. Despair is a potent force and I was wallowing in my own unfathomable slough. I was, most assuredly, not my grandfather. Medina watched me closely from his chair. I swayed, barely able to distinguish the vertical from the horizontal, peering at him through blackened, crusted eyes. He laughed, rose gracefully, and prowled towards me caressing me with that voice. I listened, hypnotised once more and then, without warning, the caressing voice switched languages. I scarcely noticed the change at first, but key words broke through. Beyond my control, my body jerked.

He paused, walking slowly round me, studying me, head tilted to one side. He spoke to one of the Chinese, holding his hand out for a syringe. He tapped it, raised it, squirted it and went back to watching me. I peered at him again. He smiled. "Hold him."

He turned the syringe in his hand. "This is Propranolol, an adrenal hormone blocker. It will make remembering much easier for you, John, so much easier."

I had no idea what he meant and I couldn't even begin to struggle. Again, I felt the prick of the needle. He spoke... I half heard him. Then he was behind me, speaking now in a language I had never heard before and suddenly – no flash, no blinding light, no alarm bell – it was there again, what I had fought to forget for twenty-eight long and solitary years.

It had been his father laughing as he showed me my mother dead and rotting on the floor of her bedroom and now, I remembered him too – the eighteen–year–old boy who stood in front of me grinning while his father took his place behind me. The curtain was torn back and the window to my sub–conscious, closed since I was eight, was opened once again. I knew without understanding what it was I had to say before he raped me as his father had beaten, slashed and raped my eight-year-old self, before the awful, tearing pain – when I had refused to speak for fear of letting my poor, dead parents down – began again.

The words tumbled out of my mouth – sentence after sentence. I was hallucinating. I had no idea what I was saying, what language I was speaking, but I knew it was the words my father had made me learn from the age of four. I could see my father's face again for the first time since he had died, his kind, gentle eyes watching me as we went through the strange, unexplained lesson again and again and again. I saw everything through a thickening haze of fatigue, sickness, pounding heart, hunger and remembered pain. I came to the end of the first speech my father had taught me and paused – something else was there too. I opened my mouth and croaked again in what must have been Mandarin as the two men beside me stiffened and listened intently, one putting a digital recorder in front of my mouth as I spoke.

Medina saw this and shouted at them to stop. They ignored him. He strode toward them shouting. I kept speaking. The Chinese man to my left raised his gun, pointing it at Medina. I knew I was hallucinating now as I could hear pops and bangs in my head. I stopped talking. The pops and bangs continued. They all heard it now unless they just were creatures of my mind. But mummy would wake up soon and I wouldn't have to go back to the school I hated so much.

The man who had thrown me the water in my attic room ran in shouting at the two Chinese holding me. They raced to the door and as it opened, I realised that the pops and bangs were real. This was the rescue. I staggered towards the door, but couldn't make it. I tripped on the rug and fell giggling to the floor. I wanted to remind Harry that this was just like when we had first met. I struggled to roll over and tell him and Medina's blow with the fire iron missed me by an inch. Then Harry was behind him grabbing at the iron and the woman was striking at Harry and then there was a crack and a sucking of air out of the room.

"Flash bang," yelled Harry.

Medina turned away his face contorted with anger. He grabbed the young woman and together they ran to the far side of the room where a portion of library wall came away revealing a dimly lit passage. They got in and with scream of pure rage he pressed a hidden button and the door swung to leaving the book filled shelves juddering.

I could hear a hissing in my head and I shook it to clear my mind. The hissing continued. I swayed to my feet. Harry was staring at the wall where Medina had left.

"Oh, Christ. Poison gas!"

He stared round wildly and then leapt to the door. I assumed he was leaving me like he had before, but instead, with Medina's fire iron, he hammered at the glass on what, even in my state of delirium, I realised was a smoke alarm. He broke the glass and water began to hiss down on our heads. He grabbed and pushed me until I was directly beneath a jet. Blessed water. I turned my face up towards it and started automatically to wash myself, letting the water run into my mouth, over my head, streams of white appearing under the dirt. Harry stared at me in amazement and then started to laugh. I realised I was laughing too.

The door crashed back on its hinges and there was a gas masked, crouching man in combat fatigues, covered by a Kevlar waistcoat, waving a machine pistol at us. We held our hands up above our heads. The crouching man was yelling at us. We knelt. This wasn't a rescue. This was the end. The crouching man straightened to his feet, towering over us, tearing off his mask. "Fuck's sake you two morons, will you get out of here now. The water will stop soon."

It was Dave. It was the rescue. Harry helped me to the door and I staggered down the first flight of stairs.

Two flights down the battle was still raging. Dave's men were holding off the Chinese, leaving an escape route for us. But this wasn't what should happen. I grabbed Dave's arm. "No, Dave. Let me talk to them."

"The hell you talking about?"

Battle madness. He didn't want to stop this fight. "Mr Lord, cease fire!"

Dave blinked, stiffened, all but saluted and with a muttered "Sir" turned to yell at his men. "Cease fire! Cease. Fire. Now"

I pulled myself to my feet. "Harry, you speak Mandarin. Tell them that this is a stand-off. Tell them this is a fight they will not win, that these men are from our SAS."

Harry stared at me uncertainly and then began to shout across the landing. He looked at me again.

"Tell them that John Hannay will repeat the words he spoke in front of Medina provided they leave this house immediately. Do it Harry!"

Harry spoke again and there was silence – then a single word.

Harry nodded at me. The man who had thrown me a bottle of water stepped forward with the recorder. I pulled myself upright and recited the second half of my father's lesson once more. The other Chinese came out, guns held loosely in their hands, staring up at me. I finished. I closed my eyes.

"What have I said?"

Their leader shook his head and now, guns held more tightly, they backed away down the stairs carrying their wounded. Dave's men stepped forward.

"Dave."

"Yes, John."

But the world was spinning white again. Dave wrapped me in a blanket, swung me over his shoulder in a fireman's lift and my last sight of that cursed house was an upside down, bouncing view of the stairs and the flames beginning to lick at the wall hangings a floor above us. Outside in the street I forced my eyes open once again, squinting round blearily in the bright, white light. Good God, I was still in Mayfair. The sun was still shining. People were still walking around, leading normal lives with normal worries and normal homes, wholly unaware of the existence of the house of perversion and torture on Mount Street. As Dave swung me round into the back of his van I saw Anna walking towards me smiling and behind her… No.

"Anna, no! Anna!"

But my voice, I realised, was hardly above a whisper. No one heard. No one noticed. At that moment I was just excess baggage and the Rolls Royce which had raced silently off the road and on to the pavement, caught her in the centre of her back and tossed her high into the air.

CHAPTER ELEVEN

I opened my eyes. The light was too much. I closed them again. But there had been something blonde there. Robbi? I opened my eyes again slowly. Blonde, yes and something black and then a long, pink tongue licked my nose. A pink tongue that smelt of dog food. I began to focus. A Golden Retriever was smiling at me in an amiable, interested, doggy way, his tail waving elegantly behind him. He backed away and sat on the foot of someone slumped in an armchair by the bed. The someone woke and spoke. "Oh, Rufus."

I watched her from half open eyes. I think her smile must have taken four seconds to be complete. "Hello, John Richard."

I swallowed and croaked. "Hello, Roberta Jane."

She looked tired: black rings beneath her eyes, lines beneath the rings. She stood up, stretched, pulled a thermometer from a sterile jar, placed it in my ear and took my wrist in her hand – Roberta Nightingale. She looked at the results and smiled again. "You're getting better, Sir John. Another two weeks and we may even have you back on solids."

She kept smiling at me. I managed a lip twist back and croaked again.

"How long have I been out of it?"

"Five days. You've been very ill. We – we thought you were dying."

"We?"

"You're at your Uncle Marcus' – which reminds me."

She walked to the door. "Aunt Mary? Aunt Mary? He's awake."

I heard the footsteps coming up the stairs and Aunt Mary's heavy breathing as she came in. "Well, well, well, finally. What a relief! You, young man, have given us all sleepless nights – Roberta more than anyone. The girl's a natural nurse. How's his temperature, dear?"

"Right down, Aunt Mary."

There was a catch in her voice. Aunt Mary smiled. "Well, John. Well! I don't know where to start. Roberta hasn't left your bedside for five days. I'm not sure whether I've been more worried about you or her! Talk about determined too. We were confronted with her and her enormous brother on our doorstep on Tuesday evening. She'd managed to extract our address from the office. And she had you up here in your old bedroom, bathed, sterilised and in bed before we knew what was going on. Then she demanded a doctor. Then she refused to let him take you to hospital. Then she told Marcus that no one could know you were here until you were ready to talk. Then she moved in."

Robbi smiled at this and kissed Aunt Mary on the cheek. "I did say pretty please, though."

I looked at them looking at me. I closed my eyes. "I'm going to doze for a little, if I'm allowed."

I slept.

* * *

I was woken by the late evening sun streaming in through the window. I blinked, squinted and blinked again. Then I heard a giggle.

"I thought if I opened the curtain, you'd wake up."

I swallowed. It didn't hurt that much.

"What happened to Roberta Nightingale?"

"She got bored and buggered off with the doctor."

She walked towards the bed. I smiled up at her contentedly. Then I remembered. "The bomb!"

"What bomb?"

"Don't muck around, Robbi. The bomb Medina threatened to set off."

"Relax, big boy. We had it covered."

"What do you mean, 'covered'?"

"Do you remember anything of that last day at Medina's?"

"Bits."

"Well, when we got you in the van you were shaking and muttering and then you suddenly got the strength of about three men and screamed at Dave."

I groaned. "Did I? Oh dear. What did he do?"

"He was quite mild considering. He held you down and then he yelled at me. And then of course Robbi saved the day." She huffed on her fingernails and buffed them on her shirtfront.

"Robbi."

"Yes?"

"The bomb."

"Yes."

"Robbi!"

She smiled that mischievous smile. "You know, it's been so boring having had no one to wind up for the last week. All right, all right, keep your stubble on. Incidentally your pubes look dead funny – all short and bristly."

I breathed out and tried to look exasperated. "So?"

"So, I realised the word you were saying was 'bomb'. I told Dave. He said fuck a lot and then Palmer grabbed his little computer thingy and ran inside and Dave said fuck a lot more and ran in after him and they came out about five minutes later carrying all sorts of hardware and stuff and we drove off. You were out for the count by then, but Palmer was looking very pleased with himself and Dave had stopped saying fuck."

I sighed and tried not to grin stupidly. I changed the subject. "Where's Palmer now – and Anna?"

A shadow crossed Robbi's face. "Don't you remember the car?"

"What car?"

She grimaced. "The Rolls Royce that drove at on her on the pavement. You tried to warn her. I heard you, but no one else did. I was just watching you and by the time I looked round…"

Yes, it was there – a faint, awful recollection of a body bouncing off a car bonnet.

"Jesus, no, Robbi. Is she dead?"

She shook her head, tears brimming in her eyes. "Nearly but not quite. She was flown back to Sweden in a private air ambulance. I've phoned every day. She's still in Intensive Care."

I managed another breath. "Palmer?"

"He's laying low."

"Harry?"

"Laying even lower."

A distant noise sounded from the stairs below. I raised an eyebrow. God that took so much effort. She smiled. "Dave."

I waited until a big shadow filled the door. I held out the hand without the drip and he shook it gently.

"How do you feel?"

"Better, thanks."

He nodded slowly. "You don't look it and you aren't."

He stared at me for a few seconds. Robbi sat on the bed beside me watching her brother. He looked from her to me. "So? What now?"

"Now? Now I'm going to go home, Dave."

I took more breaths. I was so tired. "I'm going to have to talk to some government people I should imagine, although Uncle Marcus will probably hold them off for a while. I doubt that Medina will have any more forces together yet so I want to go home before the next round – there's going to be a next round, Dave, whatever happens to poor Anna."

"I know." He looked at his huge hands, turning them over and examining them as if he'd never seen them before. "You got lucky this last time, John. I've kind of done this for a living as you might say. Amateurs sometimes get lucky because they do things that professionals don't expect. Next time they'll be expecting it and you. And, unless I am very much mistaken, Medina's also got whatever the information was he needed out of you so all that's left now is his final revenge and, correct me if I'm wrong, John, but he *will* want revenge."

I nodded. "You're forgetting one thing, Dave. He's not a professional either."

He nodded in turn.

* * *

Two days later, I was sitting by the French windows in Aunt Mary's drawing room watching her and Robbi weeding the entirely weed free flower beds when the hall door opened to admit Uncle Marcus and a tall, elegant man in his late sixties wearing civil service mufti – hacking jacket, corduroy trousers and brogues.

"Sir Ian Hamilton," said Uncle Marcus.

I nodded. This was to be expected – an unofficial visit from the retired head of MI5 was easier to manage than an interrogation by the awkward squad of SO15. I pulled myself to my feet to shake his hand. Robbi saw the movement and came running in like a nanny who thinks her charge is about to wee on the rug. She smiled at the new arrival and went across to kiss him on the cheek. "Hallo, Ian."

"Roberta, my dear. How are you now that your patient is on the mend?"

I shook my head. Clearly it was all getting beyond me. This seemed to have become the Roberta Lord story and I just had the walk on part for which I had always hoped.

"Anyone care to tell me what is going on?"

Uncle Marcus smiled. "Well, while you were upstairs attention seeking, Roberta thought I should make contact with Ian as she was convinced that you were still at risk."

"Did she? Am I?"

Sir Ian took up the tale. "Well as you may imagine I really do loathe being bothered by beautiful young women with sob stories and I have to say that my first thought was that she should have been sectioned. But when I looked into it a bit and started to investigate Mr Medina, I have to say that it all started to look very strange, very strange indeed."

He stood up and started to pace the polished floorboards. "There are some things I can't tell you, but having done some digging that I must admit someone should have done before, I can say that Dominick Medina may be a considerable threat to the country. He's involved in some serious Foreign Exchange trading."

Finally, a subject that meant something to me; I could contribute to the conversation. "How serious?"

"Ah yes, one forgets you were the star City trader. Let's just say that he is not quite in the George Soros league, but that if he had his hands on a few billion of liquid assets he very well could be."

"Betting against Sterling?"

"Yes, in a big way. Of course our political masters claim that the low value of Sterling against the dollar and the Euro is all a part of their world beating, post Brexit strategy, but as ever, they have little or no idea of what they are doing and the word economics is merely a four syllable word tacked on to philosophy and politics in their inadequate degree courses."

Sir Ian paused at the open French windows with his back to the room. "Afternoon, Mary, garden's looking in fine fettle."

He swung back round. "Now where, young man, would Dominick Medina get his hands on a few billion in liquid assets?"

I kept a blank face.

"The point is that he must be stopped, John. Your co–operation is requested, please."

He studied me for a full five seconds. He wasn't satisfied with what he saw in my face, but he was far too much of a professional to show any annoyance. I decided to dissemble. Apart from horse riding, fencing with foils, and ballroom dancing, it was one of the few extracurricular talents I had developed since the age of eight.

"I understand sir. I'm ready to co–operate whenever you want. If you don't mind, though, I did want to spend a couple of days at my place in the country – show Roberta round to say thank you to her for nursing me – see what needs doing. You know."

Robbi and Uncle Marcus hadn't stirred. Sir Ian nodded. "You're going to get a visit from a, er, civil servant, tomorrow. He'll be a pain. It's his job. Put up with it please and try and sound co–operative without saying too much."

He walked towards the door. He looked back at me over his shoulder. "Just like today, eh? Bye Roberta, Marcus. Give my apologies to Mary for not staying longer."

We waited for the click of the front door. I looked up. "Sorry, Uncle Marcus."

"Nothing to apologise for, dear boy. Ian's a wise old stick though, so watch out for squalls tomorrow."

He sighed and crossed his legs, hitching the trouser up to avoid bagging at the knee. "John, we knew something awful had happened to you when you were eight and I knew Ian then and I discussed it with him. My father, when he finally retired, passed on some bits of your story you may not even know about so I know all of this goes back to your grandfather, but I think it's time we exchanged information."

He cleared his throat. "And I don't want you to get hold of the wrong end of the stick on this one, John, but you pushing everyone away from the age of eighteen is what has led to this current debacle."

I stirred uneasily. He waved a hand at me dismissively and steepled his fingers. "You know that my father was your grandfather's lawyer and you and I inherited each other. What you don't know is that my father was witness to a meeting chaired by your grandfather at the beginning of the Second World War. At that meeting your grandfather made his five closest friends swear to protect his son – your father, Peter John – and his heirs from the Medina threat. Without their permission I cannot reveal their names – and anyway one of them is extremely hard to track down at any time of the year although I've just put out the word for him…"

I sat forward. "There was more than one, then? I know one of them was Valdemar Haraldsen. Anna's told me her part of the story. The trouble is she didn't know why she was looking for me, just that she had to find me."

Uncle Marcus un–steepled his fingers and decided to cross his ankles instead. "All I know is that the five of them failed to protect your father. I don't know why, I'm afraid.

"I do not believe your mother knew of the existence of this group. When she moved out of Fosse Manor and into the flat, I believe the protection failed almost completely. I say almost, because you are still alive. Now dear boy, your turn."

I gathered my thoughts into a thread and started my story, not from the beginning, but from the most recent postscript and what damage Medina could do if... There was another long silence at the end.

"Well. Goodness gracious. If it weren't for the fact that Roberta is clearly quite sane and you are sitting here looking like death warmed up, I would be calling for the men in white coats."

He swirled the dregs round in the bottom of his teacup. "And this treasure, this gold; you believe that he will use it for what, John, if he can find it, that is?"

I shrugged and guessed. "He's a fund manager, not one of the very big ones, but certainly big enough to do some massive damage to Sterling if he really went for it and in doing so, wreck what's left of the British economy."

Uncle Marcus looked expectant. "Do you mean some kind of cyber-attack or something on the currency?"

I shook my head. I always forgot how ignorant even intelligent people were about the City's activities and processes. "No, not at all. He could do it by simply trading cash – bog standard, fractional reserve banking and margin–based leveraging. If he's got $10 billion in liquid assets, he could easily leverage it up to $30 billion. With that he could do serious damage especially if he has ways of getting out some disinformation out into the markets."

"I think I can speak for both of us in saying we have no idea what that meant, except that we have to take your word for it that he could screw up the economy."

Uncle Marcus' car arrived before I had to explain and he departed to his office taking Aunt Mary to a lunch with friends at Fortnum's. Despite the heat of the day, I began to shake and shiver. I felt the black delirium begin to sweep over me and once again I was back in that haunted library and then further and further back and in my mother's flat with the torturers. Robbi sat beside me, bathing my head with cold flannels, stroking Rufus and taking my temperature and pulse.

It passed.

She sat on the floor propped against the sofa. I lay propped up on the cushions. We argued. Two hours later we were hunched over papers spread across the dining room table and still we argued. But by the time the others returned I think I was winning. Robbi had called Palmer. I had spoken to Dave. I had also spoken to my 'wealth manager' and arranged to transfer some money – quite a lot of money – into a special account in Robbi's name. That was mainly what we had been arguing about. Robbi didn't want any of my money.

CHAPTER TWELVE

At nine forty–two the next day, when the doorbell rang, we were prepared. In the hall Robbi greeted the visitors, introducing herself as my assistant, walking through in front of them into the drawing room where I was sitting in an armchair looking pale and not particularly interesting, with Marcus Wethers reading legal papers at the table.

Now this was a shock. A thin civil servant had entered. He hadn't changed a bit – thin all over, thin nose, thin lips, thin shoulders.

"Hello, Hannay."

"ffitch? What are you doing here? And who, may I ask, is your friend?"

"Superintendent Walker of SO15."

Superintendent Walker could have doubled for a 1960s B Movie, American G–man – five foot nine inches, crew cut hair and a face that looked as though it had been badly sculpted from Breccias. Robbi walked over to me holding out some papers – blank as it happened – and my phone. She leaned forward giving them a look at her long, long legs above her short, short skirt. I took a photo of the visitors while their view was distracting, pretended to skim the blank papers and passed them and the phone back to her.

Robbi swung back round. "Tea or coffee, gentlemen?"

Orders were placed and as she left the room, I performed introductions. "Julian ffitch, Marcus Wethers, my lawyer. ffitch and I were at school together, Uncle Marcus."

ffitch stared at me. He had never liked me at Eton and I can't say I could blame him. I had found him pretty loathsome and hadn't bothered to disguise the fact. Marcus Wethers cleared his throat. "Gentlemen, I won't insult your intelligence by pretending you weren't expected, but I am a busy man so I'd be grateful if you could inform me what you want to discuss with my client so I can get to my office."

ffitch bridled. "I am here representing Her Majesty's Government and I expect your client to answer some questions fully and immediately."

We continued to stare at each other in silence until Robbi came back in with the coffee, put more papers in front of me and went to sit at the table. I looked at her neat notes.

1. Palmer says fffffffffitch works for the Treasury – Political Adviser on currency reserves and trading.
2. He says there is no Superintendent Walker at SO15 (That's Special Branch in case you didn't know).
3. He also says he looks like an Alan Cummins from MI5.
4. ffffffffffffffffffffffffffitch hasn't looked at me once. Is he gay?
5. Did I mention that I'm not wearing any panties?

I didn't dare look at her. ffitch started. "We have had a series of complaints about your behaviour in relation to someone who is working closely with HMG and whose co–operation we value greatly."

"Who's 'we', ffitch?"

"That is not for you to know at this time, Hannay."

Uncle Marcus interjected before I could tell ffitch to ffuck off. "Mr ffitch, Superintendent Walker, are either of you gentlemen aware of the legal niceties involved in negotiations of this nature?"

He raised his eyebrows at them. "This is not the first time that my client has been subject to groundless accusations by Mr Dominick Medina."

ffitch fflinched.

"My client is happy to share as much information as he can with you concerning Mr Medina, however you should be aware that I am about to take counsel's advice on whether to proceed with an action against this gentleman in regard to his extreme physical harassment of my client."

ffitch ffought back.

"I can inform you, Mr Wethers, that HMG would not take kindly to such a course. The nature of Mr Medina's work with my department is highly confidential and of vital interest to the country."

"ffitch, you are full of shit." I'd had enough. I had been drugged, starved, tortured, half killed; my friends had been attacked – one was still close to death in Sweden – and now this egregious little…

"You come round to my lawyer's house, uninvited. You refuse to say which government department you work for. You do not ask for any facts and you make entirely unsubstantiated attacks on my good name. You bring a gentleman from Special Branch – or whatever you called it just now – who says not a word and you expect me to co–operate with you. Get out! Get out, ffitch, and do not come back."

I was shaking. Uncle Marcus pressed the bell beside him and his driver appeared immediately. They all stood. The Special Branch officer was trying not to smile. I decided to rattle his cage too. "I hope to speak to you again at your convenience – ah – Alan."

He blinked at that, nodded and stood up. ffitch was white with rage.

"Come along Mr ffitch. We can resolve this later."

He hustled him out of the door. Robbi raced upstairs and reported back from the landing window. "ffffffffffffffffffffffffffitchy witchy has got into a big black car. Cummins/Walker is on his mobile. He's coming back in, John."

She bounded up to the top floor as the driver opened the front door to admit him. Marcus Wethers was smiling at the papers on his table. He looked up as we came in to the drawing room. "Yours I believe, John."

He passed me Robbi's notes. "I am afraid I have to go to my office now. John, no more tantrums, please. Goodbye, gentlemen."

Robbi swept back in having changed into a light and demure summer frock. She kissed him on the cheek. "Take care, Uncle Marcus."

"You take care of him, young lady."

"I will. Hello again, Alan."

Cummins sighed. "I suppose if I ask you how you knew that, you wouldn't tell me."

We nodded. I picked up my phone and called Sir Ian Hamilton. It took no more than a few moments for his identity to be confirmed. In the meantime, I had gathered my thoughts. "There are some things I don't think I can tell you without endangering friends. Please take a seat."

Cummins nodded. "Whatever you can."

I told him about the family feud. I told him about my kidnapping. I told him about the Chinese. Cummins was interested in the Chinese.

"Hmmm. OK, first off, a seriously injured Chinese man was found in a ditch not far from Newbury and then, a couple of days later, a gentleman from the Chinese embassy brought two friends (also Chinese) into A&E at the Royal Worcestershire hospital. Looked as though they had been shot with a 9mm pistol – probably a Glock 22. Know anything about either of these incidents?"

I shrugged again. Cummins sighed.

"It would be very useful to have some information, any information, about these Chinese gentlemen."

He looked from one of us to the other. "Then there's Mr Dominick Medina's eight bedroomed house in Mount Street. Bit of a mess, I should say. The smoke alarm appears to have gone off in his library – nearly ruined his priceless collection of incunabula – I had to look that word up, you know. Anyway that wasn't so much of a mess as that caused by the fire on the stairs. Anything you can tell me about that?"

He looked at us. "Please don't both shrug at the same time again."

Robbi looked at me. She shrugged first and then I shrugged. "Was that better?"

Cummins smiled. "Sir Ian said you'd be difficult."

He leaned forward in his chair, resting his elbows on his knees and cupping his chin in his hands. "Roberta, your brother Dave is known to us for various reasons. You two seem to have involved in him in this affair. Remember that Regimental Sergeant Major Lord will have divided loyalties. The Regiment is very important to him and he is very well thought of by the Regiment."

"That sounds like a threat, Major Cummins."

"Alan, please, Sir John, and no it's not a threat. I can imagine why you asked for Mr Lord's help. He is very resourceful and he's one of only a handful of men in the world who could supply that quantity and quality of men and materiel to take out a house in central London and get away with it. Roberta you're not supposed to look proud you know, it's a bit of a give–away."

At least this exchange had given me the time I needed to think. If I told him that I didn't know what the Chinese and Medina wanted from me, then I could dissemble some more and… "I think that it's something to do with a huge horde of gold belonging to a friend of my grandfather's. I think they think I know where it is."

"And what is this to do with the dangerously ill Anna Haraldsen?"

"Anna got on to the story from her end. Her great grandfather was the gold prospector friend of my grandfather. I think this hoard could be a great deal of money. Billions. I think that the Chinese now have enough information and have gone home to find the treasure. I have no idea what Medina's relationship with them is."

Cummins stayed silent for a while, looking at where Rufus had adopted his normal position on Robbi's feet.

"I imagine that Mr Medina has need of a large amount of money for some reason."

I managed not to shrug this time and asked a semi–intelligent question instead. "What's he worth?"

"On paper? Several billion – in liquid assets, less. He is, ah, let's just say, very close to the present administration. You saw that from your friend ffitch. There is going to be a great closing of ranks around Mr Medina."

"How come you're not taking up your position in those ranks?"

Cummins stood up. Rufus stood too, shook himself and went across to sniff his trousers. Cummins pulled the dog's ears absently. "Three reasons – all in your favour. Your lawyer, Sir Ian Hamilton, and a distinct worry about anyone who is so close to government and keeps the kind of friends Medina does. We do not understand how he gets his influence."

I smiled. "Oh, I can tell you that in two words."

Cummins looked the question.

"Hypnotic induction."

"Hypnotism?"

"If you like. He does a fine line in it. You can look as dubious as you like, but that's how he does it and I can tell you that he's pretty damn good at it too."

Cummins had gone very still. "Really?"

"Yes."

"So you claim that he uses post hypnotic suggestion, like that Darren Brown bloke."

"Derren not Darren. Something slightly more profound than that, but in essence yes."

I dissembled again, staying as close to the truth as I could without giving anything of value away. "Which is why I am not being as helpful as you think I should be. I believe that, when I was eight, Medina's father planted a post–hypnotic suggestion in me. Whatever it was, he now wants it and it looks like he'll go to pretty much any lengths to get it out of me."

Cummins stared at me. "You're telling the truth, aren't you?"

"Of course he bloody is." Robbi sounded outraged.

"Alright, alright, sorry. John, you're not going anywhere, are you?"

"Is that an order?"

"Not exactly."

"Well, I have no intention of returning to the flat, but I was thinking of going to my place in the country when I'm better."

Cummins looked from one of us to other and this time it was him who shook his head.

CHAPTER THIRTEEN

Robbi found it extraordinary that I had accounts at Fortnum's, John Lobb, Henry Poole, Turnbull & Asser, even Selfridges, but not at Harrods. I tried to explain the weird psychology of class, but the distinction between Fortnum's and Harrods evaded her. Next morning, we were ready to go after the deliveries had arrived – hiking boots, lightweight trousers, rucksacks, et al. I found myself booking train tickets from Waterloo to Salisbury, when we could have gone direct home by Great Western trains from Paddington, but that's what paranoia does to you.

At Salisbury I bought tickets for Bath. At Bath I bought two singles for Swindon and at Swindon, two tickets for Kemble. At Kemble we waited in the vague and unjustifiably optimistic hope of a bus, abandoned the hope and hired a taxi to Foss Cross. At Foss Cross we walked. It was mid-afternoon by now and the early summer sunlight was blindingly beautiful. We climbed two stiles, followed a path that I had walked or ridden down for many of my childhood years and finally arrived at the corner where the footpath met the little lane that led to the home farm in one direction and the manor on the other. An ancient Ferguson tractor with a trailer was chugging towards us.

I knew that tractor. I had driven it as a child.

I put my rucksack down and waited. Robbi looked at me and decided to sit on the grass verge. The tractor clunked, clattered and juddered to a halt three feet in front of me. The driver leaned forward, put his elbows on the steering wheel and frowned. He looked at Robbi, looked back at me and spoke. His voice was a rumble.

"Well, well, well. Young Master John."

"Hello, Mr Cartwright."

A slow, big smile came across his face. "Well, well, well. You'd better come with me back to Home Farm or the Missus will have my hide. How are you, young lady? Are you the one who's goin' to set this young man on the straight and narrow?"

Robbi stood up and walked towards him with her hand outstretched. "I'm Robbi and for the moment we're just friends and I have no idea if he wants to be any more than that or whether I want to be any more than that myself. He can be somewhat difficult."

"Always was, Miss Robbi. Always was."

I winced at this neat summation of our relationship and my life in general. Mr Cartwright shook his head at me. "Want to get up on the trailer?"

We walked round to the trailer. A Border Collie opened an eye and watched us.

"That's never Bessie, is it, Mr C?"

The old farmer chuckled. "Aah. She is. No more than a pup when you last saw her. Jump up now."

Bessie sniffed me, wagged her tail once, and turned her attention to Robbi, thumping her tail on the trailer floor in appreciation and then leaning in against her, a paw in her lap, as the old tractor coughed its way back to Home Farm where Jack Cartwright backed the trailer into the yard by the kitchen door with the effortless ease that comes with over sixty years of tractor driving. The farmyard was still immaculate – bailer and muck spreader under the eaves of the barn and the corm silo spray cleaned. Swallows darted in and out from the eaves and the House Martins were perched in their mud–balled nests at the far end of the farm beyond where the kitchen jutted out into the yard. Mr Cartwright climbed down, shouting out to his wife.

"Mother? Mother, come out here and see who's come for tea!"

Joan Cartwright bustled out of the door, flour on her hands. She stopped dead and stared at Robbi sitting in the trailer with Bessie's head in her lap – and then she noticed me. "John Hannay. Young John. How are you my dear? I hope you're better than you look, I must say."

I jumped down and went across to be hugged. "Hello Mrs C."

"You look dreadful, John. You come straight in and have some tea. I'm just baking. You too young lady, if Bessie'll let go of you."

In the dark old kitchen, Mrs Cartwright opened the door of the solid fuel Aga and pulled out a tray of steaming hot scones. Mr Cartwright retrieved clotted cream from the fridge and jam from the Welsh dresser and we sat down. Mrs Cartwright was intrigued by Robbi. "So, how long have you two known each other then?"

Robbi started counting. "Gosh, it's not much more than a couple of months, John, isn't it?"

"Where did you meet?"

Jack Cartwright grunted. "You may as well let her ask away. I'll get no peace otherwise. It'll be Jack this and Jack that and why didn't you ask them then? Long and the short of it, Robbi, she wants to know how much you know about John. Like an old mother hen over him she is whenever she gets the chance."

Mrs Cartwright bridled. "Well, someone has to be."

Robbi looked at me. I nodded. These were old, old friends of the Hannay family. Jack's father had been the tenant farmer on Home Farm in my grandfather's day.

"I know all about John and his history, Mrs Cartwright. I'm supposed to be nursing him at the moment and the last time I let him out of my sight I got him back looking like this... only a lot worse."

Jack looked at me and sighed. "You always did take on more than you could handle, John."

I shrugged and snaffled another scone. Robbi snaffled two and looked at Jack Cartwright enquiringly.

"Well, I'll give you a f'rinstance. When he was twelve, he came down here for the summer and stayed on his own up at the Manor. He used to go out running and a couple of lads from the village decided to have a go at him 'cos he was posh."

Joan Cartwright seethed. "Wayne Johns and Peter Venner. Little horrors. No better now than they were then neither."

"You don't have to tell the whole story, Mr C."

"Yes, he does, John. Shut up. Carry on, please Mr Cartwright."

"She's got the measure of 'im, Mother. Well, these two little devils ambushed him and give 'im a good hiding. So, what did 'e do? Came straight round here..."

"Blood all over his face and his shirt – which he was going to wash off with warm water, if you can imagine…"

"I was twelve."

"Shut up, John!"

"And he asked me if I would teach him to box…"

"Mr C. used to be an amateur boxer."

The story continued, embroidered by time's passing.

"… So, by the end of the holidays, he was getting pretty good. I told him he wasn't good enough to take 'em both on, but he didn't listen. Next thing I knew he was back here in a police car. Young Billy Thornton – PC Thornton as he was then – could hardly keep a straight face. John had gone round to their houses with a note challenging them to a fight behind the school. One of the little buggers told his mum and she called the police, but by the time Billy got there, John had one of them in tears and was kicking the other in what Mrs Cartwright don't approve of me calling 'the nuts'."

Robbi was laughing now and Mrs Cartwright was smiling approvingly at her.

"Well, now you've thoroughly embarrassed me and Robbi has finished all the scones, I think we should get ourselves to the manor before it gets too late."

"Jack'll give you a lift, won't you, dear?"

We walked out into the farmyard, Jack with his hand on my shoulder and Mrs C with her arm round Robbi.

"Thanks, Mr and Mrs C."

"You're a bit too old for that, John. You know our names."

I smiled at Robbi. I bowed, she curtsied and we spoke in unison. "Thank you, Jack. Thank you, Joan."

At my request Jack dropped us by the Copse and I unlocked the padlock on the old gate and led Robbi up the hill, through the circle of beech trees, across the open mound in the centre and down the slope to the fence with the gap by the third post – and there in the centre of the little valley sat Fosse Manor, golden yellow in the early evening sun. She stood fixated. Eventually and without turning round she spoke. "Come on, race you." She slipped through the fence and ran away across the sloping meadow. I ran after her realising for the first time that she moved like an athlete – none of your elbows in, hand flapping stuff. I stopped running and lumbered for a while, before walking with what remaining dignity I could muster. At least I had the key to the garden door.

Robbi scaled the wall.

This wasn't going as I had imagined.

She was sniffing a climbing rose on the west wall when I managed to push the door open. She peered at me from under her hair. "Come on, come on. We don't have all night."

I breathed deeply. "Well, we do, actually."

She was bouncing up and down like a particularly irritating puppy. I found the kitchen door key and let her into the dark scullery corridor flicking on the light switch and checking the Aga was on. Robbi ran ahead into the kitchen, muttering. I walked slowly behind, feeling that wonderful familiarity, leaving the door ajar and opening the leaded windows in the kitchen. Robbi was already in the back corridor exclaiming at the panelling.

"Right, drawing room and morning room. Left, library and study, straight ahead dining hall."

She disappeared into the drawing room. I followed again, pushing past her to open the French doors on to the terrace. Robbi sighed and then bounced some more and then was out of the door running. I heard her light footsteps and the opening of doors and then the sound of her running upstairs. "Open the windows!"

She yelled back something indistinct and the day suddenly caught up with me. I wobbled and sat heavily on the terrace and put my head between my knees, tasting the bile as it came up into my throat. The sickness passed and I leaned back against the warm wall. There was the sudden sound of running feet and she was beside me. "God, I'm so selfish. I should have told your friend Farmer Jack to drive us up to the front door. John, are you alright?"

I nodded, not sure that I could speak. My heart was racing. I stood incautiously and the world rocked again. Robbi pushed me against the wall. "You're too big for me to carry, John. Five steps and you'll be inside. Come on. Come on, you can do it."

I got into the drawing room on rubber legs and collapsed on a sofa. "Push it towards the window," I croaked.

Robbi pushed with manic strength. The sun came into sight. My heartbeat began to slow and I could get breath into my lungs.

"Robbi?"

"Yes, John."

"I think I'll stay here for a while if you don't mind. Could you please remember to shut all the doors and windows?"

CHAPTER FOURTEEN

I woke to a shower of drops. Robbi was shaking damp hair over me while pretending to dry herself. I looked at my watch – seven thirty-five. I'd slept for eleven hours. "You're a pain."

"I'm a pain? I'm not the feeble one who falls asleep at the drop of a hat. We've got no food, no transport and it's Sunday. So, we're buggered. We'll starve to death and in years to come they'll find our skeletons."

I wiped the drops of water from my face. Half an hour later, after I had showered, shaved and dressed, we heard a bark at the French windows.

"Bessie," cried Robbi, opening the door. The Collie wagged at her excitedly. Jack Cartwright's voice followed.

"You two decent?" He came in with a basket in his hand. "Joan sent me round: eggs, bacon, bread, butter and milk. That's for you." He held up his hand to stop our thanks. "But she says you have to be at church for ten thirty. She's been on the phone."

I groaned. "Spare me, Jack."

"Sorry me boy, but I only sees you once in a blue moon. Her I have to live with. We'll pick you up at ten."

"What's wrong with church, John?"

Robbi spread an enormous slab of butter onto a slice of Joan's newly baked bread.

"I'll have to read the lesson"

She hooted. "You'll have to what?"

"I'm supposed to be the squire. It's tradition."

"Squire? You? OoooOoooh."

I left her to her third cup of tea and went to the dressing room off the main bedroom suite. It felt wrong. The dressing room, I mean. It felt wrong. I was distracted though, by the need for a respectable suit that might fit my newly skinny frame. God, was this how women felt all the time when they were dressing to go out? The feeling drifted past me and away as I found an old charcoal grey suit and joined Robbi by the front door. I heard Jack's car in the drive and went back in to the house locking windows, doors and setting the alarm. In the car, Jack passed a walking stick to me over the seat. He'd remembered my limp, of course. I nodded. I might need it. Joan looked over her shoulder. "I'm not sure if you'll approve, John, but the vicar is a lady,"

"Fine by me. She nice?"

"Very."

You may think me hypocritical – as a non–God believing person, I mean – but I'd always loved our small Norman parish church with its silly, nineteenth century, gothic–revival, architectural fripperies. We parked beside the village hall next to the church. I wasn't surprised to see the crowd. Joan would have been on the phone all evening.

The vicar was nice – Dorothy. Yes, I would read the lesson – yes I knew 1 Corinthians 13. Hello, Mr Danvers. Good morning, Colonel. Morning, Mrs Trudgeon, you're looking well… It was as if I had never been away. Robbi smiled politely at all comers. We followed the crowd into the cool, white dampness of the old church and I felt Robbi's surprise as I led her to the front and the family pew.

"You really are the squire, aren't you?"

"Lord of the manor actually. It's one of those meaningless titles."

"Chyeah."

The service started and I let the litany flow over me.

My turn came and, stick in hand, I climbed up to take the reading in front of the lectern. I looked down at the congregation. A shadow passed in front of the open west door. I strained my eyes to see who it was.

"Thank you, Dorothy. Good morning ladies and gentlemen. I apologise for turning up unannounced, but it's a pleasure to be back with you. I'll only be here for a couple of weeks, but I hope to be able to return more permanently very soon."

The shadow at the back of the church crossed the sunlight. Whoever it was had left. I waded into Corinthians:

> Though I speak with the tongues of men and of angels, and have not love, I am become as sounding brass, or a tinkling cymbal. And though I have the gift of prophecy, and understand all mysteries, and all knowledge; and though I have all faith, so that I could remove mountains, and have not love, I am nothing...'

So, I was still nothing.

Afterwards, outside the church, it was handshakes

and hellos you haven't changed a bit. I told anyone who would listen, which was everyone, that we were staying at least a fortnight. I told Mrs Trudgeon that Robbi was nursing me as I had been ill and that no, we weren't engaged. I told the Colonel that I would have the home meadow mowed and rolled for the village cricket match in August. I told Nick from the pub that I would need a bar set up for the match and finally I managed to catch Jack's eye and we escaped.

Back at the manor I studied the lock on the heavy oak front door. There was a new scratch on it that I was sure hadn't been made by me.

"Food, John Hannay, food!"

"All in good time, young lady. Follow me."

She followed. At the door of the outbuildings, I reached up for the keys in the false brick and pushed open the big doors, turning to watch her reaction. She peered into the gloom and then saw the shrouded car. I pointed at it. She walked forward pulling off the heavy cloth.

"No way! No way! You've got a Roller.

"A 1958 Bentley Continental actually. My grandfather bought it not long before he died."

"But does it go?"

"It's a Bentley. Of course it goes."

It took seven minutes to drive into Northleach. The mini–mart was open for basic provisioning and I followed obediently behind Robbi, holding a carrier bag, as she sniffed round the corners off the Market Place, familiarising herself with this new environment. She was examining the small ads in the post office window when I saw a familiar, pale and glabrous head in the shop next door. I knocked on the window. The face had disappeared and all that was now visible was a bottom, quite a large bottom encased in what must have been waist size 38 blue jeans. I knocked again.

"Fuck off, we're closed."

I grinned. Robbi looked a question. I tapped on the window again.

"I said we're fucking clo......"

The large bottomed one had swung round revealing a large, gently rippling stomach, mostly covered with shirt.

"Fucking hell. It's Hannay."

The figure crashed through the empty boxes he had been stacking. He unlocked the door, glanced at Robbi, did a double take and then adopted a theatrical stance shading its eyes and peering up and down the square. He took Robbi's hand and stared deeply into her eyes. "Where have you left it – the guide dog, I mean?"

I groaned. Robbi giggled.

"You see, and I want to be very honest with you here, most of his women (and there have been many, many, many of them, all with quite dreadful STDs) have been either blind, or deaf, or both or deficient in mental acumen. Which of the above are you?"

"Not one of his women. Who are you?"

He pointed at the sign over the door.

"Oh. Hello, Andrew Barraclough–Wines."

She walked past him and went into the shop, looking at labels on bottles. I followed.

"How's business, Andy?"

"Good, good. Your loan's paid off and I made a profit in the last quarter. Damn good in fact. Yes, er, damn good."

His voice tailed away into a murmur and he looked away from me. I smiled uncertainly, surprised by this turn of fortune. I had loaned him the money not really expecting to see it again as he had never before shown the remotest aptitude for business. We had both grown up here, which made him one of the very few remnants of my pre–Medina childhood, and had a relationship based, on his side, on insult and mockery.

"So how goes the family history? Any breakthroughs in the family feud? Found your nemesis yet? Your Moriarty, my dear Sherlock?"

Robbi looked up sharply. I smiled at her reassuringly.

"It's OK. I've known Andy since I was a baby. He knows as much as anyone."

He shifted uncomfortably. Something wasn't right. My antennae were up, out and waving. He turned to Robbi and started flirting, but it was mechanical, forced. After a minute he turned and probed once more. "So, is this the beginning of the end for the big vendetta John?"

"I don't know, Andy. Could be. To be honest, I don't care anymore. I'm going to leave the country for a few years. I'm just here tidying up for a couple of weeks and then I'm off."

"So you think your man is down and out, then?"

"Not out, just down long enough for me to get away."

Robbi was pretending to look around the shelves, watching me out of the corner of her eye. Barraclough stirred himself, turned on his charm and had her laughing in a matter of moments with neatly chosen insults about my sexual prowess. I smiled in a superior manner.

"I'll bring the motor across. Don't turn your back on him, Robbi. He has dirty, public schoolboy habits."

I parked the Bentley outside as Barraclough came out with his arm round Robbi.

"Bye Andy. Really glad the business is on the up and up."

"Er thanks, John. Anyway, best of luck getting Medina."

"Thanks, Andy."

I saluted him. Robbi kissed him on the cheek, laughing as he tried to pat her on the bottom. We pulled away. "Robbi. Pull down the sun visor and put some lipstick on in the mirror."

"I don't have any lipstick."

"Just slit your eyes so it looks as though they're half–closed and tell me what Barraclough is doing."

She stared at me for a second and then leaned forward peering at herself in the mirror. "He's watching us. He's got his phone out. I think he's giving someone the number of your car. What's going on, John?"

"Didn't you hear him?"

"Obviously not. Wait."

She sat back and thought. "Oh God! He mentioned Medina by name."

"There was someone at the Church. Came in and left while I was doing the reading and there was a scratch on the front door lock which wasn't there before."

She swivelled round towards me. "And you weren't going to tell me any of this?"

"I just didn't want to believe it. I think I'm paranoid enough as it is. When's Palmer due?"

Robbi glanced at her watch. "Could be any time now. I'll call him."

She dialled. "Hey, Palmer. How you? Good, good. Where are you? Just a sec. He's just left Burford on the A40 and he thinks you live in the twee—est part of the world he's ever seen."

"Tell him to take a left on to the B4425 at Upton and follow the road to Aldsworth. Then right towards Eastington. It's a very narrow lane. We'll find him along there. What car is he driving?"

"Mondeo. What car are we driving? You'll know us when you see us."

Palmer convulsed with laughter through the windscreen when he realised it was in us in the Bentley. I gave him the finger and beckoned him onto the farm track. No one appeared to be following us, but we were scarcely inconspicuous.

CHAPTER FIFTEEN

I finished the story leaning against the bonnet of the Bentley. Palmer hadn't stopped walking round and round the car, touching it, stroking it and finally moving me away from the front of the car and lifting the bonnet to stare at the engine.

"Palmer, have you heard a word I've said?"

"Do I look stupid?"

We both opened our mouths.

"Shut up. Right, Medina has two (probably) people in the area. One of them is spying on you. He could be a sniper. You have put out disinformation to the effect that you are here for two weeks. They have heard this. They should call for back up and plan on doing something when they arrive. That's what I would do. We should, therefore, try and take them out tonight and watch for further arrivals."

He followed me to the copse where Robbi and I had walked through to the house the day before. I unlocked the old gate and Palmer drove the Mondeo up the rutted track and into the shelter of the trees. Back at the house we talked, dozed, ate, ate some more, washed up and eventually went to sit on the steps of the drawing room to watch the summer sun setting over the west wing of the house. The evening was heavy with the scent of the climbing roses on the garden wall and the muted chatter

135

of the swallows swooping over the pond for insects. Night fell.

Palmer stood up and cracked his knuckles. "Time to move."

We donned our old dark clothes, pocketed the weaponry and the electronic devices and walked over the paddock and into the Copse, where a Tawny Owl hooted in mournful surprise as we trod on the dry, dead leaves in the wood. Within 15 minutes we were driving past the off license in the town. We dropped Palmer in the street, parked the Mondeo on the slight incline in front of the butchers and waited for him. He was back within the minute giving us instructions. "Front door's easy. I've already disconnected the alarm. We may as well go straight in there."

We did as ordered. Palmer looked at the staircase at the back of the shop, bending down to test the bottom step and stepping back to shake his head. Pressing his hands against the side wall he placed his feet over the banister rail and began to work his way up the walls. I waited until he reached the top and followed suit. Half way up cramp struck. I made it… just. Robbi was up in seconds. Breathing through our mouths we crept along the wall to the first door. In the moonlight we could see Andy Barraclough sprawled on the bed, fully dressed, a half–drunk glass of wine still held in his hands. He snored.

The next door along the landing was closed. Palmer dripped oil into the hinges and the doorknob and slowly, slowly turned the handle. I stepped across the doorway and leaned against the wall to steady myself as Palmer lowered himself carefully to the floor and gently pushed the door further open.

Nothing – then slow, deep breathing. I peered in – pitch black. Palmer pulled down his night vision goggles and slithered forwards spreading his weight to stop any boards from creaking. My eyes had adjusted to the darkness now and I could make out a figure lying on its side on the bed. Palmer was by the bed now. Slowly he came into a crouch. The figure moved suddenly – very fast. Palmer moved faster, striking once, hard, into the back of his neck. I raced in, clamped my hand over his mouth while Palmer whipped cable ties round his ankles and wrists. I moved my hand and before he could take a breath, Palmer slapped a strip of gaffer tape across it.

"Check on Robbi."

I backed into the corridor, my heart pounding. I breathed deeply. Robbi was in Barraclough's bedroom doorway looking back at me. I joined her in the bedroom as she lifted the glass out of his hand. He didn't move. I leaned over him and gently pinched the bridge of his nose – his breathing stopped. He gasped faintly and started to snore through his mouth – he was out of it. I went back to help Palmer.

"He's not going to trouble us for a while."

He nodded and pointed to the bound feet. Together we carried the limp body out and down the stairs to the front door.

"Time for Mr Barraclough."

"He'll be heavy."

Palmer nodded and I followed him back up to the bedrooms. "We'll just tape him while he's asleep and drag him down the stairs. Too bad if he bangs his head."

He did and it *was* too bad. Palmer gave more orders.

"John, bring the car. Have the rear door open. No lights."

I went out the back door and was ghosting back down the slope with the Mondeo's engine off in thirty seconds. The off–licence door was open and the two bodies were slumped in the entrance. We hauled and swung and they were in the back. I lowered the rear hatch door without shutting it. Palmer and Robbi pushed the car until it rolled down the short slope to the high street where I started the engine and turned on the lights. Two minutes later we were out of the town with the rear door shut. Palmer turned on the interior light and started to look at his hoard.

"Two mobile phones, another Glock and, you'll be pleased to know, a sniper rifle. Stable block, please and the guy with Barraclough is very dangerous. He was fast asleep, but he still nearly got me."

It was after four by the time we had secured our guests in the cellars beneath the stables and I crawled into the huge bed in my parents' old bedroom feeling the strangeness of the idea. This was the first time at the manor when I had not slept in my old bedroom next door. Robbi was in there now.

CHAPTER SIXTEEN

I was awoken by a very long peal on the doorbell at nine. I staggered downstairs to greet Dave. Robbi pushed past me to hug her brother as another tall figure darkened the doorway. "Nice little place, Hannay. Any good–looking maids?"

"Morning, Harry."

I proffered sandwiches and followed them out to the stables. The air in the cellar was fetid from Barraclough's vomit. I left the hatch up and the light made the two prisoners squint and blink. Dave stayed in the glare of the light and looked at them both. He smiled without humour and went to crouch by the sniper. "Morning, Paul."

The man called Paul peered up at him and then sighed. "Warrant Officer Class 1, David Lord! What're you doing here, Dave?"

"Protecting my family, Paul. You?"

"Trying to kill your family by the sound of it. Since when have you been connected to the upper classes?"

"My sister, Paul. She appears to be a friend of one of them."

"Young Robbi? "She's all grown up now, of course. God we're getting old, Dave."

Dave nodded. "John, meet Staff Sergeant Paul Browby, top sniper in the Regiment. Paul, meet Sir John Hannay, the man you were going to kill."

That rated as one the stranger introductions I could recall. I studied him – mid to late forties, I guessed. He was much smaller than Dave, shorter than me, five foot nine or ten, put together like the Meccano sets of my father's youth – all struts and metal. His brown eyes were calm, wide–set either side of a broken nose with a deep, jagged scar stretching from the neck beneath his ear, across his cheek and down to the point of his jaw.

"Where did you meet Medina, Paul?"

"Don't know any Medina. I was recruited online."

He glanced at Dave. "You know."

Dave nodded. "How's Margaret?"

Paul shook his head, his lips tightening.

"That why you took the job?"

Paul just looked at Dave steadily.

"He won't say anything, John."

I spoke to them both. "From what I can understand of this ridiculous conversation, you have been a staff sergeant in the SAS where Dave was your RSM. You have taken on a contract to kill me. I can buy that contract out if you wish as it sounds very much as though you need the money for your wife."

"She had cancer ten years ago," said Dave.

Paul looked down, then looked at Dave, nodding his head towards me. "Officer?"

"Short service – QRL."

Paul nodded at me. "Yes, sir. My wife has Hodgkins Lymphoma, fourth stage. She's in remission at the moment and this twenty k would have got her to the Mount Sion Hospital in San Francisco. It gives her a fighting chance and that's all I ever ask for."

I straightened up and looked at Barraclough. He looked away.

"Let's go and have some breakfast. Palmer, let 'em up. Andy'll need a shower."

Palmer nodded.

Robbi took my arm. "I remember Auntie Margaret, John. She was good to me after our mum and dad died. The Regiment always takes care of its own, but she was lovely. She worked off base in a pub and used to bring me sweeties."

I nodded. "Which is why you're so fat now. You realise they are all certifiable, though, don't you?"

"No more than you, uglywugs!"

She snorted with laughter at her wit leaving me grinning at her back as she ran into the house. I cooked breakfast and then leaned against the Aga rail. "Paul, did they tell you why I had to be killed?"

"Only that MI5 couldn't touch you 'cos of your contacts in government, but that you were a traitor."

I shrugged. "The man who actually hired you is called Dominick Medina. Andrew Barraclough will confirm this. He kidnapped Harry too, didn't he Harry?"

Harry looked uncomfortable and nodded quickly. Robbi took over. "His family has pursued a vendetta against John's family for three generations. He killed John's father first and then his mother. We can prove this. This man Medina hates England and is trying to destroy its economy. John says he can do it. He's very well connected and very, very rich."

Paul Browby transferred his steady gaze to me. I picked up the thread.

141

"You may have gathered that I am not exactly a pauper. I inherited this place and a bit of money and I made more money as a trader in the City. We need help, Paul."

I watched him. He shrugged – eyebrows raised. I continued.

"I would like it to be known that you have carried out your contract. This will stop them sending back up. And I want Andy to be able to go back to work at his shop, but I want him protected. It occurs to me that one of the top cancer clinics in the country is just down the A40 in Oxford. Once your wife's case has been gone through there you can take her to San Francisco. But I need you on this job until it finishes."

"How long would that be, sir?"

"No more than a month I hope, but I can't guarantee."

Barraclough cleared his throat. He spoke very quietly, all his normal bounce gone. "They approached me a year ago – Medina on the phone and a Chinese bloke in the flesh. I was broke. Your loan had disappeared and all they wanted was to know when you came back. I got the same story as Paul. They paid off your loan and then the business started to work. I did turn it round, John. I did. I'd forgotten all about them when you turned up yesterday. But I still called the number. Then Paul arrived in the evening. Frankly I was so scared I drank myself into even more of a stupor than I normally do."

I thought. I felt a degree of pity for Paul and nothing in particular for Andy, but it was my life they had been trying to terminate, no one else's. A couple of months ago I don't think I would have cared either way, but now… "I've offered a solution. Take it or leave it."

I walked out into the walled garden. I knew I was nowhere near recovered yet. Perhaps Medina had been wrong when he said I had youth. I felt old and frail. I lowered myself on to the stone bench in the warmth of the sun. One by one the others joined me – the newcomers sniffing the roses for scent and studying the pond for fish. Paul spoke first. "I'm very sorry. What more can I say? Yes, I desperately want the job. Yes, I would love Margaret to come here. Please."

I stood up and shook his hand. "Andy?"

Barraclough sat down heavily by the pond. "I've always been a fuck up and I probably always will be. I've always been jealous of you and that's what made me take their money. I wanted to show you I wasn't a total loser. Anyway, I had an entire night smelling and tasting my own puke to think about what I've done and what I've become. I'm just ashamed of myself. In case you think it helps to say all this in front of you all like a bloody Alcoholics Anonymous meeting, it doesn't. I'll do whatever you want, John and I am truly sorry."

He went to get up, but I waved him down, smiling at him.

Dave spoke. "All right, we have work to do. Let's get to it."

"Dining hall's got the biggest table, Dave."

CHAPTER SEVENTEEN

There were nine of us around the old, oak table. I couldn't see the point of excluding Barraclough. I had noticed Dave have a word with him and even at his most bumptious I didn't see Andy taking the risk of offending the omerta of the SAS. Dave looked at me and raised an eyebrow. Palmer yawned with a shiver and rubbed the palms of his hands on the top of his thighs. "Come on, John."

"Well, the one thing I am sure of is that the final moves of our endgame are going to be played out in the City of London. We know that Medina is in a position of some power with the present administration, so my guess is that he's going to use a national or international event in order to do what he does for a living – go short on a currency – in this case, Sterling."

I thought again.

"Robbi, you need to find out what the event is. Dave, you and Paul need to plan the strike against him. Palmer you need to record whatever it was I said in Medina's house – both bits of it and then get Anna's help to decrypt it. And, Harry?" I paused. He watched me nervously. "You know what you have to do."

He pushed himself away from the table shaking his head, hands outstretched, palms forward in a gesture of denial. "You have no idea what you're asking. Just remember that he managed to exert some kind of mind control over me once. I have no idea if he can do it again. I have no idea if he still has control over me now. You do realise this, don't you?"

Palmer raised a hand. As usual he had hunched down behind his laptop. "Ignoring the tosser, I've already done Robbi's job. There's a G20 meeting on July 20th in London. Couldn't be a better time and place to destroy the country's credibility."

Three weeks away. Twenty-one days. I left them to work on a plan for my demise and walked out into the kitchen garden, stretching in the late morning sun. Three weeks. Jesus! Palmer strolled towards me, phone in hand, recorder app activated. I stood quite still, closing my eyes to reach the words flowing from somewhere inside me once again. I finished, opened my eyes and looked at him. "Well?"

"Well, what?"

"Well, what do you think it means?"

"Fuck should I know? I'll send it to Anna and hope she's well enough to translate it."

Dave was beckoning to us from inside the house. He was standing waiting for me in the hall. "Time to have you killed."

"But…"

"No time for that. Paul's heading for the copse to set up. Put this earpiece in. Now, can you hear Paul?"

I nodded as I heard his breathing.

"Right. Go for a walk outside the wall. Pretend you're on the phone. You'll hear Paul take a slow breath in and out before he squeezes the trigger. Throw yourself backwards on the out breath."

I heard Paul's voice in my ear.

"In position."

"Right, Robbi, stay in the garden. When you hear the shot, come running out and scream when you see John on the floor. Paul, carry on."

"Let's just hope someone answers the phone."

I looked up at the beeches in the Copse waving at me in the light breeze, half wondering if there was another shooter already in the wood also planning my demise. In my earpiece I heard the beep of phone keys and then the ringing tone. A female voice answered. I remembered the girl at Medina's house in Mount Street.

"Hello."

"I have a clear shot."

"Wait."

A new voice – Medina, by God! "Back–up is on the way. You will wait."

"I have a clear shot. I told you I didn't need back up."

"What is the shot?"

"Seven hundred metres, five knot south west breeze, exit route clear."

"Wait."

We waited. I moved as if about to head back inside the walled garden. I had to force the issue.

"Target moving. Clear shot possible for only one more minute."

"Very well. Take him. I want to hear it. Your phone should be able to take video. Use it and send it to the Hotmail account you were given and I want a photo sent to me of the body immediately."

"The camera is running."

I heard Paul take the deep breath. I threw myself backwards. The single shot echoed across the valley and I felt the thud of the bullet in the soil just beside my arm. I held my breath for as long as I could. Then I heard Robbi running and she was at my side screaming and screaming. Dave followed, hiding me from any further threat. He felt the pulse in my neck and shook his head at Palmer. I heard Paul's voice again and breathed out very slowly.

"The photo is on its way. The video I'll send when I get broadband. A big guy just felt his pulse. He's dead."

There was silence for a few seconds, then…

"I have the photo."

"And my money?"

"It will be sent as agreed."

"If it doesn't, you know I'll come after you."

Then laughter, just laughter and the connection was terminated. Dave's voice. "We'll carry you inside, just in case someone else is watching. Paul can you hear me?"

"Copy. Wait." A pause. "There is someone – your ten o'clock."

"Is he a shooter?"

I followed the rest of the hunt on my earpiece until Paul's murmur again. "He's coming my way. Looks like only a sidearm, if that."

Dave responded. "How far from me?"

"Forty metres, still your ten o'clock."

"OK, count me down."

Paul read off the distances quietly until we heard a grunt from Dave. "You want to live, then stay very, very still."

Three minutes later they were back with us. Dave walked across to where I lay and threw a horse blanket over me. At least I could breathe now, although the air was somewhat equine. Dave spoke first.

"Search him."

Silence, rustling and a thud…

"Just a mobile phone. Nothing else."

"Which rifle did you use then? L115A3?"

Silence.

"You're going to talk voluntary or assisted, son. Your call."

Silence. Movement. Then a dull thud followed by a groan. Another thud, another groan, a slap a thud, a deep groan.

"Alright, OK."

"Well?"

A Yorkshire accent. "I'm not your shooter. I was the spotter. I have to report to someone."

"Who?"

"It's a phone number."

"Whose phone number?"

"I don't know."

"So, phone it."

"But what are you going to do with me?"

"Do you often watch people being killed?"

"No, no, no. I was recruited by a mate – he's ex-military. The shooter was not to know I was there and then I had to report on the hit by making the call."

"You'd better do it, then."

A pause while he dialled.

"Hh… Hello. Successful hit. Yes. Yes. I have seen the body."

A rustling thud and then Palmer's voice.

"He's rung off. It was Medina. I'm not likely to forget that voice. You can come out now, John."

I swung myself off the table dreading what I might see. The spotter had fainted. I picked up the phone by the body and dialled the last number. Dead. Like I was supposed to be. I looked round. They all looked back at me.

"Paul, we need to rid ourselves of the Spotter. Obviously, he believes me to be dead. Did he see your face?"

He shook his head. I pulled out my wallet. "OK. Sneak into the cellar, bung him this £100 and tell him to disappear. Make sure he still thinks I'm dead. You know, break in and cut him free. That kind of thing."

Paul grinned. "Consider it done."

CHAPTER EIGHTEEN

I woke at an absurdly early hour the next morning still worrying about other people in my life – well one other person primarily. What did she feel about me? What the hell did I feel about her apart from the fact that she was the most beautiful person I'd ever met; that she was gentle, kind, intelligent, sensitive, very brave – and funny. Yes, she made me laugh – not something for which I had ever been famous. And what did she feel about me? She'd saved my life for God's sake. I stared at my still too thin body in the bathroom mirror and remembered Dave's comment about how she liked to save birds with broken wings. Well, I may not have broken wings, but if I didn't put on some weight soon, I'd have to order a whole rack of new suits.

I went back to bed and stared at the ceiling. New suit... New rack... What was wrong with the dressing room? The thought that had crossed my mind on Sunday morning came back with perfect clarity. I sat up. What was wrong with the dressing room? I climbed out of bed and walked towards the dressing room door, opened it and walked in. The rack of suits brushed my right arm. I turned round slowly. The rack brushed my left arm. I was sure the suits never used to touch my arm. The room was narrower. I threw a pile of clothes on to the bed, went back to the dressing room and crouched down, staring at the wall. That wasn't right. I dragged more suits off the racks, tapped the walls and stared again. There was a knocking on the door. Palmer was wondering what the bloody noise was at such an unearthly hour.

"Look at the wall on the left. No, my left."

Palmer stared at me and then at the wall. He knelt and peered at it more closely.

"Oh! It's new, isn't it? Have you got a claw hammer?"

I stood up. The object of my early morning thoughts was standing in the bedroom doorway staring at me and wearing an old shirt – one of mine actually – and not a lot else by the look of it.

"I'll get it. In one of the drawers in the kitchen by the Aga, isn't it?"

She returned in a minute and passed the hammer to Palmer. He hit the wall once, by the floor. The plasterboard gave and he reversed his grip levering out chunks of the board. Behind the plaster he found a length of four–by–two and tugged at it. It gave way and together we pulled a whole section of the false wall away. I glanced over my shoulder to see a row of eyes watching us.

"This is a stud wall. It wasn't here before. Someone has put it in."

The dust settled. Dave passed me a torch and we examined the length of original wall. The plaster had been chipped at revealing… nothing.

"Pull the next section away, Palmer."

Palmer levered and the next section and struck at the plaster on the wall by the drill holes pulling bits away. He stared at it and looked at me questioningly. I leaned in for a closer look. Where he had hit the wall there seemed to be something black showing behind the crazed plaster.

I nodded at him.

He struck again. About two inches in beneath the lathe and wattle plaster there was definitely something black. He glanced over his shoulder. "Cold Chisel. Quick."

Robbi ran again. I could hear her steps as she bounded up the stairs three at a time. It took Palmer five minutes of hammering and levering and white dust flying from beneath the lathes until… there it was.

I stared.

It was a small door.

Three foot to the tip of its Gothic arch and eighteen inches wide at the base, made from what looked to be a single piece of Oak. I sat on the dust covered floor to think about this.

"It's not so much what it's doing there as where it goes. Could it be booby–trapped, Palmer? Stupid question. Course it could. Dave?"

It took him and Paul no more than two minutes to give it the all clear. Paul pointed at the lock. I nodded at him and he got to work with some bent wires and a nail on the ancient mechanism. Dave put his stethoscope to the door again and thirty seconds later they smiled at each other and turned the handle. They pushed first and then pulled. It creaked, squealed, grated and opened to reveal… nothing – just an expanse of ancient stone wall.

Harry didn't care. Harry was delighted. This was a problem Harry thought that Harry could solve. He called for drills, tut tutted over mine, demanded cash and departed in Dave's van for the DIY superstore I assured him was on the outskirts of Cirencester.

For myself I wasn't sure whether to fret or mooch. In the event I settled on fretting. With no other vehicle to hand I added Paul's name to the insurance for the Bentley – to his considerable amusement – and he departed to collect his wife from Kemble station. Palmer, Robbi and I headed to the study where the computers I had ordered were ready to be set up. Palmer wasn't bothered by the riddle of the door either. He had computers. But did he have my translation?

"Apparently the translation was the easy bit. You spoke first in Swedish and then in Mandarin. She's done the Swedish one and a rough translation of the Chinese bit. Trouble is it means nothing to her or to me."

"Show it to Robbi then, she's the Sudoku queen."

"She is?"

"Yeah, you've heard of idiots savants, well she's the idiot part."

She didn't bother to reply. She looked over Palmer's shoulder at the screen. "Well, I can only see two things at first glance. The Swedish bit isn't relevant."

"It isn't?"

"Well, it may be, but there's nothing particularly special about the words. They're random. The English is different. Look."

I looked. I shrugged.

"Well look at this line... Idiot."

Beat Strong is great Thor, no doubt, when Meginard
He braces tightly o'er his rock–firm loins.

I shrugged again. "Well, it looks like a Norse Saga poem."

Palmer grinned. He was enjoying this. "You see, cryptology is nothing to do with poetry or even a particular language. Go on Robbi."

"Well in the Swedish version there are words with two or even three letters the same. In the English version none of the words have any letters repeated – except for these two: Xaanthi and Hezgaard."

"So?"

I had never seen Palmer grin so much. "Private key setting."

"Do I really have to play Watson to your Holmes? Bloody explain, will you?"

He was bloody loving this. Which is how I came to learn that there had been a chap called Kerckhoffs who had a principle which stated that the cypher method does not need to be secret so it can fall into the hands of an enemy without inconvenience and in language even an idiot (yes, one such as me, thank you, Robbi) could understand. The encryption scheme itself didn't even need to be kept secret; it was only the key that needed secrecy, the key that contained the secret information shared by the communicating parties. In simple terms, you have Party One who wants to communicate with Party Two and they both know that Party Three is listening or reading or watching, so they depend entirely on the key for their security.

Was I with him so far? I nodded. Robbi condescended so far as to pat me on the head. Palmer continued.

"So, what we're dealing with here is classical cryptology. So, this stuff is breakable – unlike the block chain apps and public key encryption I work on. However long it takes all classical encryption is breakable. You ever hear of Caesar's code?"

I shrugged. He grabbed the keyboard from Robbi and typed. "You move the letters of the alphabet forward by 3 places. See?"

I saw.

"So, if Julius Caesar wanted to write the message, "begin the attack now" – in English, I mean, not Latin. Yes, all right, I know you could tell me the Latin for it if I would only let you. Moving on… He would have removed the spaces and encrypted it as – EHJLQWKHDWWDFNQRZ. Good eh?"

Actually, it was good. "So?"

"So, my guess is that the two words noted by Robbi should be removed and the text should be scrunched together and we should get to work on trying to find the key code."

I stared at the pattern of letters on the screen and let my brain tick over. Patterns. Patterns of thought: how might Medina's mind work? Did we need to talk to a psychiatrist about him? Perhaps someone from this so–called profession would be able to give us a handle on a man who seemed, for perhaps up to ninety-nine per cent of the time, to be able to act completely rationally and completely within the bounds of normal business and social behaviour. If we knew what kind of maniac he was we could use it against him, surely.

"John Hannay."

I shared my rambling thoughts…

"… but my problem is that I don't know any shrinks, well none that I would trust."

"I do."

I looked up, startled at the intrusion. Harry was leaning nonchalantly against the open door. We looked at him in silence.

"Well, there's yet another vote of confidence if ever I saw one. You're thinking of Harley Street quacks or the idiots who should have sorted John out when he was a boy. Well, your Uncle Harry can tell you that you're a million miles from where the real head fucking takes place."

Palmer smiled. "Army psychiatrists."

"Give the man a coconut. The guys who deal with PTSD are shit hot. Chum of mine lost his platoon on patrol in Afghanistan. Total wreck. Blamed himself and to be fair it was partly his fault. Anyhow he was a gonner, but these chaps brought him round; shell shock in the First War, Battle Fatigue in the Second and Post Traumatic Stress Disorder since Vietnam – same shit, different war. You want to get to the bottom of a very fucked up person, talk to an army psychiatrist."

"OK, where?"

"I've got a name. By the way, you got a tape measure in this manor?"

"Kitchen, top drawer to the left of the Aga."

Harry raised a hand in acknowledgment and sauntered out again. Palmer took over the Mac. I realised Robbi had been staring at me. She stood up and looked at me meaningfully. "I am going for a walk in the woods and if a certain baronet of my acquaintance doesn't follow me within two minutes…"

She left the room. Palmer glanced at me curiously. "Have I missed a stage in the development of your relationship?"

I sighed. "Probably. I know I have."

But I made sure that I left before the two minutes were up. She was sitting on the fence in the Copse from where she had first seen the manor.

"What's the matter with you, John?"

I joined her on the fence. "I'm just being a dick, Robbi." I waved an arm back at the manor. "It's just that there are so many people… and you, you know… and…" I changed tack. "You do know someone else is going to get hurt."

She wasn't to be distracted. "God, for someone who's so clever, you are so inarticulate. What do you mean by 'and you, you know'?"

I stared at the grass. It was no help. There were still twenty-eight years of pain and solitude in the way. She spoke again. "Do you realise that if it weren't for Aunt Mary and Joan Cartwright telling me to stick it out, I would have walked away weeks ago. You've spent your whole life being beautiful and haunted and fascinating, but sooner or later, John, you have to give something back. Do you understand? Stop being so bloody selfish."

Before I could say that I did understand she had jumped down and run back to the house.

CHAPTER NINETEEN

At eleven, Paul returned with his wife, Margaret. She was the classic army nom–com wife, crew neck pullover, skin–tight jeans, a sharply pretty face and a thick veneer of calm competence covering any hint of nerves. She stood in the hall with her overnight bag in one hand and the other clutching Paul's. Robbi whooped when she saw her.

"Where are my sweeties, Auntie Margaret?"

"Robbi Lord? Goodness, didn't you turn out well, Robbi."

Robbi hugged her and introduced us all. Margaret came across to me and kissed me on the cheek. "Thank you, John. Paul's told me what you've done."

I was Englishly embarrassed. Harry was leaning against the drawing room door and smiling cynically. "Johnny boy. Want to see something interesting about your little mansion? Follow me. All aboard the tour bus, if you please."

I will spare you the next twenty minutes of Harry's smugness. The answer to his question in English measurements was that the wall at the corner of the library directly below the main bedroom was exactly one foot six inches (ninety centimetres for those who think in metric) thicker than any other of the manor's walls which did little to explain the fact that the little door in my dressing room opened on what appeared to be a lot more than ninety centimetres of solid stone. Not one of Harry's new drill bits could break through.

"Just a moment."

I remembered Uncle Marcus's comments about the last tenants and how they had tried to dig up the slabs in the kitchen. I was about to call him when I thought of a short cut.

"Back in half–an–hour. Want to come, Harry?"

We drove round to Home Farm to meet Jack Cartwright. He would be back for his midday meal if I knew anything about his routine. I parked the Bentley in the farmyard. This, I realised, was silly. I texted Robbi as we walked towards the back door: 'pls buy a 2nd hand LWB Landrover.' Harry took one look at Jack and knew he had to behave. He sat down quietly and left me to ask the questions.

"Jack, do you know why Marcus Wethers was so upset about the last tenants?"

He rubbed his jaw and glanced towards Joan. "Well, I was driving the old beast back down Manor Lane in, when would it have been, mother?"

"Last May, Jack."

"Right, right. Anyways, I ran into young Michael Harker. You'll remember his dad, John, Ollie Harker. His second cousin Gerald's the one who's ruined Glebe Farm for you."

I nodded. They were a widespread local family of dubious repute and Michael was the jobbing builder. Harry shuffled, but I knew there would be no hurrying Jack.

My phone bleeped. 'wot's LWB?' I texted back: 'long wheel base'.

Jack continued. "So, I asked him where he was going and he said he'd just had a very odd meeting with your tenants at the Manor. They had told him there was a damp problem in the little room off of your big bedroom and it was making their clothes all mouldy and they wanted him to put up a plasterboard wall to cover it. They said they would pay cash and not to bother the lawyers. So being a Harker, he did it of course. He said he couldn't see any damp anywhere in that room, but he could see that someone (probably them, he thought) had been chipping away at the walls with a hammer or some such. Anyways he said they paid him and then they took him into the kitchen and said there was a problem with one of them great stone slabs on the floor and could he lift it up for them. Well even Michael Harker thought this was going too far and said if they asked John Hannay's lawyer and the lawyer told him it was OK, he would be delighted to do it. There a problem, John?"

"I don't know, Jack. All I do know is that we've never had a damp problem anywhere in the house."

"Tell me, Mr Cartwright, was there any building work done on the Manor in John's father's time."

Joan gave Harry the once over while Jack rubbed his jaw again. "Funny you should say that, young man. Harker said they asked him the self–same question. Of course, he didn't know. But… The answer is no, not in John's father's time, but in Sir Richard's day. My dad told me they had a whole heap of work done to the corner wall of the Manor – subsidence they called it. They had to dig down and underpin it or something."

Harry's languidness was fraying. "So where would your building plans be kept, John?"

"With the Land Agent in Burford. Hmmm. Thanks, Jack. Things are beginning to move. Bye now. Bye, Joan. And don't worry, I am under instructions from Robbi not to do anything stupid."

Harry joined in the polite leaving noises and I pointed the Bentley towards Burford. I hadn't been to see the agent in many years although I remembered that the father had long since retired and the son had taken over. My phone bleeped again.

'how much? need to save money for clothes for me!!!'

I appeared to have been forgiven for being selfish. I replied.

'your call'.

'not good n uff hannay. u r the boss lol lol lol'.

'f o'.

'OooooOooooh'.

The office hadn't changed much. It was on the outskirts of the town, a converted barn that, twenty years ago, had retained a degree of dignity. Now it looked tired – ill cared for. The reception area was tiny and occupied by a pretty girl in front of a computer surrounded by documents. She was slight with cropped red hair, a stud in her nose and no make–up – not Harry's type. She smiled at us pleasantly and I realised she was older than she looked.

"May I help, gentlemen?"

"Yes, please. My name is John Hannay. You won't know me as I've been away for quite a while, but your company manages the tenancies on my land and I would be very grateful for a look at some documents relating to the buildings."

As I finished the sentence the rear door crashed open and a thick set man in his forties wearing a rugby shirt with the collar up and cavalry twill trousers came striding out. The red head turned to him and gestured towards me.

"Oh, Alexander, this is…"

The man spoke in that dreadful gobbling accent of the truly stupid, upper middle class.

"No time now, Miranda. Jolly busy as you should be able to see."

He turned to me. I suppose, what with my skin–head haircut still growing out, my thin frame and shabby appearance I shouldn't have expected to be taken too seriously, but the contempt in his once–up–and–down gaze was a tad beyond the pale.

"Look we don't tend to let people walk in off the street. It's generally regarded as good manners to make an appointment. Or perhaps look for another land agent, yah?"

He strode out, the door slamming behind him. A horsey looking Sloane with a particularly fine example of what used to be known as embonpoint peered out from an inner office. She saw Harry and simpered. He put on his best Leslie Philips voice. "Well, hello, what have we here?"

He turned to me. "Lend us £20, Hannay, and I'll grab a taxi home."

I groaned, parted with £20 and turned back to the receptionist who was keeping a studiously blank face.

The door closed behind Harry.

"Miranda, if I may call you that, I'm sorry, but it looks to me as though our acquaintance is going to be short. I will no longer need the services of Mallin and Son. Was that the son?"

"I'm very sorry, Sir John."

I glanced at her.

"I'm a local girl, Sir John, Miranda Thornton."

I looked at her more closely. "I don't suppose you're any relation to Billy Thornton, the policeman, are you?"

"My dad – he's Chief Inspector William Thornton now."

"Well, well. Remember me to him, will you? He gave me quite a clip round the ear when I was twelve – not that I didn't deserve it. Good man, your dad."

She smiled proudly. "Is there anything I can do to help, Sir John?"

"Well yes, there is actually – three things if you don't mind. For a start, you can drop the 'Sir' bit. Then you can give me a blank sheet of paper and a biro and I will write a note terminating my contract with Mallin's, and finally you can, if you are able, find me the plans for Fosse Manor which show any building or renovation work carried out there in the 1930s."

Miranda vacated her seat. A sheet of paper and biro were laid on the table and I sat down to pen my brief termination letter while she went over to a large filing cabinet. She was back standing in front of me before I had even finished the letter holding a big file and a cardboard cylinder.

"You don't seem very keen on trying to make me stay with Mallin's, Miranda."

"Well, you can guess what the future is going to be like. When they see your letter, they'll only blame me, so I'll probably be on my bike anyway."

I looked at her, thoughtfully. "Let me give you this number."

I wrote Robbi's mobile phone number down for her.

"Also, drop a CV with references, to Fosse. If and when it goes sour here, give that number a call. It belongs to my, er, my friend, Roberta Lord. We're going to…"

A CV, beautifully typed and laid out, was placed before me. I smiled. Miranda Thornton was growing on me. Glancing down the page, I saw one of the references was from Jack Cartwright and that she had a BSC in Estate Management from…

"I know it isn't exactly from Oxford, but it's a good course and Mr Cartwright liked what I did for him in my placement. I haven't been able to get any real work since then."

She swallowed hard, looking vulnerable and suddenly very young.

"If Jack'll vouch for you it would be worth a trial, don't you think? You'll have to negotiate money with Roberta – Robbi I should say – because she thinks I'm a financial incompetent, but there's a lot of work to be done at Fosse."

A squeal came from behind the closed door.

"And I know about the estate. Apart from the Home Farm, there's Glebe Farm also under tenancy."

I laughed out loud. "Look, I'll be away with Robbi from late this afternoon so why don't you call her about three for a quick chat. And is there any chance you can get all my papers over to the Manor?"

"I'll pack them up now and if necessary, I'll take them back to my Dad's home for safe keeping. Um, thank you ever so much, Sir John."

"John! Oh, and Miranda, best if you don't tell anyone that I was in today, I mean apart from dear Alexander, of course."

She assented without questioning me. On the way back to the Manor, I called Jack Cartwright. He remembered Miranda Thornton very well. "Very bright young girl. Sorted out the farm accounts and gave me the best advice I've had from one of those graduate types about soil analysis and barley varieties. Give her a chance, John. I've the feeling you and she would get along well."

I found it hard to take in the scene at Fosse when I arrived. I'd become so used to solitude that the atmosphere inside the house startled me – there was an almost audible hum. To be fair, Margaret was using the Dyson, but Palmer and Robbi were in the study, Harry was in the library and Dave was on a ladder examining the wall beneath my bedroom. I sat on the bottom step of the staircase and thought about this for a while, contemplating all my possible futures. All of them worried me.

* * *

Robbi's phone rang. Damn, it was three o'clock.

"It'll be the girl from the land agent – Miranda Thornton."

She nodded and answered the phone.

"Hello Miranda. Yes, he told me. Oh, oh dear. Well, where are you now? OK, good. Yes, do bring them in now. John and I are leaving in an hour or so, but perhaps we can have a quick chat before then."

She put the phone down and came round to report. "Her boss came back, read your note and sacked her on the spot. She'd got your stuff out first though and she's on her way over now and giving Harry a lift at the same time. Apparently, her boss caught Harry at it with his secretary."

I relayed the story of our time at Mallin's to the others who slowly decamped to the front door in order to greet Harry's emergence from Miranda's ancient VW Beetle with a round of ironic applause. Harry, in no way discomfited, bowed right and left. Miranda got out more slowly and pushed the driver's seat forward to bring out the box files from the back seat. Robbi stepped forward.

"Hello, Miranda. Now I have no idea what you were on with Mallin's, but would a probationary three–month contract at £400 a week on PAYE, and your stamp paid, work for you? From what Joan Cartwright told me, one of the tenant farms is in a mess and the old shoots are going to rats – literally! Look, come on in and let's draw up a letter offer and you talk to your dad and see what you think – ooh and the first thing you'll have to do is buy a, buy a…"

Robbi found her mobile and read out: "Second hand LWB Landrover"

She walked towards me, a mocking grin on her face. "So, we're business partners now, are we Sir John? Is that the deal?"

I didn't get my twenty quid back from Harry either.

CHAPTER TWENTY

I don't care what the cognoscenti say about the Ritz or Claridges, I like the Hilton in John Islip Street just round the corner from Westminster's Think Tanks and party-political HQs. We checked in, went out, walked, ate and much later as we strolled back in the gloaming, I noticed that she had, most unusually, stopped talking until…

"You know, John, this is going to be our first night on our own when you have not been either dying or ill or being shot at"

"Good grief. Have you been keeping track?"

"I'm a woman."

"Despite your belief to the contrary, I had noticed. Can we talk, Robbi?"

"So long as you don't start apologising or explaining that it's all to do with your childhood."

She came into my suite and lay on the sofa. I lay on the floor and talked… and talked. In the event I did, of course, apologise and in the event it was, of course, about my childhood. But I really needed her to understand just how damaged I still was, that I probably would never be capable of a normal relationship… whatever that meant. Eventually I ran out of things to say. She hadn't kicked me for a while or interjected some caustic comment so maybe I was winning. She snored – maybe not. I covered her with the duvet and went and lay on the bed. The blackness drifted down over me suffocatingly and sleep was a long time coming. Recalling the events of my early life was not therapeutic. Keeping them locked away safely had been by far the better option.

* * *

The next morning on the dot of nine, my broker, sorry, 'wealth manager', Bill McElroy, arrived to go through my investment portfolio. After half an hour I mentioned bonds, which was the cue I had agreed with Robbi.

"The bond market's still very fragile, Mr McElroy."

"Bill, please, Roberta. It is. If there were another Soros wanting to sell Sterling short, there could be a complete repositioning of the currency. Sterling's already extremely fragile against the US dollar because of the endless Brexit fallout. And the dollar is in a total mess thanks to the Trump legacy and the vast amount of US treasury bills owned by China. The world really could not handle a currency upset at the moment."

She tried another tack. "What about the Renminbi then, Bill?"

"China's not my area, Roberta. But as I just said, they hold far too many US T Bills, which they couldn't sell without destroying the American economy, which would in turn destroy the world economy. The whole One–Belt–One–Road thing has really got the Yanks worried. Funnily enough though, I heard that chap Medina talking up the Renminbi at a livery dinner the other day."

My eyes left the ceiling. "Who?"

Bill smiled. "Oh, come on, John. I know you've been travelling, but everybody has heard of Dominick Medina. He's a fund manager. Said to be worth billions. Very close to government."

"Sorry yes. Dominick Medina. Funnily enough someone I was at school with was raving about him the other day. Bloke called ffitch – works as some kind of advisor to the Treasury. What's the matter, Bill?"

He had gone very still. "Friend of yours is he, ffitch?"

"Tell the truth, no. I couldn't stand him at school and he doesn't seem to have improved much."

He looked deeply relieved. "Good, I'm glad about that. I think ffitch is the most appalling little creep I've ever come across and I simply do not understand for the life of me how he has managed to gain so much influence in the field of currency regulation. He's also far too close to Medina for my money."

How to find out more without seeming too keen? I looked vaguely at the ceiling trying to sound uninterested, dismissive, bored even. "Really. He'd not take a bribe though, would he?"

"Well, that's always a possibility, but my point is that he is very, very dim and he's in a very, very difficult job and he's very, very close to someone who could make a very, very large amount of dosh if he sold Sterling short at the right time."

Robbi leaned forward.

"But didn't Soros have to have something like fifteen billion in 1992? That would mean Medina would need thirty billion or more today wouldn't it."

"Yes, you're right of course. I hear all sorts of rumours about the man mainly to do with whether or not his empire is all smoke and mirrors."

Well, well, well. I looked at my watch. "Shit, it's ten o'clock already. Bill, really sorry, but we have to scoot. Look I like what you're doing; thanks very much and er, keep up the good work."

He laughed. We shook hands. He left. Robbi and I sat down and looked at each other. She spoke first. "Smoke and mirrors. How many other people in the City would think like that?"

"A few. Bill is a shrewd guy – amazingly well connected too. Shows we're on the right track."

"But if he can't get his hands on thirty billion, what's the problem?"

"It's what I said about fractional reserve banking. He doesn't need thirty billion. He needs about ten billion, then he trades that up to the twenty. It's just derivatives."

"Just!"

I smiled and glanced at my watch again. "Come along, young lady. We have a meeting with my old boss at BTD at twelve thirty and you need an outfit."

"I do?"

Shopping with Roberta Part Two: this time we didn't go to a Sainsbury's. We took a taxi to Bond Street. Now Bond Street is a world where bored, rich women compete with other bored, rich women while chauffeurs or toy boys or sugar daddies stand or sit in attendance. As you may have gathered, I wouldn't know an Issy Miyake from an M&S and by the fifth shop I was getting anxious about the time although delicate hints were simply not working. She stood on the kerb at the junction with Conduit Street gnawing on a knuckle and causing an outbreak of hooting as a taxi driver missed the light change watching her. She grabbed my arm pointing up the street.

"It's the Yamamoti shop. I'd forgotten it was here. Come on, Hannay."

To my huge relief, the shop contained neither toy boys nor sugar daddies. I sat quietly in my very slightly over–large suit watching the discussion and looking at my watch. I leaned back in the chair, the very comfortable chair.

I was woken by a kiss on the head to hear her voice.

"Aah, isn't he sweet? You'd have thought that he'd been at it all night, wouldn't you, but you can take it from me that he wasn't."

The pretty Japanese assistant had her hand over her mouth and was giggling at me.

"So, what do you think, John? This is serious now."

Thank God – decision time. She stepped back and did a slow turn watching me all the time either directly or in the mirrors. Black trousers, white shirt – the outfit looked delicate, slightly informal, elegant, and expensive.

"He likes it."

The assistant giggled again, very happy; that made Robbi giggle and I sat there with an idiotic grin on my face. I knew it was idiotic because I could see my idiotic grinning reflection in several of the mirrors. I got out a bankcard refusing to listen to the price and went to pay. Robbi waved her arm frantically at me. Shoes? No –

sandals: of course, sandals. Why hadn't I thought sandals? It was almost twelve. We told the assistant we would collect Robbi's old dress later and I went outside to hail a cab. I leaned against the door telling the driver where I wanted to go when she came out into the street. I heard the cabbie say, "Holy fuck! I mean, sorry guv."

BTD wasn't one of the Mayfair hedge funds. It was in the City just off Bishopsgate, on New Street. Within twenty-five minutes we were sitting in the Boss' anteroom looking out over the glossy trading floor – forty or more hi–tech desks, ergonomic chairs, banks of trading screens all distributed over a few hundred square feet of some of the world's most expensive floor space. Robbi seated herself and faced the window onto the floor. She was impressed. "This is classy."

I shrugged and she turned back to watch the Floor. The inner door opened and the Boss came out in person to take us in. I watched Robbi's reaction. She registered that it was a woman and a black haired, elegant, aquiline nosed, high cheek boned, beautiful woman at that. Robbi looked down at her trousers and went all thoughtful. The Boss didn't notice her at first. "Well, well, here he is, John Hannay, the Super Trader himself, back in the flesh. Not after a job, are you?"

The door was pushed open and a man in his forties poked his head in and winked at me. "Boss, the Floor wants to know if the Super Trader's coming back?"

The Boss didn't even look at him. "The floor can fuck off and you can tell Chilton that if he misses another trade like the one he missed two minutes ago he can forget his fucking bonus."

I raised a hand at Max Jarrod, the departing trader, and the door closed. Robbi stood up and the Boss' eyes widened. She looked her up and down and then came close feeling the fabric of Robbi's new shirt... or blouse.

"I don't believe it. Is that Yamamoti? Turn round. Beautiful, beautiful. They haven't lost their touch since his death, then. Come on in. You too, Super Trader."

We went into the sanctum and I glanced at the bank of screens and the cameras which spied on the traders on the other side of the tinted window. "Robbi meet the Boss, AKA Emma Fitzgerald. Em, this is my, er, friend, Roberta Lord."

The Boss smiled at Robbi sourly. "So, have you managed to pull the King of Cool or not? When he says 'er' like that it usually means he's trying to hide something. I mean he used to have super models lining up in the foyer for him, but was the man interested? Well to be honest nobody could tell."

Before Emma could insult me further or Robbi ask which super models, I interjected. "Don't be deceived by Emma's miserable and unpleasant exterior, Robbi. Inside her, there beats a heart of misery and unpleasantness. Anyway Boss, I appreciate you finding the time to see us in between your busy schedule of eating babies and pulling the heads off kittens but, as you rightly surmised, we have a problem which you need to know about."

I leaned over her desk and turned off the recorder and bent forward to whisper in her ear. "Em, seriously, for your own sake this has to be off the record. If you've got anything else running turn it off"

She turned off the recorder on her computer and moved away from the desk.

"If there's anything that the Bank of England shouldn't know, don't tell me."

"OK. I think someone is going to have a punt at Sterling."

"Good, tell me who and we'll go short on it too."

"No Em. I'm on the side of the angels on this one and it's a lot more serious than that."

The Boss thought for a moment. "Why on earth do you think that I would help anybody but my bank?"

I shrugged. "Because you have the best judgment of anyone I have ever met when things are going too far."

Let me tell you about The Boss. In my arrogance I had permitted no one else in the City to be my boss. The only boss I had ever wanted was Emma Aubrey Fitzgerald, the greatest senior trader of her, or in my view any, time. Why? Because at the advanced age of forty–five she was the captain of a pirate ship sniffing through coastal mists hunting for her prey. She could smell the weather. She could scent when it was about to change. She knew where the shoals and sandbanks were, where the wrecks lay. In her youth, the Boss had pulled out of dot coms three months before anyone else. The Boss wouldn't touch CDSs and so avoided the sub–prime disaster. The Boss had told anyone who would listen that Bernie Madoff was a crook. All of which was why BTD was now so powerful and she was so wealthy.

She looked at me thoughtfully. "Flattery from the Super Trader. Things must be serious. How do I know you're telling the truth?"

"One, because you know I don't lie and two because I want you to come to our hotel in Westminster at five o'clock and meet someone who can confirm all this."

The Boss walked back to her enormous and virtually empty desk and checked her diary. She spoke into the phone. "Helen, move Macon to 7.00pm. If he doesn't want to do that tell him to fuck off and get me a car to take me to…"

She raised an eyebrow at me.

"Hilton Doubletree, John Islip Street."

"Got that? 4.15pm and the car will have to wait."

She put the phone down and looked at me thoughtfully. "Give me one fact that demonstrates you are not completely fucking insane."

"Dominick Medina."

The Boss' eyes widened and she sat down slowly. "You know you couldn't have… I'm turning the recorder on again now."

We stood up. The Boss smiled at Robbi with genuine warmth. "By the way, Miss Lord, in case you're interested, we never did. It's against the rules for one thing and for another he's not my type."

I was at a loss. Robbi wasn't and she gave the Boss a quick peck on the cheek. Bye Boss. See you later."

"Cheeky cow."

But The Boss was smiling as she ushered us out. By the lift, I could see a question building up. I sighed.

"Yes, I have been out with a super model. And she did come here and cause a scene when they wouldn't let her up to the floor to see me."

"Well, well, well. Who knew super models were so short sighted?"

The short, skinny BTD messenger was grinning broadly as he got into the lift behind us. I turned. "Wayne, let me just say if any part of that conversation is relayed to anyone on the Floor, I shall know and you will suffer. Believe me, Wayne."

"Yes, Sir John. I do."

"Oh, and Wayne."

"Yes, Miss."

"He's full of shit."

"Yes, Miss."

The doors opened on the second floor and Wayne fled.

CHAPTER TWENTY-ONE

We got back to the hotel at three thirty and ordered afternoon tea in the suite for four. I lay on the bed and dozed. A knock at the door jerked me back to life. I checked the spy hole and saw Alan Cummins waving at me. I started the briefing. It took over half an hour. I then outlined my (pathetically inadequate) plans and stumbled through (pathetically inadequate) answers to his far too pertinent questions until just before five o'clock when there was another knock at the door. Alan was on his feet before I had registered either the knock or the time.

"It's OK, Alan. This is someone I want you to meet."

I checked the spy hole again and let the Boss in. She nodded at Robbi and studied Cummins. "Is this who you wanted me to meet?"

"Yes…"

"Evening, Emma."

"Evening, Alan. So, if it's you they want me to meet then I guess there must be some truth in this crazy story."

"You know each other?"

"Well observed, Super Trader."

"Aah, so Hannay is the Super Trader?"

Em sat down. "G&T since you asked and I've got until six fifteen."

Robbi poured drinks raising a glass questioningly at Cummins who shook his head.

"We met on a financial problem the government was having a few years ago. Emma was very helpful and…"

"Don't tell him everything, Alan. It's such a pleasure seeing him lose the plot. John, the last words you said before you left my office were Dominick Medina. Has someone finally got some dirt on that piece of shit?"

Alan answered for me.

"Looks like it."

"Well perhaps this time we'll get the bastard."

"This time?"

"I have no idea what your involvement with Medina is, John, but some of us have been after him for years. There's something badly wrong with him and this dreadful little government is standing behind him for reasons I just don't understand."

"Well, according to John, the reason is hypnotism."

Emma snorted but then, as we sat silently in front of her, realised that Alan was being serious. Being The Boss, she didn't waste time. "How and who?"

"Well, me for a start, when I was eight. I promise I'll tell you the whole story, Em, but right now, the point is that it looks as though I may have enough cash to trade against him."

"You sure? You'll need a few billion."

I nodded although in fact I felt far from sure in any way at all. Emma sat staring at the G&T in her hand. "I'll match anything you put up, but you have to do the trading. I'll need some reassurance from you, Alan."

"You can't tell anyone, Em."

"Don't mistake my helpful and sweet behaviour this evening, Super Trader. I am not a complete fucking idiot and I still tear the heads off kittens for fun as you told

Miss Beautiful here earlier. I shall expect a very big favour in return. In fact, I can tell you what it is now. When this is all over Miss Beautiful and I will go shopping down Bond Street with your credit card."

Robbi cheered.

Alan held up his hand. "Let's be clear on one thing. The odds against us are not exactly small."

He stood up and began to pace. "First, I cannot speak to anyone in the department. They are too compromised with this government. I am, in point of fact, unofficially reporting to the retired head of the department – Sir Ian Hamilton – who is persona non grata with both the Home Secretary and the Chancellor of the Exchequer."

Good for him, was my first thought.

"I still have a staff of three whom I think I can trust although they're about to be put on to other duties as the financial analysis side of my work is being shut down."

"Idiots." Em was unamused.

"Idiots, maybe." He moved his head from side to side. "Or I'm being outmanoeuvred. Anyway, the second thing is that Emma can't ask for help because it would get back to Medina very quickly. Thirdly, we don't yet know if John has got his money. On the plus side… I don't know. Do we have a plus side?"

I shrugged. "Well, he thinks I'm dead."

Emma put her glass down.

Alan nodded. "Medina sent a sniper to kill John two days ago. So far as we know he thinks he succeeded."

Em picked up the glass and drained her G&T. "I wish I hadn't asked that question. OK, how do you communicate with me?"

I raised a finger. "Why don't you, Em, report to the top floor that you are concerned about some trades which you think have been made illegally and suggest to them that, as there could be a scandal if it comes out, you call in Alan, as MI5's financial guru will be more discreet than anyone at the Fraud Squad which leaks like a sieve? There's nothing stopping me talking to Alan direct."

The Boss considered. "OK, it'll do for a little while." She stood up and paused and then looked at me. "You, Super Trader, try not to get killed. Miss Beautiful, take care of him. He still looks as though he needs TLC. Alan, I'll call tomorrow. Need a lift?"

"No, I'm just across the river, thanks, Emma."

"Of course. Bye all."

She left and Robbi breathed out. "Phew."

Alan smiled. "I assume young Palmer is watching out for bugging?"

"Yes."

"Tell him to step it up. We need to buy time. Are you going straight back?"

"Tomorrow morning."

"OK. Lock the door and don't order room service!"

Robbi returned to the iMac and I sat on the sofa and stared out of the window. She yawned and stretched. "OK, I'll take the Yamamoto stuff off now."

I smiled at her as she went through the connecting door to her suite next door.

"Don't take it off on my account. You look wonderful in it."

She studied me, an inscrutable expression on her face.

"I like it, Robbi."

Inscrutability morphed into cynicism. I tried again.

"I, um, I like *you*, Robbi."

She turned her back on me. The door closed. I sighed and closed my eyes. How much more useless could I become? The door clicked again. I opened my eyes, bracing myself for another tirade. The doorway was empty. I looked at it. Still empty. I swung up off the sofa. Had someone broken into her suite? Was she safe? I raced to the door and stopped dead.

She was standing in the middle of the room wearing her new sandals, a gold necklace and nothing else at all. I just stood and stared and stared… and stared. Her eyes narrowed.

"Look, I know I'm not a super model, but are you just going to stand there?"

I swallowed. God, but she was beautiful. "For as long you stand there, yes."

"Oh well that's easily solved."

She sashayed across to the bed.

I followed.

CHAPTER TWENTY-TWO

Much later we had fallen asleep and I drifted up to the surface wondering if it was too late to grab some dinner. Not too bad, it was only five. Robbi was snoring lightly beside me. Five o'clock. I sat bolt upright and grabbed my phone. It said 05.01. We'd slept through the night – and I hadn't minded her being there at all! She stirred. I went to the bathroom. When I came back, she was awake and gazing at the curtains.

"What's the time?"

I chucked my watch at her. She peered at it. "Oh! Shall we go home?"

I half–smiled to myself... Home. "Not yet. We have an appointment with Harry's army psychiatrist, if you remember. Then, home."

I kissed her and she stumbled into the bathroom, scratching her backside. I er, I even liked that. I texted Paul to ask him to collect us from Kemble station at about twelve thirty. She came back in from the bathroom and interrupted my packing. I liked that a lot. By seven thirty we were ready to check out.

Harry's army psychiatrist worked out of an office off the Victoria Street end of Horseferry Road so after breakfast we left the bags at reception and walked. When we entered the doctor's consulting room, I admit I looked for the couch. There wasn't one. The office was standard issue MOD, in beige and cream. We sat in two uncomfortable chairs and looked across the desk at the hunched Scotsman who peered at us over his half–glasses.

"So, you know my remote and distant cousin, Harry Livesey, do you? Would you be an old friend of his now?"

I shook my head. "No Doctor Livesey, we only met recently on a business matter. We were both the victims of a physical and psychological attack by the same person. I think you should know that my colleagues and I believe this to be a matter of national importance and I am already working with intelligence officers. If you wish, I can provide you with the name and phone number of our contact."

"That may be necessary, Sir John. Possession of a baronetcy is not of itself a sufficient indication of integrity and this is all somewhat outwith my bailiwick. However, if you would like to explain the position I shall tell you as and when I feel uncomfortable."

It took me ten minutes to explain (with frequent interruptions from the good doctor) what I believed to be the nature of Medina's particular psychological issues. Eventually even he fell silent and listened to me without moving or making a note. When it became obvious that I had finished he swivelled his chair and stared out of the window in silence for two minutes. Finally, he spoke. "Sir John, were you in the army yourself?"

"Queens Royal Lancers – short commission."

"And young Harry was in the Guards, of course."

"Blues and Royals."

"So, I am wondering if I could advise on possible cases of PTS disorder."

"But I…"

Robbi put her hand on my arm warningly. "Thank you, Doctor Livesey. That would be exactly what we think would be required."

Livesey studied her. "I imagine it must annoy you, young lady, when people continuously assume that great beauty of itself comes at the cost of brain power."

She smiled. "John's problem is twofold, Doctor – time and security. We have less than three weeks before we have to 'manage' this person. Unfortunately, due to his proximity to certain parties, we are unable to avail ourselves of serious government assistance. However…"

She passed Alan Cummins' business card across the desk. He took it gingerly as if it might contaminate him and Robbi stood up, nudging me with her foot to do the same.

"Aye, well. I may not be the person to help you, you know, but I think I know someone in my department who may be willing to be of assistance."

By this time, I had caught up with the situation and as Robbi scribbled my phone number on the back of Alan Cummins' card I thought I could make a contribution to the conversation. "It may be very useful if whoever this person is would be willing to meet and analyse this person face to face."

"I cannot rule that out or rule that in, Sir John. Goodbye to you both. I would in normal circumstances offer my best wishes to cousin Harry, but to be frank, I cannot abide the boy. Good day. Good day."

We walked down the steps into the warm morning. "You swallowed a dictionary?"

"I dinnae ken what you mean, Sir John."

"Avail ourselves of government assistance…"

"Up yours, skinny boy. At least I didn't come out with 'matter of national importance'."

We picked up our bags from the hotel, took a taxi to Paddington and caught the first train we could to Kemble via Swindon. Back in the Manor it was the same busy, busy. Miranda walked out of the kitchen with a cup of tea in her hand. She saw me and blushed. "Sorry, Sir John, I was just…"

Robbi yelped with laughter. "Don't call him that. He's big headed enough as it is."

Miranda blushed again.

CHAPTER TWENTY-THREE

Back to the dining hall. I looked round at the others and cleared my throat. "Here's what I think Medina will do. In the next week we'll start to hear more stories about the continuing dreadful state of our post Brexit trade balance with the rest of the world and he'll start to sell Sterling. My guess then is that he'll get someone in the government to fuel the story with an ill-judged comment about China. Then the Chinese will do something to help him. By this time the pound will be well below par with the Euro and probably down to parity against the dollar. I think he'll hold it there and then sell the shit out of it as the G20 starts."

So… I tried to ignore how tenuous this all sounded.

"We find this hoard of treasure – I'm assuming it's gold because Anna's great grandfather was a gold prospector – and use it as collateral to trade against Medina. We can't talk to anyone in government, but I have assurances from BTD for funds to match whatever we find. The basic issue that MI5 and BTD are trying to get to grips with is how big Medina's fund is. If he's got fifty billion dollars, we're up shit creek. I don't think he has anything like this amount, but then, at the moment, neither do we."

Harry sat forward, half raising his hand, but I'd just got into my stride and nearly forgotten how much I hated being part of a group.

"Just a sec, Harry. Dave and Paul will see what the chances are of a strike against him if the worst comes to the worst. The problem with that is that we don't know whether the whole thing will collapse if he goes down. Finally, you, Harry, will have to go back into the lion's den. Tell him you think he's wonderful or whatever you like, and offer any help you can. It doesn't matter if he believes you or not, it will cause confusion. So, what did you want to ask?"

"Well, I'm only going to state the obvious because no one else is. What happens if Palmer can't break the code?"

"We're screwed."

"Oh, that's all right then. So, if we've finished here, I shall borrow young Miranda's car and pop into Burford for a little R&R."

Palmer was back in the library Skyping Anna. Even allowing for the Skype quality she looked ill. Her neck was in a brace and I could see the remains of bruising all over her face. I stared at the screen feeling horribly responsible.

"John, I don't know if you realised, but I can see you as easily as you can see me. Anyone tell you how dreadful you look?"

I blew her a kiss. "Touché."

"I need to rest now, but Palmer's almost there, John. Obviously it's only a transliteration"

"Obviously!"

I looked at the words and seemingly random letters. "Why haven't you been able to translate these?"

I pointed at sets of hieroglyphs below already translated letters.

"Oh, they're numbers. I was going to do them last of all."

"Do me a favour, Anna. Can you translate them. I have a feeling."

"They're not map references if that's what you're thinking."

"Well can you just do the ones round this place called Gutok."

"OK. I'll email them to Palmer when they're done. Bye."

Palmer watched me as I retrieved the library steps from their corner and slid them along the wall opposite the fireplace. On the top shelf I knew there were my Grandfather's gazetteers, dozens of them dating from the end of the 19th century and at the bottom of a pile of stained and brittle maps – as if hidden by design – was a gazetteer of China. I opened the flyleaf. It was dated 1918 and the ink stamp proclaimed that it was 'Ex Libris Clanroyden'. So this had belonged to my grandfather's particular friend, Sandy Arbuthnot, the Lord Clanroyden, a man who had been with him on so many of his insane adventures – a man, I reminded myself, who had known Anna's grandfather.

I carried my heavy, dusty prize to the nearest of the library's three long tables. This could take some time. I tried logic. I tried skimming the maps to see if anything stood out. The problem was the maps were so small and the country so vast. Eventually I went into the kitchen and had a cup of tea with Margaret unable to suppress the feeling that if something didn't break soon it was going to be all too late. I shrugged and spent fifteen minutes peeling and parboiling potatoes.

It was six o'clock and we had nineteen days left. I called Dave. "How's the shredding business, Dave?"

"Well one of the worrying things is that it's working perfectly without me and the other worrying thing is that I am bored shitless. How's things there?"

I smiled. "I just boiled some potatoes."

Dave laughed – a rare event. "You know that Alan Cummins thinks it's too risky to take out ffitch at this stage?"

"Yes?"

"Well how do you feel about doing it anyway? Want to guess where I am?"

I smiled. "You're outside the Treasury Building, aren't you?"

"Yup."

"How do you know where he is and which entrance he uses?"

"I have friends. Wait a bit. Here he comes."

"Leave the phone on."

"Will do."

I heard the engine start and then judder and stop and then Dave's voice. "Bugger."

A slam of the door and then Dave again…

"Excuse me Guv, can you tell me how to get to Admiralty Arch."

And then ffitch, faint, but loveable as ever…

"I am a busy man and I don't have time to answer stupid questions"

"Oh, OK, Guv, sorry to have bothered you."

A scuffle and a squeal and a door slam and the engine revved and Dave again. "Do not move."

"Look I'm sorry. Admiralty Arch is just up here. It's just that happen to be very busy and I work for the Treasury."

A pause. "We know, Mr ffitch. Stupid name that. Where'd you get it?"

"What do you mean?"

"Well what's with the double ff in lower case?"

"How do you know my name? Who are you?"

"Think of me as a patriot, Mr ffitch. Got any plans for this evening?"

"No. I mean, yes, I am visiting my sister. She is expecting me."

I butted in on Dave's Blue Tooth earpiece. "He doesn't have a sister, Dave."

He relayed this to his passenger. "You don't have a sister, Mr ffitch."

I butted in again. "Dave, head towards Horseferry Road in Westminster. I have to make a call. By the way, I think he'll start to get uppity in a minute if he thinks you're not going to hit him."

I heard the engine slow, the quick rasp of the handbrake and then a squeal and a bump. "He won't be causing any problems for a while, John. Call me back asap."

I called Dr Livesey, hoping against hope that he worked long hours.

"Sir John?"

He did. "Dr Livesey, you will remember that I told you of the man's hypnotic power."

"Aye, I do. I have been reading up on this. It seems to speak of a monstrous ego. An American president whose name you may remember suffered from the same problem, if suffering is the right word in his case. The colleague I mentioned would be willing to help."

"Well, we happen to have one of the people who I think is one of his subjects. It would be very useful to know if this man is simply greedy and immoral or if he's under our man's influence. And er, it happens that we have the man very near to you and we don't want to keep him out of circulation for any longer than an evening. We are at a very difficult stage."

Silence. "You don't ask for much, do you, young man."

"No, Doctor, I know."

"I called your Major Cummins. He seemed to be amused by your presumption. Call Cummins. If he calls me within the next five minutes, the answer is yes."

I called Cummins.

"Hello, what are you up to now?"

"Alan, I know you've spoken to Livesey."

"Och aye, the wee doctor."

"Look, Alan, Dave Lord has got hold of ffitch and he can take him round to Livesey's office within five minutes. We'll let him go immediately after, but we need to know how in with Medina he really is. If you phone Livesey now he'll co-operate"

Silence. "God, John."

I said nothing.

"OK, I'll do it, but I want to be there."

"It's only just across the river."

"I'm aware of that. Tell Mr Lord to wait outside. Is he in his van?"

"Yes."

"I'll join him there."

"Thank you, Alan."

I dialled Dave. "Yes, John?"

"We're on. Major Cummins is on his way."

I put the phone down and waited. Robbi called from the door. "Margaret says food's ready."

"I'm waiting for Dave to call back. Start without me."

She studied me for a moment, nodded, and turned away. She'd be back, I knew. My phone rang. "Dave?"

"Major Cummins is here."

There was shuffling, door banging, distant noises and then voices, crackling and a thud which I took to be Dave putting the phone on a desk and activating the loud speaker – and then clearer voices. One I didn't recognise. It spoke.

"Mr ffitch."

Silence.

"Mr ffitch. I am a doctor. I have just checked your vital signs and I know you can hear me so please don't waste my time and yours by pretending to be unconscious. We have brought you here because we believe you are in grave danger both physically and psychologically. For your information I am an army medic and your arrival here, while unorthodox, has been approved at the highest level. We have put the blindfold over your eyes as one of my colleagues needs to remain anonymous. Do you understand?"

Silence. A sigh. "Do you understand, Mr ffitch?"

A noise, a muffled thump, a squeal.

"I don't believe you. I have been kidnapped, assaulted, bullied. I will not tolerate this behaviour."

The doctor spoke again. "I have told you the exact truth, Mr ffitch. I would be very grateful if you would co–operate."

"You do not frighten me. I have no intention of co–operating with you. I demand to be released."

"Mr ffitch, we do frighten you. I will give you one more chance to co–operate, before we use chemical methods."

A long silence. Another sigh. And then Dave's voice. "You don't have to waste army chemicals on him, Doctor. Just give me ten minutes with him and he'll sing you a song."

"You keep that man away from me. You claim to be a doctor. If you really were a doctor, you would not tolerate such behaviour from this thug."

"You weren't listening, Mr ffitch. I am an army doctor, a psychiatrist. I am often obliged to use unorthodox methods to draw out psychological problems in my patients."

"I do not have any psychological problems."

"Oh, but you do, Mr ffitch and if you do not co–operate I will have no problem at all in sectioning you and holding you within one of our army institutions for as long as I deem it necessary. That could be for a very long time. Now I am going to give you one minute to consider your position."

I looked up. Robbi was walking back towards me holding a plate of roast potatoes that she waved under my nose. I held up a finger, put the phone down, put it on loudspeaker and muted it. I grabbed a potato. God – a hot potato. I waved my fingers frantically in front of my mouth. Cummins interjected.

"You don't seem to understand, Mr ffitch. You have stepped out of your world and into ours. Everything here is reversed. Here you are not an important person. Dominick Medina is not an important person."

The army psychiatrist took over. "You will be aware that you flinched at the mention of that name, Mr ffitch. Perhaps you can now see that our interests are somewhat wider than you had imagined. Now, I will not ask you again. Drugs or voluntary co–operation?"

A murmur from ffitch.

"I beg your pardon, Mr ffitch."

"All right, all right. What do you want to know?

"Tell us about Dominick Medina."

"He is a brilliant man. Quite brilliant."

A pause.

"In what way?"

"He has a remarkable vision of the economy. Not that you would understand, but he is the John Maynard Keynes of our age. HMG finds his advice invaluable."

"What is his training?"

"Er, finance."

"And his specialism?"

Cummins had taken over.

Palmer came out and we waved him to silence. Within a minute the entire household was crammed round my phone. ffitch was still sounding nauseatingly bumptious. "I don't believe you would understand the level of finance at which we work."

"Try me."

"He er. It is…"

And then in a rush. "Foreign exchange trading, arbitrage."

"And his academic qualifications are?"

"I er don't er… know."

"I see. How well would you say you know, Mr Medina?"

"I know him… I know him very well."

"How long have you known him?"

"I er, er…"

The doctor upped the pressure. "Mr ffitch. That's a simple question. How long have you known him? Four years, five years? Longer?"

"I can't remember. It's not important."

"What if I tell you it is the most important factor in his conversation, Mr ffitch? When did you meet him? Where?"

"I er… I…"

"Do you begin to see the problem, Mr ffitch?"

"No, I do not."

"Well now. Sir John Hannay said you were stupid, Mr ffitch, and that answer proved him right."

I stiffened. What was Cummins playing at?

"What the hell is Hannay got to do with this? The man is a traitor to his country. He should be arrested and charged!"

"And why do you say he is a traitor, Mr ffitch?"

"Because he attacked Mr Medina in his own home."

"And who told you this, Mr ffitch?

"Dominick Medina himself."

So they were that close.

"And did you think to question his statement, follow up on it, see where and when the attack took place? Did you ask Mr Medina what damage had been done to him personally?"

"I do not need to follow up on such things. Mr Medina has proved himself time and time again to be a patriot and a man of integrity."

God, what a stupid little man.

"If I were to tell you that Sir John Hannay is regarded by our security services as a man of great value and probity and that Mr Medina is regarded as a serious threat to the future of this country, what would you say?"

"I would say you were talking rubbish. Hannay is now in a sexual relationship with a common little Essex tart. He is living off his family name and is a has–been in the City."

"Can't argue with any of that", I murmured.

Robbi stood on my foot. The doctor took over again.

"You will remember what I told you about everything being reversed here. Sergeant, hold his arm."

ffitch screamed and struggled, but he wouldn't have had a chance against Dave's enormous strength. Eventually there was silence and then Dave's voice.

"Can we phone John back on a land line, my battery's going down?"

I disconnected and the phone rang immediately. I could hear Alan's voice. "… so, Doctor, was that significant?"

"Well Sir John is right in that he is not as bright as I would have expected a man in his position to be – Good evening, Sir John."

"Evening, Doctor, this is much appreciated. Would I be overstepping the mark if I said that there was some reasonable evidence that he is under the influence of Mr Medina in some way?"

"Not at all. If you had seen his face, you would have seen that he was really struggling to answer the question about when he first met your man, Medina. His problem, by the way, is egotism and self–regard more than stupidity. He is not used to being questioned. Dr Livesey told me of your childhood meeting with Mr Medina and I'm wondering if something not dissimilar, if far less brutal happened to ffitch. When did you first meet him?"

"At school. We were in the same year."

"And was he hostile to you from the first?"

I thought for a second. "Yes. Yes, I rather think he was. Doctor, one final question. If we were able to get someone into Medina's presence, how should he play it with him?"

"I haven't studied the subject in person, but my colleague Dr Livesey's comment about his monstrous ego would suggest that whoever gets in front of him should pander to it. Be very humble, praise him extravagantly, never disagree, only speak when spoken to and never volunteer any original ideas. Now if that's all, Sir John, we have to get on and plant the idea in our patient here that he has been in a motor accident, knocked down, I would suggest, by a white van. Fortunately for us, he is very suggestible."

"Good, good. Thank you, doctor. Thank you very much. Goodbye."

I pressed the off button and looked around at the faces. I picked out Harry. "Remember that, Harry. That'll be your job if it comes to it."

"What?"

"You will have to be humble and praise him."

Harry was shocked, appalled. "Me? Not a chance."

No one spoke. We watched Harry. He looked round the faces seeing no hint of weakening and groaned. "God, all right. All right! But under protest."

"Protest duly noted. Well, I suppose that all takes us forward a bit, but ffitch's interview isn't anything we could use in court."

Palmer smiled. "I don't think a court room is where this is all going to end up, John. Come and have a look at where I've got to."

"You've got somewhere?"

"Getting, not got."

* * *

A block of text was on the iMac screen:

drlhlnuvvogslkovxsakpibvtihucssnsvixifwcnsamatnw
ixkrubtzidjbrlzkshmnfrknfyfogmoxrxmmctesoyfkiyotmb
hkuztayrdodgulcrkswfonhnwatozrlohofdkfsoiptmr

"Is that Caesar's code?"

"No. We don't know what it is yet. It's part of that speech you made."

I stared at it until the letters began to merge into one another. I blinked the tears out of my eyes.

"Mmmm. Have you let the common little Essex tart have a look at it?"

"Careful, Has Been."

Robbi sat down in front of the screen, pushing her hair behind her ears. She was silent, then… "Felt tip pen."

I passed one to her. She started to ring letters on the screen, counting under her breath. "One, two, three, four, five." She ringed a letter. "One, two, three, four, five – 'L' – one, two three, four, five 'O' – one, two three, four, five 'O' – one, two three, four, five 'K' – one, two, three, four, five. No, shit, it doesn't work."

"Add another letter."

"What do you mean?"

"You've got a whole word there – 'LOOK' – so add another letter for a gap between words."

"Gotcha."

My heart skipped three beats. I knew it hadn't behaved like this before Medina's ministrations or maybe ffitch was right and I was just a has–been. And in less than three weeks' time I was going head-to-head with the world's best traders in a battle in which I would be outgunned, outmanned, out–financed and probably out–thought. Robbi glanced at me, sensing something wrong. I shook my head at her. She carried on counting.

"Still doesn't work."

She put the palms of her hands over her eyes, pressed them in and then stared at the screen again. "OK, we have the first word – L O O K"

"So maybe they changed the number of letters after each word."

She started counting again, ringing the sixth letter now.

"Yes. Got the next one – I N W A R D S"

"Seven letters now."

F R O M. Even I could count that. She stopped and cursed under her breath.

"I lost count. Eight this time: Y O U R. This is easy, Palmer."

"Not any more it ain't." Palmer was staring at the screen over her shoulder.

They stared then shook their heads in synch. The exultation seeped away.

"'LOOK INWARDS FROM'… From what for Christ's sake?"

I turned away determined not to let my anger and frustration show. I failed. "Sod it. You may as well just start from the other end."

I walked out of the house towards the semi–derelict lodge house at the top of the drive wondering if it would be worth renovating for some future and entirely mythical estate employee. I circumnavigated it, peering at the ivy climbing the chimney and the rotten windowsills until there was an unladylike yell from the manor. Robbi was running towards me.

"Own door."

I stared at her, still half–thinking of the lodge house. Why would it need another door?

She held my face between the palms of her hands and laughed at me. "Own door, John Hannay. Own door."

She slapped my cheeks on each word. The penny dropped. "You mean 'Look Inwards From Your Own Door.' How did you get it?"

"It was you. 'Start from the other end', you said. So, after a while I did just that."

I started to run back to the house. She grabbed my arm and wagged a finger at me. I was to walk slowly. I dawdled in a docile manner until she took her hand off my arm, then I ran up the steps into the house. She followed, laughing. And there it was on the screen with all the relevant letters capitalised, highlighted and italicised.

drlh*L*nuvv*O*gslk*O*vxsa*K*pibvtg*I*hucsd*N*svixi*W*cnsam *A*tnwix*R*ubtzi*D*jbrlz*S*hmnfrkn*F*yfogmo*R*xmmctes*O*yfkiy ot*M*bhkuztat*Y*rdodgulc*O*rkswfonq*U*lqingtra*R*m *O*dxtjfptkry*W*hzemplkytr*N*wkvnwatozc*D*cuaqitolh*O*xfp glohof*O*dkfsoiptm*R*

"Count nine letters backwards from the end and then the last two words read backwards. But which door?"

Harry started with the front door. He climbed a ladder. He tilted the chandelier. He tapped the walls for hollow patches. He measured the thickness of the walls. Nothing. He went to the scullery.

CHAPTER TWENTY-FOUR

I got up late. Robbi had gone for out for a run with Palmer at seven. At eight thirty I turned on my phone – there were four messages from The Boss waiting for me. I dialled.

"Sorry, Em."

She didn't even bother to mock. "Someone's going short on Sterling. I think it's starting."

"What's the Bank doing?"

"Nothing yet. It's off a whole cent against the dollar. Where's your money, Super Trader?"

"Almost there, Em. Had a breakthrough last night."

"Good. I'm going to need you here, John. Bring Miss Beautiful too, the Floor will like that."

I snorted. "Tomorrow, Em. I'll get a trading screen set up now. Oh, have you told Alan Cummins?"

"No, he's not an early starter."

"I'll call him."

I commandeered two of the computers and started to set up the trading screens. Margaret heard the cursing and came in with scrambled eggs, bacon, toast and coffee. She stood for a minute watching me as I loaded up the proprietary software.

"John?"

"Yes, Margaret."

"Do you mind if I tell you something?"

"Of course not."

"Well, yesterday lunchtime you ate an apple. Last night you ate one roast potato and you are now ignoring breakfast."

I stared at her and then at the food.

"From what Paul tells me, you are about to do something very stressful and you look as ill as I feel. Now for goodness sake, eat something before you pass out."

I picked up a piece of toast. Margaret glowered at me. I sat down quickly and picked up knife and fork. God, I was hungry. I ate ravenously under her stern eye and an hour later I was set up and watching the spot trades. Palmer watched the flickering trades on the screens for a few minutes.

"How much does it all represent?"

"In dollars? Well about one point four trillion dollars get traded on spots in a twenty-four-hour period so in the time we've been here… about a billion, I guess."

He shook his head at the insanity of the market. I didn't disagree. After another twenty minutes I released the computer back to him. The pound had only dropped another 10 points and no one else seemed to be joining in. If it was Medina, he had one hell of a short position. Robbi grabbed the mouse and started checking to see if there was any bad news coming out anywhere. I called The Boss.

"It's settled for the moment, Em. Any word on who or why?"

"No. Nothing. My spy at the Bank says there a lot of scared little bunnies there. You sure it's settled?"

"Smells like it, yes."

"Well I hope like hell that the Super Trader's nose is as good as it used to be."

My phone buzzed again – Dave. I walked out through the scullery into the kitchen garden.

"What's up, Dave?"

"I've managed to get a two-day cleaning contract for a company that's moving into the same building as Medina's company. Want to use it as a forward observation post? You know, stick in video and listening equipment and relay it to somewhere we can analyse it?"

Excellent thought. I walked round to share it with Palmer. He looked up and actually smiled. "Translation finished, thanks to Anna."

"Well, it's a bloody shame I can't work out anything from the dear old gazetteer."

I picked up the book and made as if to throw it out of the door. The sun shone through the window at an angle lighting the edge of the room and shining through the yellowing page – the yellowing page with tiny shafts of sun coming through the tiny little holes. I stopped dead.

"Palmer, tell me I'm not mad."

"No."

"Come and see this."

He crossed the library and peered at the sunlit page. "Aaaah. OK. OK. You're still mad though. Hold it there. I'll get a pencil."

I moved not a muscle. Five seconds later he was back and starting to draw rings round the holes. He stared at the pencil marks.

"Now all we need is Anna's translation."

"Yes, and someone with a brain."

Robbi was watching from the door. I raised an eyebrow in her direction as she walked forward. She shrugged.

"Well, it does look as though the gazetteer and the hieroglyphs are connected and whatever that connection is, it's bound to be the private key setting."

Palmer nodded. "We know that John here was just learning and speaking by rote. And we know that it took Anna hours to translate it. Why? She's still online. I'll ask."

He Skyped her and asked.

"Because I was having to interpret what John said and then make sense of it in writing."

"And what was your first impression of it, Anna?

"My first impression? That it didn't make complete sense."

"Why?"

"It just didn't read right. I had to interpret it. Not the numbers, I mean. They were clear."

"How long will it take for you to type the text out without any interpretation and the numbers, Anna?"

"Half an hour maybe unless the nurse comes back."

CHAPTER TWENTY-FIVE

Time is elastic. It stretched thinner and longer that day as the seconds ticked into minutes, the minutes into endless, bloody hours. By five I was standing in the drive again staring at the front door when I heard Miranda's Beetle chugging back in. She climbed out with an expression of concern on her face. "John, what's everybody been doing staring at the front door? Is something wrong"

"Didn't Robbi tell you?"

"She started to, but I had to rush off and see a tree surgeon."

"It's a thing that she worked out – a coded message for me from my grandfather which we don't quite understand."

"And it is?"

"It says – 'look inwards from your own door.'"

"But why's that your own door? That's the front door, not your door."

And there it was, just out of reach somewhere in my frontal lobes. I knew which door it was and Miranda was right. It wasn't the front door. My phone rang.

"Boss?"

"John."

John, not Super Trader. This was serious then.

"I think the top floor have been got at. If you don't have your money by tomorrow, the deal's off. Alan

Cummins is with them now, but I can read that load of bastards like an open book."

The phone went dead. Shit, shit, shit. Suddenly I didn't want to see anyone or talk to anyone or listen to anyone. Life had been so much simpler when I was on my own. I went in and up the staircase to the main bedroom thinking that I may as well pack. Maybe I had put on a bit of weight and one of my suits would fit me again. They were still hanging on a rack in the bedroom following our excavations in the dressing room and I started picking through them in a desultory manner, my brain still half–ticking over on Miranda's comment. My own door, where? In the flat – the place where I'd spent most of my life? My door. Front door? No not mine. Bedroom door? Probably – somewhere *inwards* into my childhood bedroom. I had better go up to London tonight and look.

Without thinking I opened the dressing room door and went to hang a suit on the rack that was no longer there. I flicked on the light switch and there it was. Idiot! Not 'my' own door – the 'your' was plural, the Hannay family's own little door. The little door I hadn't even known existed until a few days ago – our own little door. I crouched in front of it and opened it again staring at the solid stonework behind it, pushing my finger along the pointing, peering into one of the drill holes left by Harry's excavations. I traced the dust on the floor left from the drilling, idly drawing a finger wide line in the grey powder out from the door into the room.

Inwards from your own door: inwards from my own door… our own door. Inwards. I stood up, rubbing the dust from my fingertip. And it sank in. Not into the wall

– into the room. Inwards, not outwards. I stamped my heel on the floor. I reached up and tapped the ceiling. 'Inwards from your own door.'

"Harry? Harry?"

I stood on the landing and shouted down.

Heads began to appear – a blonde one first.

I looked down and smiled.

"'Inwards from your own door.' Our door. Not the front door. Miranda put me on to it. Our door."

Robbi was walking up the stairs staring at me. "You mean the door in the dressing room!"

"Yes, Roberta Jane. I do."

Harry raced past her up the stairs. Robbi followed more slowly, her slow smile spreading across her face. Paul was still staring up at me.

"It's inwards, Paul. Into the dressing room, not into the wall. Get the plans, will you."

He ran to the library, coming back with the cardboard tube of paperwork to where Robbi and Harry were going through the same process as I had – tapping, knocking and hammering. Robbi picked up the plan and turned it slowly in her hands. "Have you checked the interior walls? I mean really checked them to see if they're where they're supposed to be."

"No, we haven't because… well no, we haven't."

Five minutes later we were crouched round Harry in the library in complete silence listening to Paul's shouted measurements as he used the thirty–metre tape on the wall outside. Measuring internally, from each window across the width of the library to its interior wall there was a divergence. The room was narrower than shown on the plans – thirty inches narrower, or, should you wish to be metric – which of course the plans weren't – seventy–six point two centimetres.

Robbi broke away first, running up the stairs to the dressing room. I rolled up the plans again and followed the rest slowly, my heart pounding, my head buzzing. At the top of the staircase I leaned against the banister on the landing and breathed slowly, deeply, hanging on to the plans and pretending to study them as soft footsteps came up behind me.

"You do not fool me, John Hannay."

She turned me round taking my wrist in her fingers, feeling for my pulse, watching me carefully. I shook my head at her, took one more deep breath and walked into the dressing room. Palmer arrived with the cold chisel and a claw hammer from the cupboard beside the Aga.

He looked at me questioningly. I nodded and he levered up the first of the old boards, splintering its edge. The next was easier, then a third and a fourth until the structure below was revealed. The wall between the library and the dining hall below was simply massive.

"Palmer, tap the top of the wall. Exactly below where my hand is – yes, that's it."

He tapped.

"Again."

He tapped again.

"Harder, this time. Be very accurate"

Palmer shrugged and hit down hard. The stone rang – a small crack appeared in the mortar around the slab.

"Paul, there's a felling axe behind the basket in the scullery, would you mind…?"

He ran.

By the time he returned Robbi and I had managed to clear what looked like centuries of dust, dead insects and detritus from the surface of the stones. Paul stepped forward with the axe in his hands, reversed it, raised it above his head and swung the back of the axe head down hard onto the top of the wall. There was a sharp crack and one of the stones split, slithered and fell clattering into the darkness below. Robbi shone the flashlight into the void and I could just make out the top of what looked as if it could be a set of rusted rungs. Paul started on one of the adjoining slabs with the axe. He paused and looked up at me. "You know this could be booby trapped."

"It could, but as it was made by my grandfather, I doubt it. No one's touched this in years."

Anyway, I didn't care. I was frantic to know more. My heart was pounding. My vision was blurring, I rocked on my heels and then... a cool hand pressed against my forehead and I took two deep breaths. She took my wrist in her fingers and I forced my heart to slow. I breathed out and looked around in the sudden silence. Four pairs of eyes were watching me.

"I'm all right. I'm OK. Carry on, Paul."

I gestured urgently. He levered up the next two slabs revealing a black, oblong hole large enough to fit through. I knelt and lowered myself into the blackness, testing each rung carefully before putting my full weight on it. Once below the level of the surface slabs I could see that the shaft was brick lined. It was narrow and around three feet from front to back, full of dust, dirt and home to ninety or so generations of spiders.

Slowly I placed my foot on the furthest rung down that I could reach. I held a torch in my mouth while Harry shone the flashlight down past my body. I kept going down and down, counting off the rungs. I had reached twenty–four when my foot touched the ground. Directly in front of me was another door. I turned the handle, pushed it open, shining the torch ahead of me. It looked and felt like a wine cellar – barrel vaulted in brick a foot above my head.

I heard Harry's footsteps on the rungs in the vertical shaft behind me as I stepped forward, my torch playing over something that looked like a curtain. As I reached out to touch it I realised it was no more than an old tarpaulin. I could hear Harry scrabbling through the door as I pulled at it, feeling more than seeing it rustle and crackle down to the floor before me… and then Harry's gasp of amazement. Behind the tarpaulin was a brick wall of something yellow and shiny. It was at least six feet high and I couldn't tell how far back it went. Harry's breath hissed out through his teeth. "Oh Cinderella," he breathed. "You shall go to the ball."

It was gold, all gold, thousands and thousands of ingots worth, even to my untutored eye, hundreds of millions or more likely billions. Propped against the wall of gold behind where the tarpaulin had been was a sealed foolscap envelope. I picked it up carefully holding it in front of the torchlight to see if I could tell what it contained and then Robbi was beside me and then Palmer and Paul. After five minutes of hysteria and attempts to count the ingots, we climbed slowly back up. A further five minutes later I was outside in the garden on my mobile to Alan. "I think you'd better get down here smartish."

"You have a problem?"

"No, Alan, we have a problem. I'll call Em. She can come with you. Can you be here this evening?"

"That bad a problem?"

"Yes."

"Tell Emma I'll collect her in thirty minutes."

That would mean they would here by nine. "OK, we'll have some food ready."

I called Em. She sounded depressed. "Boss?"

"John?" No enthusiasm.

"Alan's picking you up in twenty–nine minutes. You're coming to Fosse. No argument. This is important with a capital imp."

"OK." Listlessly.

"Boss. Buck up."

"Fuck off, Super Trader." That was better.

I walked back into the study where they were all crowded to hear Palmer's exposition.

"Say fourteen hundred pounds an ounce – give or take. How many ounces in an ingot?"

I left them to their calculations and went into the library to open the envelope. I heard Robbi's step and held out my hand to her without looking round, slit open the flap and pulled out a single piece of paper.

This letter is from Richard Hannay and is written on 14th March 1937. My beloved wife, Mary, sits beside me as I write in the study of our home, Fosse Manor.

I hope and believe my grandson is reading this or even my great grandson, assuming that our own dear boy, Peter John, does have children. If you have found this letter, I believe that you will be under threat from the family of the man who once tried and failed to destroy me, Dominick Medina. The gold and diamonds…

"Diamonds, John? I didn't see any diamonds?"
I shook my head. "Must be in the middle of the gold."
I read on.

'… that you are looking at were put here by Valdemar Haraldsen and myself in September 1936. It is less than half of the fortune secured by his father Marius Haraldsen in the course of his long and illustrious life. The rest remains in southern China where he hid it in 1919. Together, Valdemar and I decided that such wealth was not for the use of one man or family. If you have read my papers, you will know that Dominick Medina was a force for great evil in this world, but what you will not know is that he had a son and that son was brought up by his mother in the same tradition of wickedness and evil and that now, even at the age of fourteen, he has made an attempt on my life. He failed, of course, but the vengeance that he seeks will not cease with the passing of my life.

To you, my descendant, I leave this great curse and this greater legacy, knowing that you will put it to the best of uses in the battle between good and evil and in the protection and preservation of our sacred country. Remember too that you can always count on the descendants of my closest friends, friends who have pledged their help and support to my family in this battle.

God bless you, my child. Use it well and fight the good fight.

Your ancestor,
Richard Hannay.

Robbi sniffed and wiped her eyes. I stared at the paper not really trusting myself to speak yet. I went to push it back into the envelope, but something was stopping it. I peered inside, turned the envelope upside down and another document fell out. I studied it. It was a codicil to my grandfather's will leaving the treasure to my father and so to me, witnessed by Valdemar Haraldsen and Ludovic Gustavus Arbuthnot, the Lord Clanroyden, and signed by my grandfather himself. I took a deep breath. "Can you lot come in here, please."

They filed in.

"There's a letter here from my grandfather. You can read it if you like. It explains where the gold came from – Anna's great grandfather, actually, but one thing is absolutely specific. The gold is to be used for the battle against Medina."

I looked at them waiting for the argument. But all I could see were smiles and nods of agreement. I looked at Harry in surprise.

"Oh, come on Hannay, you didn't think I'd try and run off with it, did you?"

"Well, er actually, um, yes!"

"You know Robbi's right about you – you are an idiot. I know why we're here and why we're going to have to put this Medina character down. You seem to forget that he has had me in his clutches as well. If I weren't so thick skinned, I'd be hurt. Mind you…"

Palmer was watching him closely.

"I don't suppose they'd miss a few if they just happened to disappear. What do you say to that, John?"

"I'd say go for it, but bloody hurry."

CHAPTER TWENTY-SIX

At eight forty-five, a black Jaguar swung into the drive and pulled up in front of the Manor. Alan and Emma were decanted and stood there looking up at the mellow stone house in the dusk. I walked out to greet them. "So, what's the problem, Em?"

"It's what I said earlier. Unless you have proof of funds tomorrow by nine it's all over. That fucking little shit Medina will have won."

"You call that a problem? You just come and see a *real* problem. This way."

In my bedroom I threw overalls and a pair of trainers at The Boss and asked Alan if he minded getting a bit of dust on his clothes. He shook his head. I headed for the tunnel with him behind me, leaving her to change in privacy. By the time he had reached the bottom, she was starting from the top and I waited in the cellar with my torch turned up towards the ceiling. When she joined us I turned towards the pile and pulled down the tarpaulin, turning to watch the reaction. The Boss put her hands up to her mouth and stared wide eyed. Alan took a step back as Emma found her voice. "Holy Mother of God! How much is there, John?"

Palmer's voice came from behind as he emerged from the tunnel.

"On the assumption that it is a solid block and not hollow at the centre I estimate the value at current gold prices to be in excess of four billion dollars."

"Emma Fitzgerald, Alan Cummins, meet Palmer."

They looked at each other.

"According to the letter I have just found from my grandfather there is also a cache of diamonds in there somewhere."

"Four billion, plus diamonds." Alan was peering round the side of the huge golden pile. "But what's your problem, John? Surely you now have enough to go head-to-head with Medina?"

Emma shook her head. "And how the hell does John convince anyone that he's not some kind of drug lord. I mean which bank in their right mind is going to take this? You can't just pop into your local branch and deposit it over the counter. I could get the board of directors down here to see the collateral, but apart from giving them all wet pants, I'm not sure it would help."

Palmer shuffled behind me. "Anyway, I came down here to tell you that Margaret is kicking off as the food's been ready for ten minutes and she says it's going to spoil."

Five minutes later we were seated round the old dining table. I was unsure how to effect introductions so there was tentative small talk over the soup. But with the arrival of three whole roast chickens and a pile of roast potatoes and vegetables backed up by half a dozen bottles of Côtes du Rhône, conversations opened up. Alan glanced in Emma's direction.

"Know much about the Canton of Zug?"

The Boss gave him one of her disconcerting stares and then smiled slowly. "How would you get it there, though?"

I joined in. "I am aware that the Canton of Zug is in Switzerland and that it has, shall we say, liberal laws relating to overseas companies and money, but beyond that, Alan, explain."

Alan put down his knife and fork and sat back. "What, John, do you think is the most important requirement for intelligence officers who are on the move?"

"Well given the conversation we are having, I would guess it would be immediate access to large amounts of money in various currencies."

"Exactly. Welcome to the world of Banc Aargau SA in Zug. It's handled our finances for many more years than I've been with the department."

Alan shrugged. "And how the hell do we get it there?"

Robbi raised a hand. "You know that we're not that far from RAF Benson here. Well, I've often seen choppers going over from Joint Helicopter Command – not Chinooks but definitely Pumas and Merlins. So why can't they get us a Chinook which will develop engine trouble and have to touch down in the paddock?"

Paul spoke up from the end of the table where he was clearing his plate. "Mr Lord and I can put together the team, Major. We'll need some specialist lifting gear for inside the house, though."

Alan groaned. "So, all I have to do is convince the Swiss Air Force that we're not invading them. Simple."

Emma pointed at Harry. "And you, Pretty Boy? You're not saying much. What's your role in all this?"

Before Harry could answer with one of his more sexist comments, I interjected. "Tomorrow, Harry will be sitting in front of Mr Medina, convincing him that he is on his side."

Harry slowly closed his mouth. Emma looked at him admiringly. "Well to be honest I think I would rather be slung beneath a Chinook all the way to Switzerland than play that role. Good luck."

Harry made modest muttering noises, grabbed a passing bottle and glared at me.

Alan excused himself and left the room, mobile in hand. Two minutes later he came back in looking slightly happier and holding the phone towards me.

"Sir Ian."

I took the phone.

"Yes, Ian?"

"John, on the level, can this be done?"

"Yes, Ian."

"And you really intend to let all this money be used for this purpose?"

"Yes, Ian."

"Very well. Tomorrow at lunchtime a helicopter will make an emergency landing in your paddock. You had better get Roberta's brother Dave to work."

"Yes, Ian."

There was a snort of amusement at the other end of the phone.

"All right, John, give me back to Major Cummins and please don't say, 'yes Ian' again."

"No, Ian."

I passed the phone back to Alan. Palmer raised his hand out over the table. He was staring at the calculator on his iPad. "I'm not sure, but you may need two Chinooks." He looked up at us. "It's the weight of the gold."

We all turned to look at Alan. He groaned. Emma shook her head. "Well, if this is how things are done in Secret Service land, I'm in the wrong business."

"To be honest, Boss, you've got the most difficult job. I need to trade through BTD. What are you going to tell the Top Floor?"

"That's easy." She turned on her phone and dialled a short code. "Sebastian? Yes, I do know what the fucking time is. No, you listen! Shut up, for fuck's sake. You said I had to find the money tomorrow to do the trades we discussed. Right? OK, well I have something in excess of four billion dollars in legal, tradable securities. What? Excuse me you may be in a noisy place, but what didn't you understand about the word *legal*? Now you and the board made a fucking promise. Are you going to stick by it? It's an inheritance from a very wealthy friend of mine who wants it to be used to back Sterling. Yes, you do know him. Just a second." She put the phone on mute and looked at me. "Can I use your name?"

Say it's from the family, not from me as you don't know where I am. Say you were approached by my partner."

She nodded. "Remember the Super Trader? Yes, him. Well, it's an inheritance from his grandfather. I was approached by his partner. No, I haven't seen him. I don't know where he is, but I can tell you…"

I slipped a note under her nose. "That the family solicitor has approved it and is happy (I use the word very loosely because he doesn't know you) to meet you and confirm all this. I repeat – are you on?" She went quiet, listening. "And that's your last word, is it? Is it? OK, now you listen to me you piece of shit. You can call all your toy town board members and discuss whatever the fuck you like with them, but if you don't call me back within ten minutes, I am taking my team to *you know who* because they have been after me for three years and I now have the leverage to go to them on terms that I like, not what they think they can dictate. What? You fucking what? You have the nerve to use the word loyalty to me? Buy a fucking dictionary! Ten minutes – and right now I'm phoning the team."

She put the phone down and picked up her spoon to try Margaret's sponge pudding. "Oh, Margaret. This is so good. Mmhmm. Best sponge pudding I have had in years – and the custard. You are wonderful. Fantastic meal. Thank you so much."

Margaret blushed and muttered something and the rest of the table looked at The Boss. I spoke.

"That's why she's called The Boss."

Palmer was puzzled. "But you're not phoning your team?"

Em stopped shovelling sponge pudding into her mouth for a second. "Don't need to."

Palmer glanced at me. I smiled. "If you have to call your team to approve your decision, you're no longer The Boss. They'll all go with her. I would if I were still trading. She's the best and they know it. Top Floor does too."

Palmer was still puzzled. "But if I were your boss and you talked to me like that, I'd sack you on the spot."

Em shrugged. "Oh, don't worry about that, Palmer. He's an American hedge fund manager. That was just foreplay to him. He's probably just had to go to the bog to whack one out."

Robbi snorted custard. Margaret nearly dropped the plates. Palmer addressed his pudding. Alan looked at his watch. "So, when will he phone, Emma?"

"Oh, a minute or two after the appointed time. I'm not bothered if he doesn't, but he will. Are we ready to go back to Town, Alan?"

I raised my hand. "Hang on, Emsie. You bain't leaving here until Seb phones back. We'm country folks yere and we wants to see the end of the show."

"Well, I have to say that if your cognac is as good as your food, I'll stay."

I stood up, headed toward the wine cellar and havered over the dusty cellar book until I saw a Cognac I hadn't noticed before. Now this one would shut her up. I was right. One sip out of the Balloon glass and she sat back with a very big smile.

"The fuck, Super Trader?"

She cupped the giant glass in her palms and breathed in the fumes. Her phone rang. She didn't even look at it. Two rings, three rings. I raised my glass.

"To Emma."

They raised their glasses as one.

"To Emma."

She picked up the phone. "Hi Sebastian. Thank you, Sebastian. It will be my huge pleasure to bring the four billion dollars into BTD. No, no. Of course I didn't want to have to take my team away. Yes, of course I do appreciate the risk you're taking. That's why you're up there and I'm down here."

She put the phone down and continued sniffing and sipping her brandy. This was just all in a day's work for The Boss. "Ready when you are, Alan."

Cummins stood up. She tilted her head and poured the remains of the Cognac into her mouth and swilled it slowly, savouring every molecule. "You going to have any more surprises, Super Trader?"

"If you mean Cognac, then no, but if you mean with this lark, then the answer is I think so Em, but it all very much depends on Palmer. It's the Chinese angle. If we can crack the Chinese code then we may just get some unexpected help."

She looked at him. "He'll do it." She touched him on the arm, smiling directly into his eyes and he was hers for life. I'd seen her do it before, but it was still damned impressive and with an airy wave and a "see you in the City, Pretty Boy", she was gone.

The room felt empty.

CHAPTER TWENTY-SEVEN

Dave arrived at seven the next morning in a minibus with a trailer and seven hard looking men I half–recognised from his SAS rescue team at Medina's house. Robbi greeted them warmly, collected details and walked towards me. She stood in front of me smiling. "You know you fell asleep last night before I came to bed?"

"Sorry."

"Don't apologise, you upper class dope. I just lay there and looked at you. You snored, but at least you didn't dribble."

"Unlike you at six this morning."

She smiled again. "Have I told you lately that I love you?"

I squinted up at her suspiciously. "I know you think I'm a pygmy as regards popular culture, Roberta Jane Lord, but even I can recognise the title of a Van Morrison song."

"Oh well, worth a try. Now look, I've offered the guys £5,000 each, which is a lot I know. Do you think we could afford to let them have one ingot each as well?"

I did a quick mental calculation. "Yes. Sure. Easily. Good idea after what they did for me at Medina's house. That'll appeal to the romantic in them too. And don't tell me they aren't romantic. Make sure they don't all try and cash them in their local bank branch, though for God's sake."

"Of course. Right, I'll show them the treasure now."

She took Paul and the team up to our bedroom and I took Dave aside to discuss the Forward Observation Post. Within ten minutes the gold was coming out of the balcony windows in our bedroom and being packed into small crates two strong men could just carry. The block and tackle was in place. Dave checked his watch and issued orders.

"Corporal Johnson, Corporal Spinetti, secure the perimeter. No civilians are permitted entry. I'm expecting Major Cummins so make sure he gets through."

"Perimeter to be secured and no civilians. Major Cummins to be admitted, Sarn't Major."

They left at the double. He turned to us. "Robbs, tuck your hair up and put this on. John, what was your rank?"

"Only Lieutenant. Why?"

"You've been promoted."

He passed a beret to Robbi and a cap and pips to me.

"Major Cummins wants you two and Palmer to accompany the Gold to RAF Welford. The Yanks have agreed to it. From there we'll be driven to London."

God no! I hated helicopters. An army Landrover followed by a small truck appeared at the far end of the drive. Spinetti walked forward, saw Alan, saluted and opened the gates. Cummins was in uniform. Somehow, he looked more at home in it. He returned Dave's salute. "First Chinook should be here in ten minutes, Mr Lord."

"Very good, sir. I'll see to the cargo."

He strode away. Alan looked at us and produced an army kitbag which he threw at Robbi. "You two had better get changed and pack something."

In five minutes, we were in uniform. Robbi took one look at me and let out a 'mmmmmh' of satisfaction. "Sexy, sexy soldier boy. Mind you a fireman's uniform's just as good."

"As good as what?"

She trotted off grinning mischief. I straightened my cap with as what remaining dignity I could muster. In the distance I could hear the double thwack of the first Chinook's twin rotors. Within moments the noise had become ear drum shatteringly loud and, with what I assumed was artificially created smoke pouring from beneath one of the engines, the enormous brute of a machine hovered over the paddock, its rotors thrashing wildly at the branches of the old beech trees in the Copse and polishing the grass below. Maybe the Colonel wouldn't get his cricket pitch in perfect nick in time for the annual match. It hung over the ground for thirty seconds before lowering itself cumbersomely down, the hydraulics hissing as they took the weight. As the rotors slowed, the army truck bounced across the paddock to the loading bay with the first consignment of gold and two of Dave's team. I hurried back inside to rush Palmer, giving Margaret her last briefing on the house security alarms before joining Alan on the drive. At the last second, I remembered something, ran back into the library and grabbed it, stuffing it into the army kit bag.

Trying hard, and failing miserably, not to duck beneath the rotors far above my head, I followed Robbi up the ramp. I hate helicopters at the best of times, but that Chinook I loathed. Robbi's self–evident delight in the flight and her friendly banter with the three members of Dave's team in the chopper didn't help either. Alan stared into space and Dave sat holding his gun loosely in his hands. He looked very at home and very content – his world – very definitely not mine.

CHAPTER TWENTY-EIGHT

The Yanks did us proud when we got to their base.
Massive amounts of food and weak coffee were brought
out to us on the Tarmac and Alan was whisked into a
conflab with a man in a black suit and dark glasses who
might as well – according to Corporal Spinetti – have
had the letters CIA tattooed on his forehead. There was
a quarter hour of waiting while the forklift trucks
unloaded the first Chinook and loaded the aircraft – a
BAE 146 if you're interested. I wasn't.

Alan strode towards me. "Captain, you, Mr Palmer
and Mr Lord are due in London in two hours. My car is
waiting. Carry on."

"Sir."

I came to attention and saluted, thankful that I could
at least do this simple act – right arm, hand facing
forward, long way up, short way down – without making
an exhibition of myself. I followed Dave to the car and
as we raced towards the perimeter track, the second
Chinook from Fosse was lowering itself clumsily down
beside the jet to unload the remainder of the hoard.

It took one hour and forty–eight minutes to get to
Westminster which meant it would still only be just after
four by the time we checked in and I knew that Robbi
knew that the shops in Bond Street didn't shut until six.
On the other hand, I reasoned, if we went now, we

wouldn't have to go in the morning, so with every appearance of willingness I girded my loins and hailed a cab...

* * *

... So, the next morning at nine we were back in Bond Street. As the shops weren't open until ten, I took refuge in Claridges and ordered a massively expensive breakfast while Robbi window–shopped. She returned twenty minutes later as the food arrived, told me of all the shops we were going to visit and ate half my food. I paid. We left. Do you mind if we pass over the next two hours? I admit that she looks utterly wonderful in very expensive designer dresses and suits, but please, is there anything more soul destroying than going shopping with a woman? Dave called me on my mobile. "Get my bloody sister out of those shops. I'm waiting at the hotel."

"You tell her yourself. I have no influence over her."

He growled and five seconds later Robbi's phone rang.

* * *

Dave's plan was simple. He had given a bung to the foreman of the contractors repairing the utility ducts in the service area above Medina's office in order to let his team take over for one day. Robbi, Palmer and I were taken up from the underground garage hidden in three wheeled dustbins. Harry was sitting on the floor in the corner of the room looking subdued. Palmer was first across to him.

"How did it go?"

"Could have been worse. At first I thought he wasn't going to let me see him, but he did. I acted like a nervous schoolboy, just like Cousin Livesey said I should. God, the man's ego – not Livesey (although to be honest his is pretty enormous) – Medina's. I mean cousin Livesey said not to underplay the humility. So, I told him how I had missed his company and the rest of the world seemed very dull and that Hannay was dead and the group of hangers–on was staying on in his house without any idea of what to do and you could see the man swelling. I had to sit in the corner of his office while he showed off in front of his minions…"

Dave interrupted. "Measurements, Harry."

"So, he chucked me out for one meeting – with your man ffitch, John, by the way – and I paced the office floor looking distraught until I was let back in."

We watched as Harry paced out the measurements of Medina's office one floor below. Johnson and Spinetti stuck tape down where Harry indicated. Within minutes, Palmer had drilled into a duct, slid in a thin metal sheath, pushed a fibre optic camera into the sheath and connected it to a monitor. He pointed at me. I nodded and sat in front of the monitor trying to make sense of the scene when the camera found the vent that revealed the Medina Trading floor below. I could count about twenty traders – not as big an operation as I had thought it would be. I could see the senior trader walking across the floor with his head set on, watching the screens and glancing towards Medina's office from time to time. I swivelled the camera round to see the whole floor and the traders in order to get a feel for their esprit de corps. I jumped. Dave had put his heavy hand on my shoulder. I looked round. "Where's everybody gone?"

He looked at me kindly. "Robbi said you could concentrate, but I hadn't really understood what she meant until now. Know what the time is?"

"No?"

"It's five–thirty. You've been staring at that monitor for two hours without moving. Everybody's gone – just you and me left. We've got to take the monitor with us. Palmer's got it all sorted. Microwave relay on the outside wall there to a base across the street where you can stare at it all you want. What was so interesting anyway?"

"They didn't laugh."

* * *

Back at the hotel I joined Robbi in the shower, which wasted half an hour and several litres of water and then went downstairs to meet Palmer in the bar on what hotels love calling the Mezzanine Floor. Palmer put his iPad down and looked at me. "So, what did you see on the monitor?"

"I'm not sure, Palmer. But… Well, put it this way, I think I know what to do if all else fails."

"And that is?"

"We kill Medina."

He thought about that for a few seconds. "You think that it will all wind down if he's off the scene?"

I nodded.

"So would you care to share with me the steps that led to that conclusion?"

"They weren't so much steps as impressions."

"Fuck's sake, share the impressions, John."

"They didn't laugh."

"You want to kill Medina because they didn't laugh."

"Look, I watched that floor for two hours and there was no sign of any rituals, no jokes, no backchat. It just felt wrong."

"So, this is to do with Medina?"

"I think so. The head trader must have glanced towards Medina's office every five minutes. All the traders were deadly calm."

Palmer shrugged. He didn't understand. The City runs on two things – greed and fear. I had watched that floor for two hours. That's quite a lot of trading time: time to make mistakes, to make some scores. I've seen grown men smash desks up when it goes wrong and dance on the desktops when they get a big hit. Greed and fear have always been hard emotions to conceal especially under that kind of pressure. I looked at Palmer. "No jokes, no piss taking, no backchat. Nothing. *You* know what I mean, Robbi?"

She nodded. Palmer twizzled the ice round in his glass and then glanced across the room. "Harry, over here!"

Harry swaggered between the tables leering at the women and sneering at the men. He put his arm round the waitress who was at the next table. She looked up in irritation, paused and smiled. "Would you be so kind as to get me a large glass of the most expensive brandy you have and charge it to the dark haired, miserable looking gentleman sitting at that table."

He pointed at me and I nodded at the waitress. He sat down and grinned pure mischief. Robbi put her chin on the back of her hands and studied him.

"What? What?"

"You, Harry Livesey, are from the Dark Side."

"I know, I know and you, Roberta Lord, are a Child of the Light. You should pop over to my side for a while some time, it's such fun."

"Are we to take it that you've been out with Medina?"

He sniffed his brandy enjoying the suspense he was creating. We all sat and stared at him.

"God, you lot are creepy. OK, All right. Well, I can tell you I haven't arse licked like that since prep school." He sobered. "I can also tell you that he still scares the shit out of me and more. Thing is, he's decided to throw a party next week to celebrate his daughter Mei Chen's eighteenth birthday. He got in the most frightful temper – weird it was. He was just shaking with rage. You know the reason? His normal caterer couldn't do the whole job. He's got food, but no booze. So, before he could say anything, clever little Harry had a brilliant idea. I told him that when I was down at your place, I met a chap who ran an off–licence in Northleach who seemed to have a fab selection of wine. I could call him. And then he started laughing. I tell you he is so on the edge. I think he could flip out at any time. He said 'do you mean, Andrew Barraclough?' I asked him how he knew him and he just kept laughing and laughing and finally he leaned across, patted my hand and told me I was a very clever boy and I should book Barraclough for the party straight away. Then I made a very big fuck up."

"What did you do?"

"I offered to pay for the booze."

We stared at him for a second and then Palmer started laughing, Robbi joined in and I just sat and smiled until I thought about Medina. "When is this party?"

"Tuesday night."

"You'd better go in Andy's place then."

"Who me? Fuck off Hannay! Why's it always me taking the risks?"

"What risk? What's he going to do to you at a party?"

Harry stared at me for a long while and cupped his brandy, swirling the viscous, amber liquid almost to the rim of the balloon glass. "Maybe that is the best thing to do. Buy a few crates off Andy, whizz 'em into the City and then… and then?"

I finished his sentence. "You won't have brought enough tonic water for the G&T so you disappear just before the party kicks off. He knows you're a disgusting letcher so he'll think you're off at it again when you don't come back."

It took three more brandies before Harry had calmed down and then he started on our French waitress.

CHAPTER TWENTY-NINE

Robbi was singing somewhere nearby. I rolled over in bed and looked at the curtains – at least it was daylight. I found my watch and peered at it – five thirty – what was she doing up at this hour? And you know it's remarkable, but she spent half an hour more putting on make–up and dressing for the Boss than she ever had for me, but at a quarter to seven we were in BTD's foyer. I could see the Boss in her office and it looked like the floor was already at work. She looked up, saw us, and beckoned us in.

"Morning Super Trader, Miss Beautiful. John, you've got your old desk and two junior traders – they're bright but way, way too bumptious for my liking, so sort 'em out. I'm on a video conference with Bank Aargau in five minutes so if you could kindly fuck off."

While Robbi headed towards the Ladies I walked back through Reception and in the main door. It was almost three years since I had last worked here, but it looked as though very little had changed. I walked towards my desk, nodded at the two very young men who had drawn the short straws and ignored the ironic cheers and catcalls from my erstwhile colleagues. I noted how the sound level dropped as I sat down. They stood up to introduce themselves to me.

"Good morning, Sir John. I'm…"

I held up a hand. "Why did you call me that?"

"We understood that you liked to be addressed by your title."

"Which one of the monkeys told you that?"

"Sorry, Sir Jo…"

"You call me Sir John one more time and you can resign yourself to a life selling AIM shares on a retail floor in Birmingham."

I noted the noise level on the Floor drop even further and smiled inside. Robbi was crossing the floor. She glanced at my boys with a polite lack of interest as I performed an introduction. "Gentlemen, my administrator, Roberta Lord. Roberta, that'll be your desk. Could you check the RNSs and run some analysis on the Renminbi? You two, start running analysis of trading against Sterling for the last month."

"Shouldn't one of the analysts do that, John?"

I just stared at him without blinking until he got the message. The phone bleeped and before I could move, Robbi picked it up. "Yes, Miss Fitzgerald, he'll be there directly."

In her office the Boss was still sitting in front of the big Video Conference Screen. She stood and stretched. "Just finished with Bank Aargau. They hated the fact that my Hochdeutsche was better than theirs. Fucking Schweizerdeutsch – sounds like ducks quacking. Anyway, it's all sorted. They were confused as to why an aristocrat such as you – aristocrat, hah! – would put his entire fortune at risk, but I just explained that you were, like all English aristos, clinically insane."

I thanked her with two fingers, turned to go and

stopped feeling suddenly stupid. "Did you ask them what the value of the gold was?"

She nodded. "Three point five billion."

"Oh, good."

"John, that's Sterling."

"Oh. Christ! Sterling! That's…"

"Four point five billion dollars."

I went back on to the Floor to try and talk sense into my juniors. I stared at them. They stared at me and I began to realise that when the Boss said these boys were arrogant, she may have been understating the case somewhat.

"Have you started the Sterling analysis yet?"

Without a word they passed me a sheet of paper. Automatically I checked its origination; just I had guessed it had come from the Analysts' office. Very deliberately I tore the paper up into little scraps in front of them. I sighed. This was one of the reasons I had got out of trading. The constant macho posturing, the screaming rows, the humiliations – it was both tedious and soul destroying. I wasn't angry yet, just irritated. These two had just demonstrated that they were over–cocky, lazy and could not be trusted. They would, therefore, be ignored. I stood up.

"Roberta, could you come with me. Bring your Renminbi file."

I walked the ten steps to Jarrod's desk. "Roberta, Max Jarrod, Max, Roberta Lord."

Jarrod extended a hand. "Morning, Roberta. OK, what gives?"

"Maxi baby, we have four point five billion bucks which we are going to leverage the shit out of and then we are going to do some serious currency trading with it. Can you get me to twenty billion from the five?"

"Should be able to, yes. What's the currency we're going for, John? This sounds like Soros territory."

"Can't tell you yet, Max. It's all a bit hush–hush."

Max leaned forward and whispered. "You've got some inside info haven't you, you naughty boy?"

"No, nothing like that. Look, we're in the big league here, right? Well, this is a lot bigger than the big league. Nuff said, OK? You deal with me or with Roberta – no one else."

Robbi passed him our cards and he put the numbers into his phone while he kept talking.

"What about the children?"

We all looked at the two boys who were smirking and staring across at us without a care in the world.

"They are out of it. I gave them their chance and they didn't take it. They can sit there as long as they like, but they don't work for me. Just ignore them."

Jarrod explained. "They are both sons of some big investors so they think they can get away with anything. To be fair, they're bright though."

"Not interested. By the way, who in the analyst's office has the initials DB?"

"Donald Bartrum. Now he is bright. Working class kid, brain the size of a planet."

"Trustworthy?"

"Oh absolutely. Worth ten of those little fuckers any day. Ooops, Sorry Roberta, force of habit."

Robbi touched his arm. "Max I've worked on a retail floor; nothing can shock me!"

* * *

Max was right. Don Bartrum was a breath of fresh air. I took him into our confidence.

"Don, there's something big going to happen to Sterling soon."

He nodded. "I have been wondering about that for a while, John. I sent a note to Miss Fitzgerald on the subject last week and, funnily enough, she told me to expect a visit from you."

He grinned unexpectedly. "She also told me to 'keep my f–ing mouth shut and I might learn something.'"

"Sounds like the Boss. So what have you been seeing, Don?"

"Well, it's like this, and I apologise in advance if some of it sounds like my pet hobby horse. Right… we're not an important currency any more. We're way down the manufacturing and export leagues since Brexit. Everyone knows this, so why would the Chinese have a pop at Sterling?"

"I didn't know they had."

"They were doing it through third parties."

"Third parties? Would any of these be in the UK?"

"Possibly. Possibly. I'm still working on that. Why? Do you know something?"

I sat for a few seconds, drumming my fingers on the table top, then leaned across and picked up a phone.

"Em, it's John. Can I take Don Bartrum inside on this?"

"Hmmm. Put him on."

I handed him the phone and noted the nervous way he held it. "Yes, Miss Fitzgerald. Yes. Yes, I understand. Thank you."

He put the phone down.

"What did she say?"

"She said I could come inside, but if a word of your presence here or this project leaked, she would personally remove my testicles and make me eat them."

"Dear Em."

We filled Don in and watched while he sat back running his fingers through his thick, muddy brown, untidy hair. "Phew. I need to think about this. If I'm not wrong this makes sense of a lot of different things that have been niggling me for the last six months. You know, things that just haven't made sense. Mind if I go off and play with my little spread sheets?"

"No, be our guest. And Don, double your security on this and nothing to leave the building."

"OK."

"Here are our phone numbers. You only talk to us about this unless it is really desperate, then you call The Boss. If you can't raise her then in an emergency call Jarrod, but he doesn't know what you know."

He stood up to go. "Oh, and the final thing, Don. Those little idiots on the Floor who asked for the research this morning, they are nothing to do with me. Do not talk to them about any of this and on no account let them see any of what you're doing."

"Now that, John, would be a pleasure."

Back on the floor, the children were on the phone. They looked at me expectantly. I said nothing, but clicked on my mouse and studied the trades. Interesting. Very interesting. Half an hour later, Robbi touched my shoulder. I looked up.

"The boys are saying you've been ignoring their questions for the last thirty minutes. I have explained that when you concentrate you block out all external interference."

I glanced across at them. They were definitely getting pouty.

"Look, John, I know you weren't amused at our little jape, but you should accept the fact that we were right to do it this way. Bartrum's a bit of an oik, but he's bloody bright."

I looked at Robbi. She shrugged and motioned to me that I should say something.

"You know who I am and you know my reputation?"

They both agreed that they did.

"So when I ask you to do something, why do you think you know better?"

I held up a hand as they started to speak. "That was a rhetorical question. You don't get second chances at BTD. The Boss has put you here to work for me. You ignored a direct order. You want me to go and tell her? That was also a rhetorical question. You do not work for me anymore. You can sit and twiddle your thumbs or download porn or whatever it is that you normally do, but…"

I stood up and leaned forward with my knuckles pressed down on the desk and raised my voice for the benefit of the Floor. "You do not work for me and you will never work for me. You think I have come back in here to play some stupid power game with a pair of overgrown, ill–educated children? Well think again and do not ever try and speak to me again when I am concentrating."

A ripple of applause and cries from the old guard of 'The Super Trader strikes again' went round the floor. I didn't acknowledge it. I just kept my eyes on the two young men. Interesting, judging by the pouting, they still hadn't learnt their lesson. "Roberta, got time for lunch? The canteen's good. You coming, Max?"

My phone rang and I sat down again. "Alan, hello. Problem?"

"Afternoon, John. No, but I'm having the tapes from Medina's office looked at by our army psychiatrist."

"When?"

"Can you do today?"

"Yes, just going to grab a spot of lunch and we can be with you by three."

I put the phone down. The children had made a decision. "We have decided that we have to report you to Personnel. We think you may be a bit out of touch with the way in which employment law has changed since the days when you thought you were important here, but you simply cannot talk to us in the way you just did."

I stared at them, amazed, then looked at Jarrod. He shook his head in despair and the three of us walked away with Jarrod telling everyone we passed how the boys were going to report the Super Trader to Personnel. A wave of laughter followed us. The Boss beckoned me in as I passed.

"Well?"

"I won't work with them Em. It's not just that they're rude and arrogant; it's mainly that I don't trust them. They also disobeyed a direct order."

She nodded.

"Oh, and they're reporting me to Personnel."

The Boss was dumbstruck – a rare sight. "What for?"

"Shouting at them."

"No."

"Yes."

She snorted with laughter. "Send them in."

I went back out onto the Floor, whistled at the boys and pointed at Emma's room. They got up and made their way through the desks with the traders humming the Death March. As we waited for the lift to take us to the Canteen, I heard her voice enquiring of them what they had done to incur my displeasure. The lift doors closed.

CHAPTER THIRTY

"Is that what you were like, John? Is that what it took?"

She was sitting beside me in a black cab heading across London.

"Of course. That's why I left."

I hadn't liked myself at the end. I hadn't liked how good I was at it. How I could go on the attack without even thinking. How I could spend ten hours working at the screens and only stop when Em came and hit the off–switch. We were a hell of a team. I traded. She protected me. And she never let me down. I let her down when I left. And she forgave me for that too.

"If it all works out, Robbi, she'll make a fortune on this deal and you know what we have to do, don't you?"

"Get her to stop."

"Yep, although God knows how we'll do it. She lives on adrenalin, espresso and brandy."

"How long did it take you to recover?"

"Oh, it was easy for me. I'd been planning to open my restaurant for some time and I just walked out of BTD and into No 44. I did it for a year flat out, then a while later, after my chef, Alessandro, got our Michelin star I let him buy out half my shares and then those phone calls started. And then I did nothing… and then I killed a man and then…"

"You met me – the most perfect woman in the world and the love of the rest of your life."

I didn't disagree.

Alan was waiting for us as we paid off the taxi. He took us through the security doors, along a bland MOD coloured corridor, up two flights of stairs to a small, stuffy, windowless office. Palmer was slouched in an office chair in front of his laptop with his fingers hovering over the mouse pad. Dr Livesey was perched on a stacking chair to his left and to Palmer's right was a third man – mid forties, overweight in an ex-rugby forward kind of way. The three of them were staring silently at a video recording of Medina's office on fast forward. Occasionally one or other of them would point at the screen and they would all nod. I waited. Who was I not to respect concentration? After five minutes they noticed us. Livesey offered a sour smile – more at Robbi than at me. The third man spoke.

"It was Mr Palmer who saw it first. We've now verified it and the timing is remarkably exact."

Ah, I knew that voice. It was the doctor who had supervised ffitch's interrogation. I nodded like a dog on the back shelf of a car. Robbi was more direct.

"What is *it*?"

"Oh, sorry. The visual reference to Medina. Exactly every five minutes the man whom I understand to be the Senior Trader looks at his office – Medina's office that is. Now, look at this piece here."

Palmer fast forwarded to a point where the senior trader left the floor. We leaned forward as he played it forward at six times normal speed. The rhythm was broken. Some of the traders kept glancing across to Medina's office. Others stopped working and leaned back. One even opened the Financial Times.

"Now watch this."

Palmer spun back and ran the whole hour at 16 times normal speed.

"God!"

Across the hour of filming the rhythm was exactly the same. While the senior trader was there the concentration was absolute, when he left, the link to Medina was gone and the rhythm was broken except the one time when Medina came out of his office and stood behind the traders. Palmer slowed the tape to twice normal speed. None of the traders looked round, but all of them returned to their calm behaviour. Palmer froze a frame with Medina in shot.

"I can't enhance it completely when there's not much there in the first place and I can assure you that F.R. software isn't anywhere near as good as it claims to be, but it should be able to fill in some of the missing bits."

We waited for the computer to render the picture and thirty seconds later the image was clear. Medina's face was glowing with triumph. This was his creation. I murmured something to myself. All heads turned towards me. "Sorry, just thinking aloud – 'And God saw every thing that he had made, and, behold, it was very good.' Genesis Chapter One."

Dr Livesey looked approving. "You'll be telling us next that you're a Wee Free, Sir John. But you're right. We have been discussing whether this man has a bad case of malignant NPD or a massive schizoaffective disorder."

"NPD?"

"Narcissistic personality disorder."

Alan was interested. "I thought that narcissists were insecure and believed they were flawed."

The second doctor patted his arm. "You've been reading Wikipedia again, Major. Have you not heard of Donald Trump?"

I entered the academic fray. "Trump was conditioned by his father and Medina was too. And his father was taught by his mother and there was also a huge hatred of England in there for reasons which I can fully appreciate."

The second doctor cocked an eyebrow. "You mean the Famine?"

"No, I mean that for just those very few years between 1171 and 1998 – during which Ireland and the Irish were treated abominably by England and the English and it always has been inexcusable."

Alan was surprised by my vehemence. "I forgot you were an historian. But the Medina family has never been Irish nationalist. This is all about power surely. Doctor, how can this kind of mania or whatever you want to call it go down three or more generations of the same family?"

"Well, Sir John may have a point. There is some evidence that the condition is hereditary. In any event if the son is strongly influenced by the father, then any inherent propensity will be massively exacerbated. If you think of Trump, remember the book by Mary Trump on him and his father, Fred."

I could see Livesey preparing to argue when Palmer twisted round from the screen. "Does this change your view of what has to be done, John?"

I looked directly at him. "No, Palmer, it doesn't. He needs to be removed.

CHAPTER THIRTY-ONE

Back at BTD the next day, feeling like home already and no sign of the idiot children, thank God; spent ten minutes with The Boss; watched the trades; spoke to Don Bartrum; thought about bringing Jarrod inside; decided against it at this stage; noticed the children had come in looking as though they might be considering apologising; turned my back on them.

There was nothing much more I could do here. Robbi was discussing trades with Jarrod so I walked over to The Boss's outer office, nodded at Helen, her secretary, picked up Who's Who and turned to "A."

> 'Ludovic Cospatrick Arbuthnot, 18th Lord Clanroyden... Family home, Laverlaw at Ettrick in the Scottish Borders... London Residence, Lord North Street, Westminster.'

Well, what do you know? Just round the corner from our hotel. I phoned Sir Ian.

"Morning, John. What is it to be this time, the Crown Jewels or the Royal Art Collection?"

"Both will do fine, thanks, sir, but actually something a lot simpler. Do you by any chance know Lord Clanroyden?"

"Ludo Arbuthnot? Yes, he was a couple of years above me at school – Westminster. Why?"

"Well, he was a friend of my grandfather and I very much want to ask him a question."

"Very well. I trust that you aren't going to ask him anything which could get him into any of this current fracas?"

"No, no, no, not at all. I found a book in the library that was given to my grandfather by his grandfather. Um, could I ask you for his London number to see if he's in Town? I'd rather do it direct if I may… to er sort of give it back if you know what I mean."

"I'll call you back, John."

By the time we had returned to the hotel – via Bond Street yet again, I'm sorry to say – I was staring at the phone number Sir Ian had texted me – the phone number of the descendant of my grandfather's closest friend. I tapped in the numbers and waited.

"Clanroyden residence."

"Good morning, my name is John Hannay. Lord Clanroyden's grandfather and mine were close friends and I very much wanted to have a quick word with his Lordship."

"Just one moment, sir."

"Oh, hello? Could you tell him I would like to return a library book my grandfather borrowed?"

"Certainly, sir."

There was a long silence and then a light, aristocratic voice. "A library book, is it? Is this really Dick Hannay's grandson? Peter John's boy?"

"Yes, sir, it is."

"Good Lord."

"Lord Clanroyden, I'm sorry to trouble you, but I'm afraid I need to ask you a couple of questions – about my grandfather. Do you have any time today? It's quite urgent, I'm afraid."

"One moment, my boy. Lockhart, when's the meeting at the British Museum?"

I heard a faint voice then Lord Clanroyden once again. "John, how soon can you get round here?"

"Five minutes sir. My partner and I are staying just round the corner from you."

"All the better. See you soon."

Robbi came out of the bedroom looking curious and more elegant than when she had gone in. It was another dress. I backtracked desperately through the shops we had just visited in an attempt to impress her.

"Balenciaga?"

She clapped her hands in pleasure. "Clever John. I'll make a toy boy of you yet."

"Come on, you patronising clothes rack, we have an appointment with a Lord in five minutes."

I ran her down the corridor to the lifts. In Lord North Street the butler answered the door, bowed politely to me and blinked when I pushed Robbi in front of me.

"This way, Sir John, Miss."

I stepped over the threshold and stopped dead. I had been here before. My first thought was panic – was this another of Medina's traps? I followed Robbi up the staircase, too disturbed by my thoughts to be disturbed by the entrancing sway of her hips. But surely not a Clanroyden, the grandson of my grandfather's closest friend. I studied the little butler to see if he offered an insight into his master, but I could see nothing behind the smooth glossiness. My heart raced and missed two beats. I would never admit it publicly, but I was beginning to wonder if there had been any permanent damage from my stay with Medina.

At the top of the stairs, we were ushered into the library. Now this *was* a library, more incunabula than at both Fosse and Medina's house and all with that patina of usage. I love libraries and the calming smell of old paper. I peered at an eighteenth-century edition of Boethius' Consolation of Philosophy that I had tried (and failed) to read as a young (and pretentious) man. I turned, hearing footsteps. Clanroyden was slight, straight–backed, bright eyed, with an almost elfin quality about him. And I knew him. I was sure I knew him.

"Ah, you like old Anicius Manlius Severinus do you, John?"

"To be honest, sir, not really. I tried to read him when I was young, but…"

"Less of the sir, please John. You used to call me Uncle Ludo. And, if I may be so bold as to ask, who are you, young lady?"

He must have seen my jaw drop as he paused in his greeting to Robbi.

"Uncle Ludo? Yes. Yes… I do remember an Uncle Ludo."

I stared at him while he, in turn, observed me closely. "You have a fire in the room downstairs and a sword hanging over the mantelpiece."

"Well done my boy, only it's a Claymore. Belonged to one of the early Clanroydens who was a damn sight more warlike than me. Now, young lady, leaving John to work out what I have to do with him, who are you?"

I could see Robbi stopping herself from curtseying and I came to her rescue.

"I'm so sorry, this is my partner, Roberta Lord."

"Delighted to meet you. Lord, eh? Lord. Do you have relatives in the army?"

Yes, sir. I come from an army family, but it depends on which generation you mean. My brother David was an RSM with 22 SAS Regiment – he's now with L Detachment; my father, Fred, was a sergeant with second Battalion, the Gordon Highlanders and my grandfather was RSM in the Scots Guards – Reginald Lord."

"That's my Lord! Splendid. I was a very green subaltern under him. Scared me to death. Well, well, well and you're his granddaughter? I can tell you one thing, you're a damn sight better looking than he was."

A clicking of high heels announced the arrival of Lady Clanroyden. "Angela, Angela, look at this. Remember I've told you about Reggie Lord, my RSM in the Guards, well this is his granddaughter, Roberta, and this here, skulking by the bookshelves, is young John Hannay, back from the dead."

I bowed my head. Angela Clanroyden was a slender, beautiful woman in her sixties with a ramrod straight back and the high colouring that comes of many years of life outdoors – probably in the saddle. She nodded at me thoughtfully and walked towards Robbi with her hand outstretched and scrutinised her. She turned to her husband.

"My dear, isn't it wonderful? Most beautiful girl I have seen in many a year and not a hint of coquetry or immodesty."

She turned back to Robbi who was colouring up under the compliment. "I suspect that you are probably utterly fed up with people telling you how beautiful you are, but it can't be helped. You are. Now, correct me if I'm wrong, but isn't that Balenciaga you're wearing?"

Robbi nodded mutely. Lord Clanroyden clapped his hand to his head. "How she does it I have no idea. Spends half her life on a horse, the other half in Fortnums, but seems to know every blasted thing there is about haute couture."

Angela Clanroyden released Roberta's hand, walked across to me and put her cool hand on my face, turning it from side to side. "Well, I can still see some of your grandfather and a lot of your poor mother in you now you're all grown up, John, but I have to say you are looking a sight worse than when I last saw you. Aren't you taking care of him, Roberta?"

A shadow of anxiety crossed Robbi's face. "I try Lady Clanroyden, but he is very difficult to control."

"Oh, you'll never control a Hannay, dear, you just have to learn to find them wherever and whenever they get into too much trouble, patch 'em up and send 'em back into the fray. His grandfather was uncontrollable into his eighties."

I found my voice. "Did you know him?"

"Of course I did, John, and your father, and I grew up ten miles away from where your mother lived. We went to their wedding didn't we, Ludo?"

"We certainly did, John. We tried to keep in touch, but your father kept himself very much to himself and discouraged contact quite strongly. You don't know about the 'promise' do you, John?"

I shook my head, still dazed by these memories.

Aah, well. That's the point of all this, dear boy."

"The point of what?" I was way, way out of my depth and beginning to thrash around wildly, desperate for the shallows.

"I see a brow furrowed in confusion. All will be revealed, John. All will be revealed. However, for the time being just let me say that when your mother died, I offered our services, but Marcus Wethers was doing a fine job and he kept me informed until you were eighteen. Since when we've kept a watching brief, but we rather lost sight of you a few years ago. In fact, Wethers called me the other day, but we keep missing each other. Ten to one you're what he wants to talk to me about."

I had no idea of this. "I had no idea."

"Don't worry about it, my boy. We even went to your restaurant, although I can't say it was my kind of food. Marcus and Mary looked on you as the son they never had, you know. I trust Mary approves of you, young lady."

"I think I was a bit of shock at first, sir, especially as I'm common as muck. It's a long story, but I took John there when he was very ill and demanded a bedroom and a doctor for him. They took it ever so well and I think Aunt Mary's an absolute sweetie."

Angela laughed. "You're common as muck and Mary's a sweetie? Dear, dear, if you're common, then God only knows what that makes us? I have to say too I've never heard Mary Wethers called a sweetie before. I'm lunching with her tomorrow so I'll be sure to tell her that's what you think of her. Right, must be off. Very good to see you again, John, and lovely to meet you too, Roberta. I do hope you will both come here again and again. Ludo, don't be late for the British Museum meeting."

"Yes dear."

He turned to me. "No idea how long you two have known each other, but have you discovered the 'yes, dear' approach yet? Works wonders. Right, what's this library book you're going to return?"

I pulled the gazetteer out of the carrier bag and passed it across. Clanroyden pulled half glasses out of his jacket pocket and peered at the book. "So that's what it's about." He looked at me quizzically over his half–glasses. I said nothing. "Well you've inherited either your father's taciturnity or your grandfather's wisdom. Let's see which. Does the name Haraldsen mean anything to you?"

I nodded. Robbi interrupted. "It's like getting blood from a stone with him, sir. Yes we know who both Valdemar and Marius Haraldsen were and we are friends with Anna who is Valdemar's granddaughter."

"Less of the 'sir', Roberta – Ludo will do fine, thank you."

Clanroyden smiled at her and turned back to me. Robbi stuck her tongue out at me behind his back, looked at me sharply and stepped forward. "Ludo, I think John needs to sit down. I assume the name Dominick Medina means something to you?"

"Oh good Lord, yes."

"Well this idiot here deliberately put himself in his clutches for a week and although he won't admit it, he is nothing like fully recovered."

She pushed me into an armchair and perched close to me, her arm round my shoulders, looking up defensively at Clanroyden. I managed to slow my breathing.

"So that's why you're looking all beat up is it?"

I nodded. "Sorry, I'm just not too good with shocks at the moment. I'm fine really. Robbi worries too much. If you have ten minutes, I'll explain."

Fifteen minutes later, I finished. Clanroyden had brought a library chair across, placed it in front of me and had not moved a muscle while I spoke. He stood up, stretched and picked up the Gazetteer from the table where he had placed it. He leafed through it slowly holding the page up to the light to see the pinpricks and then turning all the remaining pages over. As he went to close it, he stiffened. "Where's the map?"

We both looked at him blankly. He came across to us holding the back page open.

"Here, see. There should be a large-scale map in a paper sleeve inside the back cover."

"I don't think it's on my library shelves and when I picked the book up, judging by the dust, no–one had been near it for years."

"Just one moment." He moved his library ladder down the wall of books and after three false starts stepped back down waving what looked like a leaflet. It was the map. He unfolded it. "Take this end, Roberta."

The two of them walked away from each other holding a side of the surprisingly large map. It must have nearly six feet wide and four deep. As they pulled it taut the sunlight spilled through the window rendering the old map translucent except where… except where…

"Stop. Don't move."

They both froze as I pulled myself up and peered at the map. "Pin pricks. Look."

They both held on to their edges and peered at the back of the map. "Hang on."

I almost snatched the thin paper from them and hurried to the window with the paper billowing over my face. I pushed the piece I had seen up against the glass and the sunlight streamed through the tiny holes. I peered over my shoulder at them.

"See them?"

"Yes, yes."

Clanroyden was fascinated. He was in the process of trying to read the place names on the map near a grouping of the holes when there was a discreet cough from the doorway.

"Excuse me, my Lord, but his honour, Judge Kenwright has arrived and luncheon is ready."

"Damn. Look I can't get out of this. It's a long–standing appointment and I need to talk to him. You can stay here or take the map with you, but I want in on this, John. I claim squatter's right and anyway you need to know about 'the promise.'"

I smiled at his eagerness. "It would be a pleasure. We have to get back to Fosse this afternoon, but we'll be back in town the day after tomorrow."

"Excellent. Dinner here, eight o'clock, informal. Lockhart, tell Cook. Off you go now.

* * *

On the train I pinched Robbi's iPad – she had given up waiting for the promised 'first class buffet service at your seat' and gone to buy two cups of what could laughingly be called coffee – and started trying to round up the loose ends. I made a list and leaned back to try and find some perspective. I closed my eyes to aid thought... And then I was struggling through an old mansion with a huge sword hanging over me as I hunted in panic for Robbi. I could hear her voice in the distance and I knew I had to reach her before, before...

"John, John... John Richard."

I forced my eyes open. Robbi's face was close to mine. She was stroking my cheek.

"You wouldn't wake up, John. You've been muttering in your sleep all the way. Swindon's the next stop. Are you OK?"

I kneaded my face and focused on her.

"I'm OK, Robbi."

"No, you're not."

Woman with a mission... She asked Paul how I looked in the car. She took me into the kitchen to ask Margaret and the library to ask Palmer. I fully expected to be driven round the estate to find Miranda and ask her and then there would be Jack and Joan, of course, let alone Dorothy, the vicar. The upshot was that a bath was run for me and then I was pushed on to the bed to rest before dinner.

CHAPTER THIRTY-TWO

I drifted up to the surface and opened my eyes to stare at the ceiling. How did I feel? I thought for a few seconds. I felt good: hungry, but rested… good. I heard a murmur beside me and turned quietly to study her profile for a while. She fitted in quite well now – I mean it was a very big bed so we didn't have to touch or anything – but it was actually OK. Good for my nightmares too. I rolled my eyes at my stupidity, watched her beautiful profile for a while longer, looked back at the sunlight on the ceiling then turned my head the other way to look at the alarm clock. The little red numbers said 05:22 – thirteen hours sleep, worse than a bloody teenager. Robbi snored softly.

I slid out of the huge bed and thirty seconds later clad in a pair of tracksuit bottoms and a Tee shirt was tiptoeing down the stairs of the sleeping house. Wondering if anyone had got anywhere with the map, I entered the study first and then the library. The map and Gazetteer were both lying on a side table, untouched. I picked them up, settled on the kitchen as being warm and close to food, sat at the worn old table sipping a mug of tea and spread the map.

After ten minutes of photographing and manoeuvring I managed to get maps from gazetteers scaled to the same size in Photoshop and was busy trying to overlay one with the other when I heard the patter of feet on the stairs. It was Robbi, obviously, wearing one of my shirts which did little to disguise the fact that she had forgotten to put her underwear on – again. She stopped dead in the doorway, rubbed the sleep from her eyes and came across to sit on my lap.

"Next time you wake up and sneak out, leave a bloody note, Hannay. What are you doing?"

I put my arms round her and dozed against her back while she started to move the mouse. I should have guessed she'd be able to do it. I was just getting comfy and thinking that maybe I should have stayed in bed with her, when she spoke. "Ta da!"

I peered over her shoulder. She had managed to create a scale for the photos and had not only superimposed the Gazetteer image exactly over the map, but was slowly rotating it.

"Slower. Slower. Stop there. Back."

We both stared at the screen. Four of the holes lined up exactly. Robbi yawned. "So, what does it mean?"

"God knows, but you know what?"

"What?"

"I think that you could catch your death of cold sitting here without your string vest or Y Fronts on. I think you need to come back to bed."

"You *are* feeling better, aren't you?"

We came back down an hour or so later to find Palmer hunched in front of the computer while Harry moved the maps round. They were comparing notes and nodding at each other. I was ignored.

At 09:13 Paul parked the Landrover in front of the house and entered followed by a yawning Dave. At

09:44 a Black Jaguar appeared at the end of the drive and I went out to greet Alan and, to my considerable surprise and my greater concern, Sir Ian Hamilton. I called out to Robbi to warn Margaret of the increase in numbers. Sir Ian was urbanity personified, a veritable Whitehall archetype.

"Lovely spot, John. What a fascinating palimpsest of architectural styles."

Palimpsest. How I wished Robbi had heard that.

The dining hall looked more crowded than I could ever remember. I passed round the briefing sheet I had prepared. Out of the corner of my eye I saw Sir Ian raise his eyebrows and shake his head slightly. Just what I needed – negativity from the outset. I started in.

"OK – the known knowns. One, Medina was working with the Chinese. Two, they were at the very least semi–authorised by the Central Committee. Three it had been planned for a long time."

Alan raised a finger. "How do you know that?"

I nodded in Palmer's direction. He glanced up from his screen. "All right, it is supposition, but when I was checking him out, I found that Medina was part of a British team advising on the re–opening of the Shanghai Stock Exchange in 1990. He appears to have been back there several times since then, most recently in 2016. Any record of this, Alan?"

"Just a minute." Alan spoke into his phone and waited. "Really? You sure?"

He put the phone down and glanced at Ian before continuing. "Well, it seems our friend may indeed be very well connected over there. He attended a few formal ceremonies of the People's Armed Police and was actually one of the very few foreigners at a demonstration in 2006 when they revealed the existence of The Snow Leopard Commando Unit – they were the guys who sorted out any 'problems' at the 2008 Beijing Olympics. Next?"

I shrugged. "It's more for Palmer. Have you got anywhere with the information on Medina's iPhone?"

Ian slowly straightened, incredulity increasing with every degree of verticality. "You have Medina's mobile phone?"

Alan stepped in. "Not exactly, sir. It was in my first report. John picked it up when Medina broke into his flat and returned it to him when he was incarcerated. In the meantime, Palmer managed to break his security and download the content."

I studied Ian directly. Was this negativity out of character or was it that I had just not seen beyond or behind the urbanity of the professional civil servant?

Palmer spoke, either ignoring or not noticing the undercurrents. "I think it's his appointment diary and calendar, Alan, but it's a bloody nightmare. I doubt we'll have it done in time to be of any help."

"Pity. Next loose end, John?"

"ffitch – I have no idea of where he stands or whether he is a danger to us or himself. I admit to personal feelings of intense dislike."

"If I may, Alan." Ian leaned forward in turn. "ffitch is very irritating I grant you, and, as you have pointed out, not very intelligent, but I think he's a red herring. I don't think you should let him distract you."

I shrugged and glanced towards the door. Yes Margaret?"

"Sorry to interrupt, John, but could you clear the table for lunch?"

"Of course, of course; shall we have a break and get some fresh air?"

I looked at Alan. He looked at me. We strolled outside. "Are we in trouble, Alan?"

He sniffed a climbing rose. "Honestly, John, I don't know. Something has changed. He gave no indication of any problems on the drive down. Then he took a call and from then on he's been just been like this – very negative."

"Any chance you can get hold of his phone and find out who the call was from?"

"Shit, John, he's my boss."

He mooched away from me deep in thought. Dave was walking toward us from the French Doors. "I'm serious, Alan."

"I know you are, John. Mr Lord, what can we do for you?"

"Major, John – what are we going to do about Sir Ian?"

"We're discussing that now, Dave."

Alan walked away a few steps. Dave looked at me meaningfully.

"Alan?"

"All right, all right. Let me think."

Dave and I turned away. "We need Ian's phone, Dave. Someone phoned him on the way here this morning and we have to know who."

I started to suggest a plan, thought twice and stopped. The plan was ludicrous even by my standards. My heart skipped one too many beats. I breathed carefully. Robbi was walking towards us. I smiled at her waiting for a response. Instead, she grabbed Dave's arm and whispered urgently. "Ian's been got at. How can we find out who it was?"

I walked on. I heard Dave mutter at her and then her running steps and an arm slipped through mine. "Oy, mister, correct me if I'm wrong, but we had sex this morning, didn't we? Is this the same old story? Posh man meets poor, innocent Essex girl. Posh man takes advantage of poor Essex girl's innocence. Essex girl falls in love. Posh man shags Essex girl. Posh man loses interest. Essex girl dies of broken heart. The End."

I listened to her idiocy contentedly. "Sounds about right. Only you got one stage wrong."

"Posh man shags Essex girl lots of times?"

"Yup."

I wrapped my arm tight round her and whispered my 'plan' into her neat little ear. She shrugged, nodded her head and hurried off to brief the others. In the event it turned out to be easy… ish.

I walked back in and shut the high Georgian windows in the dining hall. As it faced south, they would act like a greenhouse. Ian sat on in the heat talking quietly to Alan, seemingly oblivious to the equatorial temperature. And then Robbi took a hand… "God, John. It's so hot. Can't we open the windows?"

Ian went into courtesy mode and started to rise. Robbi stuck out her hand to hold him down, jumping to her feet as she did so and knocking her glass of water sideways, over his feet, trousers and jacket: a flurry of apologies, a visit to the kitchen for cloths to dry the trousers and Harry literally leapt into action. He grabbed Ian's jacket, rummaged in the pockets, found the mobile and threw it at Palmer who had his laptop hidden under the table. There was an agonising hiatus while Palmer scrabbled for the right connection and then the exasperating wait while the details were downloaded. Robbi hissed from the door waving her arm behind her back frantically.

"Palmer, for fuck's sake."

"Finished. Harry, catch!"

Palmer slung the phone at Harry who fielded it brilliantly, left–handed, and dropped it back in the jacket which he flicked over the back of the chair as the door opened and Ian was ushered in by Robbi. I walked to the windows and opened them. Alan spoke and I am sure I heard a tremor in his voice. "Can we continue? I have to get Ian back to Town in reasonable time."

I went for safe ground. At least safe so far as Ian was concerned… "When I was held at Medina's there was a woman." Robbi straightened. Oh bugger. I soldiered on bravely. "I saw her three times, each time in the company of Medina."

Harry interjected. "And one time was standing right in front of you." He started laughing. Shut up, Harry. I did not need this. I risked a half glance at Robbi as Harry continued to blunder on. "You should have seen your face. You looked terrified."

Robbi relaxed… a bit. I described the woman and her demeanour. Harry joined in with more physical information than was strictly necessary, but sufficient for Alan to text a description to his team at MI5. I turned to Harry. "What did you make of their relationship?"

"What do you mean, relationship? She didn't even have a mind of her own. I mean, when I tried to speak to her, she looked straight through me."

Robbi sighed loudly. Palmer stood up. We all looked at him. "Oh, sorry, but if the next bit's nothing to do with me, I'd like to get on with the decryption."

He headed for the study. It took a further half hour of discussion, before I ran out of things to say. "To summarise if I may: Alan will come back to us re any plans for how we deal with the Chinese; Palmer will complete the decryption of Medina's calendar; ffitch we will leave alone; Alan will try and get a fix on Medina's woman. In the meantime, Robbi and I will be based in London. We shall be in the Threadneedles hotel from tonight as I don't want to stay in my London flat."

Robbi looked up, but I avoided eye contact again and continued. "I think the trading fun should start tomorrow or the day after."

Ian stretched his legs out. We watched him warily. "Thank you, John, and thank you also for your hospitality. May I just remind you though that you are all doing this for the benefit of the country and not for revenge for past wrongs, however bad they may be. If, therefore, anything should change in the next few days I would ask you to bear this in mind."

Alan was glaring at me, but there was no way I was going to let this one past without comment. It would have been out of character if nothing else. "I'm not sure

I understand you, Ian. I have just put over three billion pounds at the disposal of my country."

"Please don't think that is not appreciated, but, obviously, the proper way would have been to involve the Treasury and the Bank of England."

I took a long, deep breath. What the hell was going through his narrow, Whitehall mind? "And, therefore, let Medina know that we know what his game is?"

He fiddled with his half glasses in a way in which I found intensely patronising. I wanted to rip them off him and shove them down his pompous throat.

He cleared his throat, almost theatrically. "Cards on the table: I am unhappy about the power that this group of private individuals has and which it has already demonstrated. If you are willing to give me assurances that you will do nothing from now on which is illegal then I am reluctantly willing to agree to the continuation of the plan provided it is under the direct supervision of Major Cummins."

Oh well if a lie was all it took. "Ian, I would be delighted to be under Alan's supervision and you have my word that I will sanction nothing illegal."

"Mr Lord? Sergeant Browby?"

"Sir."

"Your positions please?"

"Sir, we would do nothing that would bring dishonour to the Regiment, sir."

Ian nodded once. "Very well. Major, can we get going, please?"

Dave and Paul came to attention as he stood. Good move, I thought. If anything would convince him of his authority over the group it was the demonstration of formal respect from the two men who could have killed him with scarcely a second thought. We all shook hands on the drive and watched them leave. Harry kicked at a piece of gravel. "That went well."

Palmer peered out of the front door. "Have they gone?"

"Yes. Did you crack the phone?"

"No problem."

"Well?"

"It was ffitch."

"ffitch?"

"ffitch."

"Fuck... Palmer?"

"Yes?"

"Is there any way we can stop Ian being able to use his mobile phone until tonight? I have an idea about how to manage him."

Palmer scratched his head and following Harry's lead, kicked at the gravel. At this rate I would have no drive left.

"Well, I can report the phone stolen – I've got all his access details. That'll mean they'll put a block on it until he unscrambles what's happened."

"Do it."

"John, are we really moving to the Threadneedles hotel?"

"No, dear."

"Whatever. We're supposed to be at Ludo's at eight for dinner."

"It's only four now. Paul, would you mind...?"

"Of course not. Anyway, Margaret says she's going to buy shares in Waitrose with the amount of food we eat. Do you mind if I drop her off on the way in?"

"Not at all."

Robbi snapped her fingers. "God, John, I'm so sorry. I forgot to tell you that a Herr Hoffman from Bank Aargau phoned this morning. He said you had his number."

"He may have left to go home and wind his little Cuckoo Clock, but I'll call him from the car."

We had nothing to pack apart from the newly repaired Gazetteer and the map and a bottle from the cellar I had been delighted to find. Once we had decent reception on the A429 I called Switzerland. As a rebuke for my racism, Herr Hoffman was still at his desk. I apologised for the delay in returning his call and waited to see what bureaucratic nonsense I would have to put up with now.

"Yes, Herr Hoffman. No. No I did not realise that. Well, er, yes. You have my account details. How much? Aah. I understand, Herr Hoffman. I am not able to get to Switzerland this week, I fear, so if you would please transfer the amounts… Yes. No, I am very grateful to you for bringing this matter to my attention, Herr Hoffman. Thank you – and to you – good bye."

We made the 17:19 by the skin of our teeth, changed at Swindon and sat in the familiar first-class carriage, looking at each other across the table. I spoke first.

"You know how you only want me for my money?"

"Oh dear, is it that obvious?"

"'Fraid so."

"And?"

"Oh, no reason."

Robbi kicked me under the table. "Hannay!"

Do you know what the overnight interest is on all that gold of ours in Bank Aargau?"

Robbi leaned across the table until her nose was nearly touching mine. "Do you know what you said then?"

"Yes. I said do you know what …"

"You said 'ours'."

"Slip of the tongue."

"You just don't care about money, do you?"

"If I say not since I met you and you start snivelling again, I'll say 'mine'."

"How much?"

"How much what?"

"Hannay!"

"One hundred and sixty-four thousand pounds. And if they have that gold as collateral for thirty days, that's almost five million quid."

"Five million… and it's 'ours'?"

"Yes, dear."

"Oh, John Richard. Alright, I do just want you for your money now."

CHAPTER THIRTY-THREE

We walked up the steps outside the Clanroyden's house in Lord North Street and I glanced at my watch. For the fourth time that evening Robbi murmured: "just for your money, big boy, just for your money."

I held up a finger and paused. Big Ben started its chime and on the first sonorous strike of eight I rang the doorbell. Lockhart answered immediately. Good evening Sir John, Miss Lord." He indicated a huge bowl of lilies. "Lady Angela was delighted with the flowers, Miss Lord. Lilies are her favourite at this time of year."

Robbi glared at me as Lockhart led the way into the drawing room. "You might have told me."

"I would have if you weren't after me just for my money."

She pinched the back of my hand, walked into the warmth of the room with a happy smile on her face and stopped dead. "Aunt Mary, Uncle Marcus, how lovely." She ran across the room and hugged the one and kissed the other. I followed in my more decorous fashion as Clanroyden entered. "Splendid, splendid and you've brought my map back… and the Gazetteer. Splendid."

"I thought this might appeal too, Ludo." I held out the bottle I had brought from my cellar together with a photocopy of a page from the cellar book. Clanroyden studied the bottle. "Goodness Gracious. What do we have

272

here? Glen Grant 1936. Now that's a single malt and a half." He pulled on his half glasses and peered at the photocopy. "'Gift from Sandy Arbuthnot, during his visit July 14th to 21st 1936'; my dear boy, well goodness me, what do you think of that, Marcus, eh? My grandfather gives his grandfather a bottle of Scotch as a present and seventy–five years later back it comes. We shall tipple on that after dinner. Aah, here you are, my dear."

Angela entered with her graceful step, patted me on the back as she walked past and took Robbi's hands. "Well Roberta, I can tell you that Mary was quite touched at being referred to as an absolute sweetie. She appears to reciprocate the feeling."

Robbi was blushing again. "I'm sorry Aunt Mary, I didn't mean to… It just slipped out."

Clanroyden turned to the butler who had brought in a tray of drinks. "When you've quite finished gawping at Miss Lord, Lockhart, perhaps you would be so good as to serve drinks?"

Lockhart was unfazed. "Very good, my Lord, and Cook says ten minutes, if you please."

I decided to get my bit in now before it was too late. "Ludo. I do apologise for breaching protocol, but may I ask another favour. I saw some rods in the hall and I wondered."

"You want to join us for a day's fishing?"

"Not exactly; I was rather hoping you might be willing to ask Ian Hamilton to go with you and I thought that if you called him before dinner, he might say yes."

Marcus looked at me thoughtfully. "This important, John?"

"Yes, Uncle Marcus. Very."

Clanroyden looked at his watch. "You have five minutes to convince us, John."

I sipped my drink and walked slowly to the fireplace. In the event it took no more than three minutes to explain why I wanted Ian out of the way. Clanroyden looked at Wethers who nodded.

"Just to be clear, John, you are not saying that Ian has anything to do with Medina."

"No Uncle Marcus, I don't think that at all. He's just being somewhat obstructive. I can't even blame him for doing it. It's just he's always led a Whitehall life."

Clanroyden glanced at his wife who nodded impatiently and pointed towards the phone. "We don't want Cook getting angry, Ludo, just phone him quickly."

Clanroyden sighed. "Very well. I like Ian anyway. Damn fine fly fisher too."

He dialled. "Ian, Ludo Arbuthnot. How are you? Listen I tried to call you earlier on your mobile, but couldn't get through. Oh, is it? Oh, bad luck. Bloody things. Look I'm frightfully grateful to you for putting me back in touch with young Hannay. It was wonderful to see the lad again and I think I was able provide him with some information for whatever he's doing – sounded like the sort of hare–brained affair his grandfather would have gone in for. Anyway, the reason for this late call is that I've got my normal stretch of the Meon for the next few days and I've just had a rod drop out and wondered if I could prevail on you to join Marcus Wethers and me for the day tomorrow. Yes, yes, below Wickham Mill. You think you can? Excellent. Excellent. Look, I'm having dinner with Marcus now, so if you can call back and confirm I would be most grateful. We'll collect you tomorrow morning at seven if you're on."

There was that discreet cough from the door. We all looked round. "Dinner is served, my Lord."

Over dinner etiquette was put aside at Angela's orders and I sang for my supper. I'm afraid it did not bode well for Cook. When I told them of the gold in my cellar there was a stunned silence. Marcus Wethers recovered first. "And it was worth how much?"

"Three point five billion sterling plus."

Ludo found his voice. "You're not putting all this money up to fight Medina?"

I nodded. Marcus Wethers gulped at his wine. "But... but you could put it to all sorts of good use, John, surely! Ludo, make him see sense."

Ludo shrugged. "Sounds mad to me, John."

Why did I feel so defensive? It was my money and this was a good cause; no, the good cause – the right cause. "I'm putting all this money up to stop Sterling being destroyed and the British economy from being wrecked."

I was climbing on to my eighteen–hand hunter again. Uncle Marcus smiled at me. "Now, now, young John. Just because you are putting a three and a half billion fortune at total risk there's no need to get snippy."

I deflated and smiled. "I've brought a memory stick, Ludo, so you can see what the pin holes on your map mean. Have you got a laptop anywhere handy?"

So after dinner, a laptop was produced and Robbi demonstrated the way in which the pinholes spelt out hieroglyphs and how they demonstrated where the Chinese gold was hidden. Ludo sat back and studied me. "So, when are you going into the Chinese embassy?"

I stared at him – bloody old mind reader. "Tomorrow, please."

"Well, I'm leaving here too early to call anyone, but if I can get reception, I'll call the ambassador tomorrow. Interesting man. Sits on my committee at the Royal."

CHAPTER THIRTY-FOUR

We had left the Clanroydens by ten thirty. They had an early start and I knew ours would be even earlier. It was. At five thirty Robbi was trying dresses on and asking me idiotic questions. I think she eventually settled on some creation by Alexander McQueen, but to be honest I neither knew nor (particularly) cared.

We were at BTD by six thirty ahead of The Boss and the annoying children I was delighted to note. We sat down with Jarrod in a meeting room and filled him in. "And before you ask, Maxie, you do get to keep your commission."

He nodded. "And the Boss gets hers and you lose three and a half billion."

"Something like that, Max. Something like that."

The Boss walked in. "Heard you were here, John. What's the matter with Jarrod? Been out on the piss? You know the rules, Max."

"I've just briefed him, Boss."

She laughed. "Oh well that explains it. Jarrod – one word of this gets out and you are beyond dead. Now, you and John get your act together on this one and we'll not only make a shit load of money, we'll wipe out a particularly nasty piece of work, and we'll save the British economy into the bargain. And will we get any thanks for it? Will we fuck! But we'll know and everyone in the Square Mile will know and they'll know in Frankfurt and on Wall Street and we'll be the fucking underground heroes of the financial world. And will be happy with that?"

She gripped Jarrod's shoulder. "The answer, Maxie, is too fucking right we will be. You, Miss Beautiful, the Super Trader and the Boss – what a team. What a legacy. What a memory!"

She released his shoulder, beamed at us all and swept out. Robbi exhaled. The door swung open again and her head came round. "By the way, if you were thinking of relying on the matching funds from BTD, don't. I wouldn't trust Sebastian as far as I could…"

The door swung to behind her. I stood. They looked at me. "I'm going on to the Floor for a few minutes. I need to get a feel for things again."

Robbi studied me. "I'm fine – honest."

I walked down the stairs and made my way through to my desk. The children were there now. They watched me warily. Why the hell were they still here? I ignored them. My phone rang – Ludo.

"Yes, Ludo…"

"John, this isn't perfect and I had to use your Snow Leopard reference to get even this, but the person you need to meet will be there at four pm, not a minute before and not a minute after. Can you do that?"

I had no idea whether Alan Cummins would go along with this. "Yes, Ludo, and thank you."

"Bye now. Ian's a happy fisherman."

The phone went dead. Robbi had arrived and was looking at me. I dialled Alan Cummins. "Alan, do you know where Sir Ian is today?"

"Fishing. Why?"

"But do you know exactly where?"

"No. Why?"

"He's with Ludo Arbuthnot and he's on the Meon just below Wickham Mill."

There was a silence. "Ludo is a friend of the Chinese ambassador, Alan. He called him this morning. As a result, I'm afraid I need your Chinese prisoner – four pm at the Chinese Embassy or no deal with them. Mobile phone reception on the Meon is non–existent and Ian's phone seems to be out of order. We have to do it, Alan. It all kicks off on Monday with the trading."

I waited. I'm sure I could hear the drumming of his fingers on the table. I sat back and breathed out. I had made my play. Now it was in the lap of one of those gods that Harry and I didn't believe in.

"Meet me in ninety minutes."

"Where?"

"I don't know. Somewhere between the City and the West End."

"Clerkenwell Green." I pressed the 'off' button on the phone.

One of the children coughed. I ignored him. Robbi looked at me sternly. I sighed. It was the quieter one. Child Number One had disappeared. "What?"

"John."

I looked at him. This sounded more encouraging.

"I er… I want to apologise."

"Apologise for what?"

"Disobeying a direct order and in general for being a dick."

"Do you know why I ordered you to do the research yourself?"

"Because you wanted us to learn about the background to the trading you want to do."

"Good. Did you work that out by yourself or did The Boss tell you?"

"She didn't say much beyond telling us that if our fathers weren't big shareholders in BTD she'd have thrown us out."

I nodded. "Tell me, what did Inhuman Resources say to you?"

"Do you want the long or the short version?"

"Short will do."

"They told us to fuck off and grow up."

"And your little friend. Where's he?"

"Um, he's gone to see his father to complain about you."

I sat up straight. "When?"

"What do you mean?"

"When did he go and see his father? This is important."

"He'll be with him in about ten minutes."

"What's his father's name?"

"Peter Mathers. He's a senior partner in a very big firm of City lawyers in Gresham Street."

Would he know Medina? Shit, shit, shit! Why hadn't I thought of that possibility?

"Call him now. Invent any excuse you want, but get him out of there – *now*."

I called Dave. "Dave. Where are you?"

"Old Jewry on a shredding contract, why?"

I turned back towards the boy. "Have you raised him? Is he leaving the building? 6, Gresham Street?"

I spoke into the phone again. "Dave, there'll be a young man coming out of 6 Gresham Street. You're five minutes away."

"On my way. Description?"

"Five foot ten. Black hair. What's he wearing?"

"Navy blue pinstripe."

"Got that, Dave?"

I chewed my thumbnail and waited. My phone rang.

"I see him. You want him?"

"Yes, please, Dave. He's an arrogant little shit so you may need to scare him."

I put my phone down and looked at Child Number Two. "I don't know who or what you're texting, but if you send it you will cease working for BTD with immediate effect. What's your name?"

"Giles Vernon."

"Well Giles Vernon you have just earned yourself a second chance at BTD. There will not be a third chance. It is now four minutes past twelve. I trust that you have no plans for this weekend."

Giles Vernon swallowed. "May I make a phone call?"

"No. And, Giles… No, really does mean no. If making the call is more important to you than working at BTD, then please go ahead. But if you want to work here then forget the thought of private phone calls, emails, texts, or even leaving here before next Thursday. Until this project is over I own you. It's one week of your life. May seem a long and boring time to you, but for The Boss, Max, Roberta and me it is probably the most important week we will we ever live."

He took a deep breath and nodded once. "Yes, John."

I looked at him dispassionately. He was still very young. What was I like at that age? I thought back. Nope, nothing like him. Just like me now, only tougher, nastier, quicker, more ruthless. There was a bustle at the door. Dave came in holding Child Number One by his jacket collar. Child Number One was not happy. Before he started, I held up my hand.

"Mathers. Listen. For once, just listen. Giles here has been given a second chance to work on my project. The reason is that he apologised and appears to understand his – and your – stupidity in not doing the research I asked you to do. Now, do you wish to continue working here?"

"Not for you, you pathetic has–been with your stupid blonde tart."

I winced. Dave leaned forward to put his mouth beside Child Number One's ear. "I may have misunderstood you, but did you just call Miss Lord a stupid blonde tart?"

"Yes, I did. And you can fuck off too whoever you are. I don't take any shit from anyone least of all a fat twat like you."

"So I'm fat am I and my sister's a tart is she"

The floor watched with interest. This was certainly livening up an otherwise mundane Friday.

"Your sister? Her? Ha ha ha. So she really is just a common little slag."

I winced again. The child had a death wish. I put my head in my hands and waited. Dave walked round to put himself in front of Child One. He sighed. "You know I'm quite a reasonable man. Some people don't believe that, but I really am. So, you're going to apologise to Roberta. You don't have to apologise to me. If you think I'm a fat twat, that's fine, because I can easily prove you wrong just by taking off my shirt, but calling my sister a tart and a slag... well she can't disprove that easily, can she? So, you just apologise and I'll say no more. Honest, not another word."

I saw Emma come out onto the floor with a smile on her face. I raised an eyebrow at her. She shook her head still smiling. Child Number One didn't even pause. He leaned upwards eyes at Dave's mouth level. "Fuck you, you fat fuck and fuck your sister too which you probably have."

"Still time to apologise, son."

"Fuck you."

Child One swung a fist. Dave swayed back letting the blow go under his nose. Child One jabbed with his right. Dave just blocked it with one of his palms. "John, I don't want to hurt him. What do you want me to do?"

I looked at Robbi. She stood up. "Mathers. Please just apologise."

But Mathers was on some other coke–fuelled planet. He tried to hurl himself past Dave, straight at Robbi. She didn't even flinch. Dave's arm shot up and Mathers slammed into it. He rocked and slid to the floor, unconscious. The Boss walked forward applauding. "Thank you, Mr Lord." She clapped her hands together. "Right, listen up! I can now tell you a little bit of what is going on."

Dave bent to pick up Child number One.

"Leave him there for the time being, Mr Lord. OK. Here's what's going down. The Super Trader here…" She waved a hand in my direction. "… has inherited an amount of money with nine zeros in it and he is putting it at BTD's disposal to make a huge trade next week."

The Floor murmured its approval. "But, children, and it is a big but. Not a word of his presence here, nor of the project itself can leave these walls. No one outside the Floor apart from Don Bartrum knows a thing about this. Hush–hush isn't in it. Are we clear?"

She waited for the yesses to subside and continued. "So, tidy up here. A few of us will be working the weekend, but for the rest of you, Monday morning, squeaky clean and bushy tailed. Three days and we will own the world."

The Floor cheered. Child Number One stirred. The Boss kicked him. He groaned and opened his eyes and stared up at her blearily. "That bastard assaulted me."

"Actually, you stupid little shit, you assaulted him and attempted to assault Miss Lord and we have the whole thing on CCTV. For that you will be punished. In the meantime, what do you want to do with him?"

Dave glanced at me.

"Keep him on ice until next Thursday."

He nodded and pulled Mathers to his feet. "Stopped seeing red now, have you, son?"

Mathers struggled to get free. Dave reached his hand out and pressed a finger into his neck. Mathers' legs buckled and he went down again. We looked at Dave. He shrugged. "Carotid artery. Pressure point."

The three of us watched the inert form. Extraordinary.

I snapped out of it. "Dave, I need you to be outside the Chinese embassy in Portland Place at one minute to four this afternoon, on foot. I'll explain later. Oh, and Boss?"

"Yes, John?"

She was still grinning delightedly at the crumpled figure on the floor. "I wanted to discuss PR and Press. Fleet Street's going to be all over you."

"Like a rash. It had crossed my mind. Got time to prepare a brief?"

"Will do."

"OK and I'll sort the top floor. For all we know Mathers Père may well be on the phone soon and if he is you can kiss goodbye to any lingering hopes you had of BTD coming in with any money."

Dave made one call. He looked at me and pointed at the body on the floor. "Sorted. Right, what about this arvo?"

I told him, wrote my Press brief, grabbed a sandwich and left for Clerkenwell Green with Robbi.

CHAPTER THIRTY-FIVE

Alan Cummins was standing in a queue outside a small sandwich shop just up from the Marx Memorial Library. I think subconsciously that was why I wanted to meet him here. Clerkenwell has a long history of subversiveness. Alan raised his right hand in the internationally recognised drinking gesture and we both nodded. I held up two fingers and mouthed, 'black, no sugar' at him.

Two minutes later he was walking towards us carrying not three, but four cups of coffee in a cardboard tray. I looked round and saw the official black Jaguar waiting on the corner of Aylesbury Street. I nudged Robbi and we headed in its direction. Alan clambered awkwardly into the driver's seat and passed coffees round. I looked at the small, compact figure carefully opening his two paper tubes of sugar and pouring the contents onto the frothy Cappuccino where it created a little hollow in the cinnamon and chocolate topping. I sipped my puritanically black, sugar free coffee and waited to hear my fate.

"This is an unusual situation, Sir John."

I said nothing. Either he told us who he was and what he was able to do or we were all just wasting our time. I looked directly at Alan, gained his attention and looked at the other man. Alan cleared his throat. The figure glanced up from his careful stirring. "I do apologise.

When you spend too much time strategising, you sometimes get ahead of yourself in temporal terms."

He sipped his coffee and his glasses steamed up. He took them off to wipe them and Robbi passed him a tissue. "Thank you, Miss Lord. It is a genuine pleasure to meet you in the flesh. You too Sir John, but…". He waved a small hand, splashing coffee drops off his wooden stirrer on to the leather upholstery. "… in a different way. What I should say is that Alan has been briefing me on your activities and I have been studying you two for so long that I feel as though we have met many times, become friends, had discussions over lunch, visited each other's houses. Alan worries that I live too much in my imagination don't you, Alan?"

"Yes, sir."

"My name is Holroyd. I am Alan's superior…". He smiled impishly. "In many ways." He stirred some more and watched the swirling mixture turn from white to brown. "Alan has been playing what outsiders might regard as a double game. He has been reporting to Sir Ian Hamilton, but Alan is not a fool, despite all appearances to the contrary, and he has recognised for some months that he could be… aah… hung out to dry. I do not, therefore, intend to dissemble." He paused and I waited for the dissembling to commence. He smirked. "You're waiting for me to dissemble, aren't you?"

I smiled and I could sense Robbi suppressing a grin. He peered at us between the head rests then drank his coffee slowly, leaving a residue of creamy foam over his upper lip as he lowered the cardboard cup. Robbi passed him another tissue. He nodded his thanks.

"I could arrange to have your Chinaman at their embassy at 4.00pm, but I have to ask you… is your strategy good? Are you confident of your outcome?"

I rubbed my chin. "How well do you know the City, Mr Holroyd? I ask only because I don't want to sound patronising, but…"

"Well enough. I'll ask if I don't understand."

"Sorry I didn't express myself clearly enough." I started again. "Look, may I ask what your job description is?"

"Good question. Good question. Um, I'm a civil servant. Do you know who Mr Vincent Wolf is?"

Robbi nodded. I raised my eyebrows at her. She didn't take her eyes of Holroyd. "You tidy up messes." And to me… "Harvey Keitel in Pulp Fiction. You need to get out more."

"If I got out more it wouldn't be to go to a Tarantino movie."

Robbi hadn't taken her eyes off the little man. "He thinks he's cultured 'cos he likes someone called Sonny Rollins."

Holroyd looked pleased. "Pre or post Williamsburg Bridge."

"Pre – hard bop."

Robbi switched her gaze to Cummins. "It's not fair, Alan. He does this all the time. Talks about someone no sane person has ever heard of and then finds someone else who has heard of the same someone and they get all hoity toity about it, but when I know about Tarantino and Pulp Fiction, it's not culture."

She looked at Holroyd again. "So, Mr Holroyd, before John tells you why we have to go to the embassy, I want you to tell me whose mess you are cleaning up."

"Whose do you think, Miss Lord?"

"The Civil Service's."

"Excellent answer. And why not the government of the day?"

"Because governments come and governments go, but the Civil Service goes on forever."

"Except that it can't breach the second law of thermodynamics."

I smiled. I decided I liked Mr Holroyd – liking wasn't trusting, of course. I continued. "Very well. On Monday I believe we are going head-to-head with a very powerful man who not only appears to have this government in his pocket, but at least one of your civil servant colleagues."

"Oh, more than one, John, more than one."

I had a sudden insight. "How long have you, not you, Mr Holroyd, but you the Vincent Wolfs of the Civil Service, been tracking Medina and his like?"

"Well now, put it this way, John. If your grandfather hadn't succeeded in disposing of Mr Medina's grandfather in that Highland mountain chimney in 1923, our sniper would have been obliged to shoot him, which would not have been as we would have liked it. It could have revealed the hand of an outside body and we do not like to reveal that hand."

"Which leads me to wonder what is going to happen to us now that we know you exist?" I studied his face for clues, but he just shook his head.

"You are concerned that you will be swapping one would be murderer for another. But whom do you know, John – a man called Holroyd? Do we know a man called Holroyd, Alan?"

"No sir."

I shrugged mentally. This was getting way too metaphysical for me. "The long and the short of it is that Medina may not have as much money as he wanted, but he has a hold over this government and, judging by the way Sir Ian Hamilton changed positions at our last meeting, BTD would not have a chance if the Bank of England stepped in. I want to give the map to the treasure to the Chinese embassy in the hope they will support Sterling or at the very least remain neutral. This is all going to come to a crisis on Tuesday or Wednesday and I think we need even the tiniest edge we can find."

He stared at his now empty cup. "It is rare for me to meet people outside our own little charmed circle, John. But you and Miss Lord interest me greatly." He looked down at his now empty cup with its strata of drying, creamy chocolate foam on its sides. "I think I am being honest in saying that I wanted to meet you in order to convince myself that the Chinaman should go to the Embassy, but the ulterior motive, if such a motive exists of course, was to see you face to face, to be the first Holroyd, if you like, in three generations to meet a Hannay. So, now that I believe I have succeeded in puzzling and confusing you, may we drop you off anywhere?"

"If you're going west, Regent's Park, please. We can walk down to the Chinese embassy in Portland Place from there. Just to be clear, I will go in first offering them a password. I will be there at one minute to four and you'll have to have your Chinese prisoner there at four exactly and give him to Mr Lord who will come in with us. Mr Lord gave me these."

I passed across a pair of handcuffs.

In Regent's Park Robbi insisted I buy her an ice cream and then we walked hand–in–hand like any normal couple with normal lives and normal problems until we found a patch of grass near the zoo where we sat leaning against each other, back-to-back, analysing and re–analysing Mr Holroyd's comments, talking to each other over our shoulders, avoiding drips of melting ice cream falling on to Robbi's dress and basking in the warmth of the July sun.

I started checking my watch at three forty-five as we sauntered out of the park, dodged across the deafening chaos of the Marylebone Road and walked down through the Nash Crescent into the top of Portland Place. At five seconds after one minute to four we walked up the steps and into the Embassy. I had no idea what to do so I said the only two words that I could think would get us in. "Snow Leopard."

A slight, short Chinese official stepped forward and beckoned me as the main door behind us opened again to reveal Dave and the man whose motorbike I had shot up on the lane to East Garston all those weeks ago. I stood my ground watching as Dave was ordered to leave. He held up his arm revealing the handcuffs linking them together. I looked at the official who had stepped forward to greet me and held up the key. The official shrugged and led the way into an interview room. He seated himself behind the desk and spoke in accentless English.

"My ambassador received a call this morning. Who was it from?"

"Lord Clanroyden."

He nodded.

"Well?"

"I have exact directions to the place your people are looking for."

"What place? I do not understand you."

He looked at the handcuffed man beside Dave. And again I was playing catch–up to Robbi. She leaned across in front of me. "Dave, I think you can release your man now."

I passed him the key and the man was released. He stood up and bowed to the man behind the desk. I cleared my throat. "I am sorry I hurt you. I was trying to protect my partner."

He bowed to me and left the room. I reached into my pocket and pulled out a USB pen and a replica of the maps from the Gazetteer. I spread the maps on the table and let Robbi explain how they worked. Eventually he sat back. "And what, Sir John, do you want from us in exchange for this information?"

"I know about Dominick Medina's visits to China and I know about his connection with the PAP. I have two reasons for wanting to stop his attempt to destroy our currency. The first is that although, thanks to the enduring legacy of the Brexit mess we are now a small country with little influence worldwide and our present government appears to be even more idiotic than usual, there are many good people here whose lives would suffer greatly if Sterling became worthless. The second reason is that Medina's grandfather tried to kill my grandfather. His son succeeded in killing my father and my mother, and the grandson has tried to kill me. It has to stop now. All I am asking is that you do not support him in his run on Sterling. I do not see what you gain from this apart from the pleasure of seeing us humiliated."

He studied me for a while. "What makes you think that is not in itself a good reason to support this Dominick Medina? Have you heard of what you call the Opium Wars? Are you aware of the humiliation your government made my country undergo?"

"Very well aware, sir, yes, but I do not think for a minute that means anything to you now that you are the most powerful country in the world. What is to be gained by this action especially with the success of your belt–and–road policy?"

He studied the papers on his desk. "Are you trying to tell me that the mighty cannot derive pleasure from mocking the weak? History would not be on your side, Sir John. You, Sergeant Major Lord, what do you think we should do?"

Dave shrugged. "There is only one thing to do, sir."

"And what is that?"

"You fight for the honour of the regiment and you do nothing that would damage the honour of the regiment, sir."

He nodded. "And you, Miss Lord? You are a woman in a family of fighting men? Do you have a soldier's view or are you, like Medina's Mei Chen, just a beautiful plaything?"

He allowed an expression of something like contempt or disgust to cross his face. Robbi watched him for a few seconds. I could see her puzzling at something. "This isn't a war for you, sir. It's not even a skirmish. If you need that money for some good reason, then use it. Don't waste time with this petty battle. All I can do is echo my brother. Use the money for the honour of your regiment." She stood up. "John, we've made our offer. The money is theirs. Let's go."

Dave and I followed her lead. Half way to the door she stopped dead. I nearly cannoned into her as she turned to stare at the man behind the desk. "When you mentioned Medina's Mei Chen. The way you looked."

She hesitated, searching for her words. "She's half Chinese and half… She's his daughter isn't she? And you would support that kind of monster against John?"

Her eyes were blazing. Dave took a half step forward, but she pushed him away. "Then shame on you and shame on the Snow Leopard Commando Unit. You have your money. Much good may it do you!"

She swung on her heel and followed Dave out of the door. The hallway had been emptied of reception staff. Four men in combat gear were waiting. Dave moved into his relaxed, fighting posture, pushing us behind him.

"Well hello, boys."

The four men began to circle him warily; one of them flicked out a foot in a high kick. Dave caught the foot and twisted the body behind it aside. A knife appeared, then another. Dave grinned. So this was going to be it, then. I hoped Em would make the trades without me. I pulled Robbi to me, kissed her and pushed her behind me against the wall. I could do little to help Dave, but I wasn't going down without some kind of a fight. The door to the room we had just left swung open and I twisted to face yet another threat.

Our official from the meeting room clapped his hands once and spoke sharply. The four men stepped back immediately. They bowed and one opened the front door. We stepped out into the sunlight. I looked back. The official bowed his head in my direction. I bowed back. He turned to Robbi and bowed deeply. The door closed.

I pulled Robbi to me. She was shaking.

"I thought…"

Dave patted her gently on the shoulder. "We all thought that, Robbs. The world looks good when you thought you'd never see it again though, doesn't it?"

I looked up. Dave was right. The sun had never been so golden bright, the bird song so clear and sharp, the sky so azure blue. We walked away. Across the road I saw a black Jaguar pull away from the kerb in front of the RIBA building.

CHAPTER THIRTY-SIX

We got a lift in Dave's van back to the City. I called Harry. The background noise was high.

"Where on earth are you?"

"In bloody Andrew Barraclough's bloody van, that's where, driving to set up Medina's bloody party."

I smiled. "Harry, you remember the girl at Medina's place."

"Not likely to forget her, am I?"

"Well, we think that she's Medina's daughter."

There was a long silence. I opened my mouth to check whether he had heard.

"You're kidding, right?"

"No. I wish I were."

"But she was... Good God. I mean. Seriously?"

"Anything you can find out about where she lives, whether they have an apartment above the office, anything, OK?"

"Why?"

"Hostage."

"I knew you'd say that. I just knew it. Here I am again, putting my fucking neck on the line for you. I mean how many times am I going to have save your life before you leave me alone?"

Dave growled. "Harry."

"Oh, you're there too, are you?"

"Just do it, Harry."

"Yes, Dave. Yes, John."

Robbi leaned towards the microphone. "You forgot, 'yes, Robbi'."

"Yes, Robbi. Bastards the lot of you."

The phone went dead.

* * *

It was a nightmare ridden sleep that night. I got up early and went to work on the hotel iMac. Robbi lay in bed and watched me silently. After half–an–hour I showered and came back to find her reading my notes.

"Well?"

"Yep."

At ten, people started arriving. Alan was first and by ten thirty even a dishevelled Harry had crawled in and the small suite was crowded. I passed round copies of what I hoped the schedule and roles would be for the three days of next week. I glanced at Alan and raised an eyebrow.

"I have, of course, not seen any of this and I would remind you of your promise to Ian not to undertake any criminal acts. Who or what is Mei?"

I told him of our meeting at the Chinese embassy. He looked thoughtful. "Any chance we can get any confirmation of this, John?"

I shrugged. "I don't see how. Not in the timescale, but…". I went quiet wondering whether… "No, I don't think so. Look, this isn't a minute–by–minute break down obviously; it's just an aide memoire of what all our key activities are over those seventy–two hours. Does anyone have any issues with it?"

"You mean apart from why I should put myself back within reach of that murderous maniac?"

"Yes, Harry. Apart from that."

The meeting broke into sub–conferences as Palmer made requests to Alan for electronic equipment and Dave made calls to Paul Browby and the SAS boys to set up the surveillance and the snatch team. Then it was lunchtime. Robbi had booked a table for us outside on the terrace and they all filed out of the suite. I let them go ahead and made a phone call.

After lunch we arranged to drive back to Fosse with Paul. Sunday was to be a day of rest. The team disappeared. I looked round the foyer and took Robbi by the hand. She smiled up at me and batted her eyelids. I groaned. "You are a sex maniac. Come on we're not going upstairs; we're going to see Ludo. I called him before lunch."

She studied me for a second. "Aah, proof of who Mei is, yes?"

"You really are coming on by leaps and bounds, aren't you? Clever girl."

She smiled and dug a finger into my solar plexus. I managed to get through the swing doors without doubling up in pain, although it took a degree of sustained concentration. At the Clanroyden's house, Lockhart was expecting us and we were shown into the drawing room with the Claymore over the mantelpiece. It took me five minutes to bring Ludo up to speed. He nodded in his brusque fashion.

"So, I imagine you need me to do something. What?"

"Is there any chance that you would be able to get a copy of Mei Chen's birth certificate? It's a long shot and it will probably show that her parents are a respectable couple living quietly in Sichuan. But on the off chance the real one exists, it could be a tad useful."

"More than a tad, dear boy. More than a tad."

He walked slowly up and down the room with his head bowed. The sun shone slantendicular through the double height windows at the rear of the house, casting a golden haze over the room. He stopped pacing.

"You know, I think it may exist. From all that I've learnt about the Chinese in my years of dealing with them, the one thing they like to have is a lever over you. What better lever could there be than proof of gross behaviour by such an important British financier? Very useful to them indeed. I'll see what I can do, although I have to be honest and say that in the time frame, I think it's unlikely. You staying for tea?"

I stood. "No, thank you very much, Ludo. We're heading back down to Fosse to get some sleep before Monday."

* * *

SUNDAY AT FOSSE

Paul and Margaret disappeared after breakfast leaving us alone at 'home' for the first time in weeks. We lay in the garden and I was wondering about lunch when the house phone rang. I passed it to Robbi.

"Oh hello, Jack. How are you? Yes, of course we can – before or after lunch? OK, we'll be straight round.

Bye." She stood up and stretched. "You know you're dead lucky. I was about demand more sex, but Jack Cartwright wants us round at his farm for some reason. Come on. Shift your skinny, upper class arse."

Miranda's old VW was the only transport left at the manor so we bucketed round to the Cartwrights with Robbi crashing the gears and over–revving the motor. Jack was waiting in the farmyard smiling. "Come on you two. Mother's inside with a surprise for you."

Robbi led the way into the kitchen to find Joan beaming with pride and Bessie in her basket nursing seven puppies. Robbi was entranced.

"Careful now, Robbi dear, bitches can be a bit protective."

Joan needn't have worried. Bessie wagged her tail at Robbi, positively smiling at her. "Oh Bessie, you clever girl. May I stroke them?"

"I thought she was looking a bit on the podgy side, Jack. Who's the father?"

"We worked that one out just yesterday, John. Frankie – Collie on Glebe farm. I'd forgotten until Joan reminded me. She were in season and he sneaked round, crafty old devil. She always fancied him anyway. So, point is we want you to have two of 'em."

I'd seen this coming, of course, but I had absolutely no idea how to react. Here was my future unrolling in front of me and of all the possible futures, the only one I had ever had any desire for in any shape or form, but I realised with a stab of irritation that I was terrified of it. If I said yes, then how many other yesses and noes were there coming up that would be beyond my ability to protect her from? I fiddled with the little box in my pocket I had taken out of the safe last night and looked at Robbi. She was staring at Bessie and stroking the small bundles of black and white fur in front of her apparently oblivious to the rest of us, but I could feel that every single atom of her senses was tuned in on me. My past caught up, nudged me, winked mockingly, grabbed me by the throat and careered onwards into my future holding me tight in its grip. I crouched beside her. A Collie puppy tottered towards me. I pushed it gently back to its mother. "You don't want the ones that come towards you, they'll be the sheep dogs. Full of energy, nosiness and drive."

Jack nodded approval.

"See the two little ones snuggled up against Bessie. They're the runts. They'll be the ones for us, Robbi, especially if they're both bitches."

"Reckon they are, John, although the vet's coming tomorrow. Good choice too ain't it, mother."

"So long as Robbi goes along with it, yes, love."

Joan had caught some of the tension between us. I looked up at her and smiled. "Oh, don't worry about Robbi, Joan. I make all the important decisions in this relationship."

Robbi smiled at Joan, but I could see the tears brimming in her eyes as she shook her head. Joan walked quickly to her and put a comforting arm round her, pulling her into her shoulder as Robbi began to sob as if her heart were breaking. I took half a step forward. Joan glared at me behind Robbi's back and then glared at Jack too (which I thought was a bit unfair). Jack nudged me and we walked out of the kitchen into the farmyard. He leaned against the ancient Ferguson tractor and looked at me. "You know, I've been married nigh on fifty years and I have no idea when a woman cries if it's a good or a bad thing."

"You think I know anything about women, Jack? Without a photograph I can't even remember what my mother looked like. That was the last long-term relationship I had with a woman until I met Robbi and look what happened to her. History repeats itself, Jack."

Jack snorted. "You know what your trouble is, John, don't you?"

"What, Jack?"

"You're scared."

I snorted. Jack held up a hand. "Hear me out, John. You've just met your mate. Nothing to do with the fact that she's the most beautiful woman I've ever seen or anything like that. She and you go together. Joan said it the minute she set eyes on her and I agree – only it took you months to see what she saw in the first minute. You're scared you're not good enough for her, but you're too much of a Hannay to back down. Now, don't you let this one go, John. Don't let her go."

I sighed. "Jack, had it occurred to you that if we stay together, I might be signing her death warrant?

"Oh, don't exaggerate. She's old enough to make her own decisions. She's from an Army family for God's sake. Don't you start down that path now! I'm disappointed in you, John."

I sighed again, reached into my pocket to show him the box, but before I could there was a shuffling at the doorway and Robbi came out looking small and wan with Joan behind her. Joan glared at me again over Robbi's shoulder.

"I've been told off, Robbi."

"So have I, John."

"Jack, may we leave Miranda's car here, please? We'll collect it later. I think we'll walk home… if that's OK with you, Robbi."

She sniffed and held out her hand like a child. I smiled at Jack and Joan over her shoulder and we walked away into the dusty sunlight of the early afternoon. We hadn't spoken since leaving the Cartwrights and I wasn't sure how to open the conversation. Eventually we were up by the fence looking down on the Manor. I climbed on to it and Robbi joined me, sitting on the top rail. I took a deep breath and jumped down, turning and holding her in place before she could join me on the ground. I looked up at her. She looked down at me warily. I cleared my throat. "I er… Roberta Jane Lord, would you do me the honour of being my bride?"

She stared at me, her eyes moving over my face. I wondered whether that proposal wasn't a bit too Jane Austin.

"I shall try again in twenty first century English in case your limited understanding of our mother tongue rules out more formal communication. Robbi, will you marry me?"

Still, she said nothing. I scrabbled in my trouser pocket and pulled out the small box and gave it to her to open. She fiddled with the catch and the box lid flipped up. She gasped.

"It was my grandmother's engagement ring." I looked at her uncertainly. Had I read this wrong again? God, I really was utter crap at relationships. She looked first at me and then at the box, fiddling with the ring, the diamond facets catching the sunlight. "Um, it probably won't fit you, due to you having fat, calloused, working class fingers."

She half–smiled. Finally, she spoke. "So how long have you been carrying this round in your pocket?"

"Since we got home last night."

"So this is nothing to do with you feeling sorry for me because I was snivelling round at Jack and Joan's."

Jack was right. Who the hell knew what women were thinking?

"I mean you do really want to marry me?"

"Christ, Robbi! Yes. You think it's easy making a tit of myself standing down here? Do I want to spend the rest of my life with you? Yes. Do I want to marry you? Also, yes." I stepped up on to the first rung of the fence so her face was just a few inches above mine. "I really want to go through all the crap of a white wedding in the village church; I really want to have two Collies and a clutch of little Hannays running round the Manor and I really, really want to hear people call you Lady Hannay."

I stepped back down to ground level. "Oh, and one final thing… if you start crying or bouncing, the offer is withdrawn."

Robbi sat on the top rung, still smiling to herself under her golden hair, looking at the little ring. For God's sake! I took her hand and the ring and without ceremony pushed it onto her third finger. It fitted. It actually fitted. I stood still, realising that the pendulum had swung. She studied the ring on her finger and then without warning wrapped her legs round my body and pulled me in close with her arms.

"Yes, John Richard. I shall do you the honour of being your bride and a very beautiful one I shall be too. John, I'm sorry I cried at Jack and Joan's. I just suddenly felt that I was railroading you into what I wanted for my future and you might not be ready for it and it just made me very sad and, and you really did intend to propose to me today?"

"Last night, actually, but there were people round us all evening and then you fell asleep."

"So will I be Lady Roberta then?"

"No, you'll be Lady Hannay… or 'oy you', whichever I decree."

"Lady Hannay… Lady Roberta Jane Hannay… OK, it'll do until I find a duke."

She took the ring off, put it back in its box, gave the box back to me and jumped down from the fence.

"We tell no–one until this is all over."

"God no, absolutely right; I'd be too ashamed anyway, you're so common."

"Too late, you can't wind me up now, Hannay."

"I'm going to tell Uncle Marcus, though, so he can change the will."

"But I don't want your bloody money."

"The Manor, idiot. Someone has to take care of it. You know… if."

"No, I don't know… if!"

And do you know, I've never even had a second thought about that decision. Strange.

CHAPTER THIRTY-SEVEN

Robbi had been up for half an hour. I showered and dressed in City attire. The future Lady Hannay finally chose a very expensive black outfit by Stella McCartney. I hoped she had remembered to put her underwear on.

At 07.15hrs the floor was full and I called Dave. Within two minutes the team had come up in the service elevator and were in Reception. By 07.30hrs the Floor knew this was serious.

There's a rhythm to the trading day. UK money trading starts at 08.00hrs UTC (that's GMT to you and me) and finishes at 16.00hrs UTC. The US dollar is involved in the majority of Foreign Exchange (Forex) trades and the US trading session starts at 08:00hrs Eastern Standard Time – 13.00hrs here in the UK. It finishes at 17.00hrs New York time or 22:00hrs, London time. So, the best time to trade is during the three hours when the world's two most important markets overlap and that's between 13:00hrs and 16:00hrs UK time. It being 07:31hrs now we had twenty–nine minutes to prepare for the beginning of our trading day and five hours before the fun really started.

The concern with which Dave's team was being studied had less to do with their number and much more to do with the fact that Dave, Johnson and Spinetti were in full army camouflage kit. Palmer ignored everybody and started to unpack his various pieces of electronic gadgetry.

At 07:33hrs The Boss walked on to the floor and clapped her hands for attention. Alan Cummins followed her slowly, seating himself on the edge of a desk by the door.

"Right, you will all remember Mr Lord from last week, it's just that he is now here in full fancy dress with some of his little friends. They are here solely for your security as they are specialists in electronic surveillance. The gentleman in the corner muttering to himself will run the initial checks to make sure we are all secure here. And yes, I did point out that we were scanned every week, but he appeared to find that mildly amusing. Some of you will also remember Major Alan Cummins who helped out last year on the money laundering scam we encountered. Alan works for the government – it's up to him how much he tells you about his work – and he is here to reassure you that none of you are at risk and that what we are doing is wholly legitimate. Any questions? Thought not. John, over to you."

I stood up as a third ex–soldier brought Mathers onto the Floor, looking subdued and neither bound nor gagged. "Ladies, gentlemen, as The Boss mentioned last week, I have inherited an amount of money which…"

Jarrod choked back a laugh. "Fuck's sake ST, tell 'em how much. The Floor needs a sense of scale."

I glanced at Em. She nodded. "It's in the region of three point five billion – er Sterling – which is about four point seven billion US dollars for those who can't calculate currency exchanges. Jarrod here has been leveraging it. How much have we got now, Max?"

"Twenty billion US give or take and as of Friday."

"So, we're putting this money at your disposal to make a series of massive trades going long on Sterling."

There was a collective noise – an aggregation of phews, gasps and whistles. I noticed Dave stopping someone at the door. It was our analyst, Don Bartrum.

"It's OK Dave, we need him in here."

Jocasta's hand was up. "But there's a lot of trading against Sterling. It was down a hundred and fifty points on Friday."

"Believe it or not, Casta, I had noticed. And *you* should also have noticed that London's hosting the G20 summit this week. The world's 'top' leaders flew in last night and they will all fly out on Wednesday evening making happy, oxymoronic noises about their plans to control carbon emissions in the light of climate change whilst keeping the fossil–fuel–based world economy growing. Now what you need to know is that someone is trying to sabotage the G20 and wreck the British economy into the bargain. Now we are going to stop that. If we succeed, we will make a shed load of money and can feel very smug. If we fail, we'll still make money of course, but God knows what will be left of the UK economy. And you can all sit there in your not very well tailored clothes and pretend to be part of the global market place and who gives a shit about England. But you live here, you work here, you pay taxes here – yes, Annabelle, I know you try not to – but the real point is – well I surprised myself when I first found out about all this. I thought I was pretty cool about trading and making money and fuck the consequences and live off–shore, but I found that I do care. And the more I have thought about it the more I care. Greed, ladies and gentlemen, is not good. It is destroying the world." I paused. "Now… We have discovered that there is someone who is going to short Sterling – sounds just like Soros – except that Soros didn't intend to destroy the UK's economy and the pound needed to devalue then anyway. This is just one man who wants to wreak vengeance on Britain. You don't have to believe me – Alan and The Boss will tell you the same story. Boss?"

"OK, children. We're going long on Sterling for three days. You know all you need to know. But let me emphasise one thing. No one outside this floor can know a single thing about this. No one. And, before we go, this isn't an every-woman-for-herself situation. You all share information. Clear? Get on with it then. Let's slide into this nice and gentle. Let's watch and learn in the next few hours."

Robbi tapped me on the arm and nodded towards Palmer. I watched. Palmer was staring at a spotlight over one of the desks. He waved an arm at Spinetti.

"Gareth, a word, please."

Spinetti threaded his way through the desks to where Palmer was still staring at the spotlight in the ceiling. He nodded, jumped up on the desk and pulled a ceiling tile out. The back of the spotlight was a camera. I walked into Emma's office and jerked my head at her, putting my finger to my lips. She followed me out and stared in amazement. I saw the anger begin to boil and quickly pulled her to my desk. "Em, you sure the top floor installed this?"

"Who the fuck else?"

Palmer leaned over my desk to question her. "What time does the top floor get in, in the morning?"

"Any time from seven thirty, why?"

"Buy us twenty minutes and we'll have a loop running in front of the cameras."

"Cameras? How fucking many are there?"

Palmer shrugged.

"It'll be more than one. I'll scan the whole room now for sound."

I tried to distract the incandescent Emma. "Em, can you find an excuse to check out the top Floor, see if anyone's watching?"

"I don't need a fucking excuse to see those tossers. On my way."

It took Palmer and Spinetti ten minutes to replace the three cameras they found and a further ten minutes to uncover microphones in four of the trader's phones including the one on the desk of a very nervous Annabelle. Robbi placed some papers in front of me. "What's Annabelle looking so worried about?"

"The whole floor knows she's been trading on her own account for years. Looks as though the Top Floor has known about it too."

Palmer, Johnson and Spinetti retired to the corner behind the doors where their stack of monitors made it look more like a TV Outside Broadcast unit than a surveillance operation. The Boss returned from the Top Floor looking calm. Nothing had been noticed. By a quarter past eight the Trading Floor had settled down. Individual traders were beginning to buy Sterling and we entered the slow build up to the main trading period. At twenty past nine the fan was hit. As ever, Jocasta noticed it first.

"Someone's selling Sterling."

The floor went quiet. How big a trade? Emma came out of her office and stood behind me. Jocasta called across, anxious to be in the game. "John, do we buy?"

For God's sake let me think, let me think. "Shut up Jockstrap."

Emma leaned forward over my shoulder, her breath warm on my neck. "Are you concentrating, John?"

"Just tell Casta to shut up, Em. She'll spook everybody else. Look, if we start buying chunks now it'll look very odd. Why would we react so fast? What do we know? Medina must know I used to work here. It'll only take one false move from us and guess who'll be on the phone to your friend Sebastian."

"The trouble with you, John, is that you don't understand the psychology of your average human being. The rest of us aren't ice–cold calculating machines. You need to offer encouragement. Let them buy a little now. It'll relax their nerves."

I nodded. She was quite right of course. Team player I was not. She straightened and clapped her hands. "All right, children. John's tactics are correct. If we start buying immediately, they'll smell a rat. Jocasta, buy a small amount, and you too Jeremy. Then in five minutes, you buy a similar amount, Annabelle, followed by George and young Giles here. That way it'll look like

BTD has noticed the selling and some of the traders are covering existing positions. That'll take us to ten thirty. Giles you watch the trades and everybody else get on with life as normal until one."

There was a nervous cough behind me. It was Child Number One. I looked at Robbi. She gave a tiny shrug. I looked at him.

"I'm not asking for a second chance, John. I just wanted to apologise to you and to you, Roberta. I er. I don't have an excuse, but I was coked out of my head. Do you mind if I just sit this one out and watch?"

"Where have they kept you over the weekend?"

"I have no idea, but they have a unique approach to making you go cold turkey. I don't want to go into it, but I wouldn't touch any of the Columbian Marching Powder now for all... well for your inheritance. I'm really sorry, John. I think I've been out of control for a long while now."

"Sit in with Giles. He'll bring you up to speed. And Mathers. You do nothing without asking me first."

"No, John. I won't."

"And, keep an eye out for RNSs and any government announcements. That is very important."

"Yes, John."

I went back to my screen. Time flowed over me. The selling of Sterling went on relentlessly. At one o'clock I asked Don to calculate Medina's exposure. Minimal. The pound was dropping if not like a stone, then certainly like a very heavy feather. There was an inexorability about its decline. Bloomberg agreed. Reuters agreed. The US markets opened. Their traders agreed. The Floor was getting restless. The Boss did the rounds, boosting morale, chivvying, still letting the traders buy in small packages. I sat in front of my screen waiting... just waiting.

Then, finally at thirty–two minutes after three, a trader on Wall Street made a mistake going long on Sterling. I leaped to my feet before he could correct the trade.

"Boss! Now!"

The Floor jumped into action with a frenzy of yelling and we bought every penny of Sterling out there until the market closed at Four. Sterling was back up seventy points and the mood on the floor was ecstatic – an orgy of high fiving, backslapping, kissing even. I looked at Don Bartrum as the noise died down.

"What's his exposure now, Don?"

"Over two billion USD."

The Floor cheered. I gave Em a long look. She nodded and stepped on to a chair.

"OK, children. You get the picture now. But... that was the easy bit. He'll come back with fresh tactics tomorrow and so will we. Now remember. Not a fucking word to anyone. One word of this gets out and none of you will ever work in the City again. Children? I mean that."

I slumped in my seat. Robbi was going through administration with Jarrod so I could show something of my fatigue without being fussed over. Alan Cummins put a hand on my shoulder.

"You know it wasn't that long ago that you could scarcely stand up to greet me. You going to last the course?"

"Thanks for the vote of confidence, but, yes, I'm OK. Enjoy it?"

"Wouldn't have missed it for the world – you get a distinctly Shakespearean:

And gentlemen in England now–a–bed
Shall think themselves accurs'd they were not here
feeling, don't you?"

"Not yet, I don't. Now we plan tomorrow. Let's talk to Em."

I started to get up and my arms gave way. I slumped back down. "Stand there, Alan and don't move. I don't want Robbi seeing this. I'm OK. It's just that ever since Medina's drugs any kind of stress knocks me back. The doc said there was nothing fundamentally wrong with me."

"Yes, John. I talked to the doctor who treated you after you got out of Medina's house. He told me that if you didn't take care of yourself and convalesce properly your metabolism would – that's 'would' not 'could' – be permanently damaged."

I smiled. The dizziness, pounding heart and wave of nausea had passed. I got to my feet carefully. Alan watched me and shook his head. The Boss held up a hand as we entered her sanctum and mouthed the word 'Bloomberg' at us. It gave me the chance to slump in my seat as Robbi came in with drinks. She glanced at me and clocked my state immediately.

"Yes, I'll talk to you for five minutes tomorrow at half past eight – no you're first, but that excludes the BBC and the FT. Yes, honey, I had noticed that there was some heavy selling of Sterling. Who the fuck do you think you're talking to? Can we beat them? Are you kidding? We're BTD. Speak tomorrow online. Bye now."

Her phone rang again. She looked at the number and smiled thinly.

"The vultures are hovering. Reuters."

"Hello, Jackie. Sorry, love, you need to get me on speed dial. I'm giving an online exclusive to Bloomberg tomorrow morning. Happy to talk at lunch when we see how the market's panning out. Half past twelve. Fine. See you online."

Her phone rang again. She yelled at her long-time assistant.

"Helen, no–one through unless it's the Today programme. Who's this?"

"Financial Times, Boss."

Emma smiled and picked up the phone.

"Emma Fitzgerald. Yes. Yes, oh hi, James. How are you? You're on the Lex column now, are you? OK waddya want, a succinct and pithy quote? How about Emma Fitzgerald, BTD's Senior Trader informed the Financial Times Lex column that if they got off their lazy asses and employed some economists, they would realise that the fundamentals of the British economy do not warrant the pound's current under–pricing. In words of one syllable, James. Watch. This. Space. Let's catch up on Wednesday. I'll tell Helen to let you through."

Helen stood half in the doorway her headset tilted away from her mouth.

"Simon from the BBC Today programme."

"Good. And let James from the FT come in for a meeting on Wednesday any time before they go to press."

"Hi Simon. What am I up to? I'm supporting the British economy, Simon, that's what I'm doing. Off the record now… You know perfectly well that this shorting of Sterling stinks and we have the money, the resources and the team to beat whoever it is at their own game. I'm not seeing UK plc flushed down the bog by a bunch of spivs."

She laughed.

"On the record, yes, I'll talk to you on air. When? Helen – Simon at six forty-five tomorrow. Speak then, honey. Bye."

She looked at Helen questioningly.

"It's the Economist."

Emma nodded and picked up her phone again.

"Blimey I am moving in exalted circles. What can I do for you? Oh, it's only you, Rebecca. I thought it was someone important. So did you? Cheeky cow. Right, I'm a touch busy now, Becca, what's the question? Hmmm. Your press date's Wednesday, isn't it? You'll need to talk to our senior analyst and our top trader as well. Sebastian will try and get in on the act so you might as well accept it. OK, if you can do some of your own research and you can hold the front page, I think we can promise our friends at the Economist one fuck of a story. Liaise with Helen on times. See you Wednesday, you old bat."

She looked at us across her desk and rubbed her hands with glee – the pirate captain had spotted fat new prizes hull–down on the horizon. She broke out the foretopgallant studdingsails…

"OK, John, I've got your press release. I'll have to run it by the press prevention department upstairs, but I think it'll go."

Jarrod knocked on the open door.

"How's funds holding up, Maxie?"

"Fingers crossed, we'll be OK until Wednesday. We went through ten billion this arvo, but tomorrow morning'll be slower I think, don't you?"

They looked at me.

"No. I don't. Em?"

She indicated that I should continue. "He'll come back with a massive hit tomorrow morning so we have to be faster. We need to buy like hell from the millisecond after trading starts through until ten, I reckon. It's going to be balls out, I'm afraid."

Emma glared at me. "Sexist pig." She looked at me more closely. "Miss Beautiful take him home. He's fucked and we need him to spot things like that trader fucking up on Wall Street earlier. Silly sod that he was. Must have cost his fund a packet. Did you see it, Maxie? He corrected in seconds, but the Super Trader saw it. No one else could have seen it that fast. You're still a genius, ST."

They all raised their glasses to me, but I shook my head. "Not me. Never was and there's still two more days."

I hauled myself out of my seat. Robbi took my hand, dragged me to my feet, helped me out of the building, shoved me into a taxi and got me back to the hotel.

CHAPTER THIRTY-EIGHT

TUESDAY 06:10HRS

I was just about to pay off the taxi outside BTD when I noticed Palmer gesticulating at me furiously from the pavement. I clicked.

"Driver, could you drop us round the corner at the Starbucks. I've just remembered that the canteen isn't open yet."

The driver shrugged, drove and took my money. We stood on the kerb and waited for the call. Robbi put her arm round my waist. The phone rang.

"The place is being watched. Wait there. Dave's van will be with you in five."

We waited.

By seven The Boss had done the Today Programme interview, handled the press officer, told Sebastian to go back upstairs and shouted at the traders. I sat in the small room off the Floor that Palmer had now commandeered for his kit and watched the watchers. Palmer had warned Alan and he came in disguised as a courier. Palmer handed him copies of the photos he had taken of the watchers. I wondered idly if they were career criminals or just Private Eyes. Alan studied the photos, murmured something, scanned them, emailed the results to his office and waited for the response. His phone rang. He listened and then put the phone down slowly. "Now this is serious."

"Why?"

"They're SO15."

"My, oh my. Medina is well connected, isn't he? Is this the closing of ranks you warned us about? Hang on, here's The Boss on Bloomberg."

I walked over to her office to watch The Boss do a live, down–the–line interview with Bloomberg TV. A self–important BTD press officer began to push me away with his hand on my chest – the expression on his face as he was lifted bodily from behind by Dave lives with me to this day. Em had done hundreds of these interviews and I listened admiringly to her cool analysis, then grabbed a piece of paper, scribbled on it quickly and slid it on to her desk. She picked it up and without missing a beat used it.

"And, Diane, I know when we're on to something big when I spot officers from what used to be called Special Branch outside BTD at six thirty in the morning. I'm sure it's wonderful for their overtime claims, but what does it say to you about this government's issues with Sterling? As Juvenal had it, Quis custodiet ipsos custodes, Diane."

Diane from Bloomberg's jaw dropped. She closed her mouth, swallowed twice, lost focus as she listened to the little voice in her ear and wound the interview up. Em winked at me as the screen went black.

"Couldn't have been better timing, Super Trader. That'll put the wind up the fuckers. Right. Five minutes to the off. Time to go and calm the horses in the paddock." She swept out onto the Floor and I made my way to my desk listening her to geeing her 'children' up. She climbed on to a desk showing a long expanse of elegant, stockinged thigh, much to Jarrod's delight, and counted the Floor down.

"Five, four, three, two, one. Go. Go. Go."

For half an hour it was chaos. Algorithms may have taken over the great mass of automated trading, but I am old fashioned enough to believe that top traders could control a market far better than any post graduate's computer program. I wasn't buying – I just supervised my two juniors who were wildly excited – but the other traders were yelling into phones like they were back in the Open Outcry era. I saw Sir Ian enter out of the corner of my eye. This should shut him up, capitalism at its most raw – hardly the dignified committee rooms of Whitehall in which he had exercised his craft. I saw him head towards me, but something caught my eye on the screen and I began to concentrate. I grabbed Giles' shoulder and pointed. He caught on immediately. We tracked the trades for ten minutes. I yelled at Jarrod without taking my eyes off the screen.

"Maxie, how much is there in the kitty?"

"Seven."

To Giles. "Get The Boss."

He ran. I sensed a crowd behind me. Within seconds Emma was crouched over my shoulder. I pointed out the trades. Someone in Frankfurt was getting scared of our activity and was beginning to buy.

"Crush them Super Trader! Crush the Krauts. Robbi, shout out when we're down to three point five billion."

So I crushed them, but it cost…

At twelve, I sat back. Robbi leaned against the back of my chair. "John, would you like me to wear stockings?"

"Hunh?"

"Well, I saw you looking at Em's thighs and I just wondered."

I shook my head in despair and started to reply that any normal man would want... when Palmer called. "Reuters – now."

Mathers switched channels on the overhead screen and turned the sound up. They had door–stepped ffitch outside The Treasury and he was in full pompous flow.

"Well, it is not for a mere government adviser such as myself to disagree with the money markets, but I do find it strange that a certain City trader is claiming to know more about the fundamentals of the economy than we at the Treasury do. We do not like to hear knockers, but we are also concerned if we hear exaggerated claims for the health of UK plc when we all know that there is much to do."

I turned and grabbed Don Bartrum and hustled him into the Boss's office. "Don, you've got five minutes to brief the Boss on why the fundamentals of the British economy do not warrant this shorting of Sterling."

Emma nodded at him and I left them to it wandering out on to the Floor to inspect the damage – four billion left and three hours of trading to go. We wouldn't get through the day – bloody ungrateful Chinese bastards. Jarrod was grinning at me.

"What, Maxie? What for Christ's sake?"

"Remove your panties from your crack, dear boy. Uncle Maxie has been leveraging again."

I began to smile. "You little genius, Max. How much?"

He held up five fingers. My smile grew. That meant we had eight point five billion. We could still do it. I saluted Jarrod. And then it was 12:30hrs and Emma was on Reuters. She was outraged.

"And since when, Jackie, have you been getting live briefings from junior government advisers? And briefings furthermore which are to the detriment of the British economy. Let me give you some of the facts that Mr ffitch seemed to want to omit. No, no, Jackie, no – I didn't notice your colleague interrupting Mr ffitch so now you will not interrupt me. GDP has been rising consistently for the last seven quarters. If you look behind the employment figures you will see...". It was vintage Emma Fitzgerald. Within two minutes, using Don Bartrum's key facts, she had presented a portrait of the British economy that sounded balanced, reasonable and above all optimistic. "So, Jackie, that is why we at BTD are backing Sterling against the naysayers whether they are in the Treasury or on other floors in this square mile."

"Would you care to elaborate on that Miss Fitzgerald?"

"Not without my lawyers present, Jackie. But let me emphasise that we have the money, the resources and the best traders in the world and I can assure you that BTD will make sure the British pound is not destroyed on the whim of some greedy, self-serving, so–called traders who pay their taxes in Jersey or Bermuda and contribute nothing to the British economy."

The screen went black and the Floor stood and cheered. Sebastian, who had just stormed in with the intention of, (to use one of his own delicate phrases), 'ripping her another asshole', retired unseen. I stood on my chair cheering with the rest.

And then it was One o'clock. Em's interviews had had the desired effect. Trading had slowed and whenever a seller appeared BTD snapped it up in milliseconds. For a brief period we were ahead of the game. And then...

"John, quick. Look who's coming in."

I glanced at Palmer's monitor. It was ffitch accompanied by a nervous looking Sebastian. I ran Robbi to the Reception area, chucked the 'management hidden' cameras at Dave, asked Alan to call Dr Livesey and sat down, hidden by Giles and Mathers as ffitch stormed through the door. He saw Robbi and stopped dead.

"Why hello, Mr ffitch. How nice to see you again."

Ffitch turned white and then blotchy red. He was not a healthy ffitch at all. He turned to Sebastian. "What is this slut doing here? The last time I saw her she was creeping round Hannay. Who's she after here?"

Em walked out of her office door and stood directly in front of ffitch. "Did you just call one of my employees a slut?"

ffitch turned his back on her and spoke to Sebastian. "Sebastian, I have had quite enough of this. HMG expects you to sack this woman and stop this floor's absurd and disgraceful behaviour."

I saw Sebastian draw breath and pull himself up to his full five feet five inches. Time to intervene. I pushed past Giles and as Sebastian opened his mouth, I tapped ffitch on the shoulder. He swung round.

"Hello ffitch."

"But you're dead. You can't be here, Medina said you were d…"

His voice faded, his eyes lost focus, he staggered and then slumped forward in a dead faint. To be fair, I could have caught him as he fell, but I stepped aside and he smacked his head on the corner of the desk before he hit the floor.

"Oh, now look, Sebastian, he's bleeding on your carpet."

Dave walked past me, tore ffitch's jacket off and put it under his head.

"That'll stop the blood getting on the floor," he murmured. He straightened and stepped over the body to stand directly in front of Sebastian.

"Before you say a word, sir, I would like to ask you a question about these."

He held up the ceiling cameras and the microphones.

"What? Who the fuck are you?"

"Warrant Officer Class One, David Lord, Sah!"

Dave came to attention with a stamp of his boots. At this point Sebastian lost it and started one of his famous rants. The Floor was delighted. This really was turning out to be one of the better days. "Who the living fuck cares what your rank is, get the fuck off my floor you overgrown, fucking hooligan."

Dave glanced at me over his shoulder. He was grinning with delight. I saw Alan and Sir Ian turn away, smothering smiles. "Be delighted to, Sah! When, Sah, you have told me why you or someone you employ planted these illegal devices in the ceilings in order to spy on your staff, Sah!" He leaned down until his mouth was on a level with Sebastian's eyes and spoke quietly. "You are in seriously deep shit here, son, so I would really, really think twice before opening your little potty mouth again."

Sebastian went purple and then very slowly he breathed out, his face moving through the colour spectrum until it stuck on an interesting shade of pale red. In a metaphor mixing way, it could be said that he hadn't climbed up the greasy pole of banking management without having to eat the humblest of humble pie from time to time.

Emma stepped forward immediately. "Sebastian, I realise this must come as a rather a nasty shock to you, the fact that someone has installed spying devices without your knowledge, I mean. Luckily Major Cummins here brought Regimental Sergeant Major Lord in to investigate and I believe you have met Sir Ian Hamilton before too. We were just about to alert you to this dreadful state of affairs when you entered in the company of someone who we know to be intimately involved in the attack on Sterling."

Sir Ian came to the front. Whatever doubts he had about me, he had now seen and heard the best possible evidence about ffitch's involvement with Medina. He was at his most suave. "Mr Damon, I am most terribly sorry you have been involved in this dreadful affair, I will come and make a personal apology to the board. I rather fear that these er, devices, have been put in here without anyone in BTD having the faintest idea of their existence. Do come and sit down in here and let's see what we can do." He led the stunned Chief Executive into Em's office. The usual resident of the office looked round the floor quietly.

"The game's not over yet, children. One or two of us…" she glared at Annabelle, "have had a lucky escape. Back to work, now."

The elevator doors opened. Who the hell was coming in now? Alan stepped forward and waved. It was the army doctor who had originally interviewed ffitch. I grabbed The Boss. "Em, would this be the time to get Sebastian to commit those matching funds?"

The Boss laughed delightedly. "Love it – kick a man in the balls when he's down. Seriously though… don't rely on it."

And now it was two pm. Giles called across the office. Ten points and a gold star to Giles; he had sat at his monitor for the whole time that ffitch had been here. I glanced at Mathers. He hung his head. I smiled. Giles had been buying, but that wasn't what he wanted to show me. Someone had started short selling again in a big way. I looked at the time line. The short selling had started thirteen minutes ago. Thirteen minutes ago – shit! I saw Spinetti. "Gareth."

He looked distinctly worried that an 'officer' should address him by his Christian name.

"Tell me the exact time that ffitch walked into Reception."

He started to salute, stopped, nodded and ran into the surveillance room and yelled back. "One thirty-six, sir."

So, the selling had started exactly as ffitch had arrived, when we would be distracted. "Gareth."

"Yes, Sah!"

"Check him for a bug. Now!"

"Yes, Sah."

"Giles. Get ready to buy everything now. You too, Mathers."

They leaped to their feet and saluted.

"Yes, Sah!"

I smiled, sat back and waited. Spinetti and Palmer crossed the office to my desk. Palmer had a small device in his right hand. "It's a tracker, John."

"How sensitive?"

"Oh, if they're close, which we know they are, then to within twenty metres."

"So, they know it's in the building, but not which floor or office."

"Yep."

"Gareth, can you run, and I mean run, round to Bishopsgate Police Station now and stick this thing somewhere inside without anyone noticing?"

Spinetti grinned. "Nice idea, sir."

He ran. "Gareth!"

He stopped and looked back. "Phone me the second you've placed it."

I stood on my desk.

"No one buy anything. Sit on your hands."

They sat… and watched the screens. It was all red as Medina threw everything into his final burst of shorting. Six minutes later my phone rang. It was Spinetti. The bug was placed in the police station. I went to stand up again and saw The Boss come out of her office grinning. She held up two fingers at me, mouthed 'two billion' and then punched the air. I turned to the floor. All eyes were on me. I started to laugh, cupped my hands round my mouth and yelled. "Buy!"

After fifteen minutes my boys began to lose their nerve. They were glancing at me between trades. I yelled. "Don't look at me. Trade! Trade!"

They traded… Fast… So fast I could hardly register them. Robbi leant over me. "Down to below one billion."

I pulled her down and kissed her on the lips. She stared at me questioningly. "Shit or bust, Lady Hannay to be. Shit or bust. We're dead in the water. I only hope that Medina thinks his little ruse with ffitch failed and that ffitch is being questioned by the police and that BTD is awash with cash. It's just that you and I know that it's three thirty pm and we're right out of money."

She looked up towards the door. She was puzzled. "Ludo?"

I glanced up. Lord Clanroyden was standing in the doorway looking uncertain. Robbi straightened and waved at him. He smiled and walked towards us. In his right hand he held a piece of paper. My heart began to beat faster. I breathed deeply. This was not the time to collapse.

"Afternoon, Roberta, John. My, oh my. This is a scene from the First Circle."

I smiled up at him wondering if he would say 'oh my fur and whiskers'.

"Anyone here read Mandarin?"

"Call Anna. Quick, Robbi."

Robbi grabbed a phone.

* * *

15.36hrs

Twenty–four minutes of trading left.

"John."

It was Mathers. He was grinning delightedly and pointing at his screen. I rolled my chair across to his desk… and there it was – what I had given up believing would ever happen, in a press release from the Chinese representative at the G20. *'The People's Republic of China announces today that it has reached agreement with the British Government for…'*

It was a trade deal – a big trade deal. I skim read it. British economy growing faster than expected… investment in intellectual property, Huawei issues fully resolved and hi–tech applauded.

"Get The Boss. Tell her to call every financial news outlet in the world."

I stood again, but it took real effort to disguise how I really felt. The Floor looked at me. I looked back at the Floor then grinned. "We're winning. Buy everything you can get your greedy little hands on."

They bayed like hounds.

"John."

It was Mathers again.

"What?"

"The Bank of England's intervening."

I nodded at him, sat down slowly and looked at Robbi and Ludo. Robbi took the phone away from her ear and put the receiver down slowly.

"Well?"

"I scanned it and sent it to Anna. She can't tell if it's a fake, John, but it looks real. It's a birth certificate in the name of Mei Ch'en, naming Dominick Medina as her father."

I pushed my chair back, stretched my legs out and wished my brain wasn't so fuzzy. "We need to speak to young Ch'en. Trouble is last time I saw her she was attacking either Harry or me. I'm not sure which, but I don't think it was love at first sight. Give me five minutes; the trading's almost finished."

* * *

15:55hrs

The competition to buy Sterling was heating up. I looked for Don. He was hunched in front of his screen, a phone clamped to each ear. He put one phone down and then the other and looked round for me. I raised a querying hand. He nodded three times. He still looked dubious, but I knew he thought the tide was turning.

* * *

16:01hrs

Emma came on to the floor carrying bottles of champagne. Helen followed with a tray of glasses. The Boss tapped on a bottle with a pen until there was silence.

"Children, I think we're there. We won't be able to tell definitively until trading starts on Wall Street tomorrow, but right now, let us eat, drink and be merry for…"

I looked for Robbi, but she was on the phone at Jarrod's desk with sheaves of paper in front of her. I took a very deep breath and made it to my feet without collapsing. It cost me all I had to get to the men's toilet where I leaned against the wall and felt myself slowly sliding down it until I was slumped on my backside on the floor, my head hanging, my chin on my chest. I breathed deeply and felt my heart begin to slow. Just five minutes alone and no one would ever know.

The door swung open. Shit. I managed to lift my head and saw through the mist that it was young Mathers. He raced to my side.

"Christ, John, are you OK? I'll get a doctor."

I grabbed his arm and held it. "No. You will tell no one. Give me two minutes and get me a drink of water."

Mathers looked far from convinced. I tried a new tack. "I should have asked you for your Christian name."

"It's Rupert."

"OK, after what we've been through, it would be churlish not to know it. A good day wasn't it."

He grinned... easily distracted. My heart continued to slow. "In a couple of minutes I'll be all right again. I was er, pretty badly beaten up a few months ago, and the trading... it takes it out of me more than it should."

The sickness was beginning to pass. I held out a hand and he pulled me to my feet. I leaned over the washbasin while the rocking slowed and finally stopped.

"Who beat you up?"

"Well, tortured would be more accurate..."

"John, who?"

I straightened and felt life begin to come back.

"Medina, of course, who else?"

I left him staring after me in shock. I walked back on to the Floor with a smile on my face. It took an effort, but it was worth it if only to see Robbi's shoulders go down as she relaxed, but she didn't take her eyes off me until I sat down beside her.

"John! John! Get your ass in here."

Bugger, I would have to stand up again. I drained my glass of champagne, took a deep breath and was grabbed by young Rupert. He gripped my arm and lifted me while making it look as though he was trying to hold me down and ask a question. I nodded my thanks and made it into the Boss' office. Sebastian was sitting in the corner looking subdued, but I could see the bounce was coming back. Two back-office men were staring at the mass of trades and shaking their heads. I recognised one of them and nodded at him.

"Afternoon, Jonesy boy. How far ahead are we?"

"Hello Super Trader. Well, if and may I repeat again if, Sterling doesn't drop tomorrow when people wake up, about twelve billion."

I looked at Sebastian. I could see why the bounce was beginning to come back. He looked back at me.

"Well John, will Sterling stay up?"

I grinned manically. I could feel life pulsing through my veins again. "Oh, yes, Sebastian. It'll stay up. You can bet the shop on it."

"I just did, John. I just did."

I walked back on to the floor with the suspicion of a spring in my step. They looked at me questioningly. "Don't ask me. I'm not The Boss." I paused and then with a whoop shouted, "but you've got to love trading when it's like this."

How they cheered. The doctor was beckoning me into the side office. I followed him and slumped down, the energy draining out of my body. He looked at me. "Don't put on any more of those shows, John. It doesn't need a degree in medicine to see that you're far from well."

"Spare me Doc. I have only one more day to get through. Palmer, if you tell Robbi what he said I shall, well, I shall be very angry indeed."

He glanced at the doctor and nodded at me reluctantly. "You look like shit, John, and Robbi isn't blind or stupid."

"I know."

I looked at the doctor. "So, what are we going to do with our boy?"

He shrugged. "What state's he in?"

"Medicated but unconscious."

I thought for a moment and then smiled at Palmer. "We need to get him to call Medina, don't we?"

Palmer grinned back. "Maybe you're not quite as sick as you look. Go on."

"Well, if the doc here has a consulting room which could pass for a hospital ward, we could get him in there, maybe get Alan to go and sympathise and leave him near enough to a phone for him to call Medina... Just so long as my name isn't mentioned."

Alan walked in followed by Robbi. She glared at me. I held up a hand. "Alan, we have a plan... Of sorts."

Alan listened. "That's not a plan, it's a half-baked piece of idiocy. However, in the absence of anything else even quarter baked, let's get on with it."

The doctor shuffled. "You seem to be taking my acquiescence in this 'idiocy' for granted."

We all looked at him. "All right, all right."

Alan made phone calls. I leaned back in my seat and yawned. Robbi crouched in front of me. "How bad are you, John?"

"Good enough for the end game."

I tried to look convincing. She took my wrist, felt for my pulse and shook her head. "I wish there was a medical doctor here."

"Oh yes, so do I. I just can't think of anyone I'd rather see more right now."

"You're a fool, John."

I leaned forward and pushed her hair back off her forehead. "I know, Robbi. I know."

Her eyes softened.

"I could do with some kip right now, you know."

She hauled me to my feet and with her arm round me, led me out of the office to find a cab. I slumped on the seat, made it through the hotel reception to the lifts and collapsed on the bed. She woke me and lifted my head to force feed me an omelette then pushed my head back down.

By half past five I was asleep.

CHAPTER THIRTY-NINE

I drifted up from the depths to hear urgent whispering. Sleep had restored me, but I could sense how fragile the recovery was. I turned over. Robbi was still whispering into her phone. I found my watch. Nine–thirty – four hours sleep. "Robbi. I'm awake."

She sighed and walked across to the bed. "It was Alan. He phoned to say that your so–called plan worked. They left one of those old wheel–round–pay–phones in the corridor outside the room they've got ffitch in and staged a little emergency so that the nurse watching him had to rush out. Soon as she did, he sneaked out of the room and made a call."

"And we have the number?"

"Yes."

"It was Medina?"

"Yes."

"All he had time to say was that he was in hospital. They got the nurse back in time to stop anything more. They were going to pull the plug before your name got mentioned."

I got out of bed, shaved and showered and wondered if I was feeling well enough. Robbi shook her head and wagged a finger at me. "No, no, no, no! I'm saving myself for marriage."

I laughed. At ten Harry phoned. At one minute past ten I phoned Dave. At two minutes past ten I raised

Palmer in his bedroom. At three minutes past ten we were dressed. At five minutes past ten we were in a taxi heading into the City with me on the jump seat. Palmer muttered most of the way there. Harry was hunched in a doorway in Bevis Marks round the corner from Medina's office in St Mary Axe. Dave's van was parking beside him as we paid off the cab. Palmer strode across the road. "You OK, Harry?"

"Yes. No. I don't know. Look she'll be coming out of his office in about five minutes time."

"You sure?"

"I heard one of the bodyguards talking in reception."

"Anyone see you leave, Harry?"

"Yes, I told Medina that I was going to meet a French waitress. He laughed, which was the first time today, I can tell you. BTD is not his favourite brand name in case you're interested."

Dave reached into the back of the van and passed me a silenced Glock. Robbi took it straight out of my hands, checked the rounds, took off the safety and kept it. Dave looked at her. "What?" He kept looking at her.

"He couldn't hit a barn door from two feet for God's sake."

Dave gave one of his half smiles and pulled out a sawn–off shotgun. "It would have to be a very small barn door to miss with this."

I took it reluctantly. Dave took control and walked us down the road rapping out instructions.

"Robbi – in that doorway. If she comes towards you, step out in front of her with the Glock held up so she can see it. Harry, you will be walking back up the street from here. Call out to her and say something about getting back in as you've left your wallet behind. John boy, you and me are in the doorway right by the entrance. I'll take out the bodyguards and you take the girl – but only – with the state you're in, only if all else fails. Palmer, back over here – come across the road and speak to her as soon as you can. It'll confuse her. Johnson and Spinetti might get here in time to help out, but we can't rely on it and I don't know which direction they'll be coming from. Any questions? No? Right, repeat your orders. John, again – you only use the sawn–off as a weapon of last resort. All the other guns have suppressors and frangible bullets."

We parroted our orders like good school children and went to our positions. For the record, I had absolutely no intention of using the shotgun. Dave peered cautiously up at the streetlights. He raised his pistol, rested it on the back of his left wrist and shot out the CCTV cameras opposite the Gherkin building. I'd come to hate the quiet crack of a silenced Glock. He slotted a full clip into the gun and we waited. Thirty seconds later the swing door swung and a bodyguard stepped out looking right and left.

"Amateur," whispered Dave.

And the world slowed down, the next two minutes splintering into meaningless moments of jagged, fractured, flickering snap shots. A black Mercedes limo cruised round the corner. Mei's first bodyguard stepped forward from the office building into the road to open the rear door.

Dave fired twice, once at his legs and once at his

shoulder. The bodyguard staggered, tripped on the kerb and collapsed over the bonnet of the moving car. The second bodyguard was facing in towards Mei, back to the road. Palmer ran forward. "Mei Ch'en?

The girl turned towards him, puzzled. Harry started his run from down the street. "Hi, Mei Ch'en, can you leave the door open? I've left my wallet behind."

She spun back to look at him.

The second bodyguard was turning towards Harry's potential threat, not realising that his partner was down, his gun half out of its holster. Dave fired once more. The second bodyguard jerked back against the glass door, crumpled and slithered to the pavement. The Mercedes had stopped. The front passenger door was opening. I stepped forward. I heard Palmer call out something else. Mei Ch'en stopped dead and turned to stare at him in amazement. Then she caught sight of my face in the streetlight and I saw the shock in her eyes. She ran. Robbi sprinted, grabbed her, wrenched her back.

The front door of the Mercedes was fully open now – a gun emerging, followed by a man. I took one more pace, raised the shotgun and rammed both barrels into his mouth. He froze and dropped the pistol, blood dripping from shattered teeth. I glanced round.

Dave had reached Robbi and Mei Ch'en in two quick steps. He hit Mei Ch'en on the jaw open handed with the heel of his palm. Her legs buckled and he threw her over his shoulder. Spinetti and Johnson appeared together – finally – running from the far end of the street, guns in hands. Spinetti took my place. Johnson hauled bodies. I stepped back, standing in front of the car with my shotgun pointing at the driver, unsure of my next move. I could confess now that I had been fully prepared for failure and as the adrenalin reaction wore off, I looked round feeling entirely surplus to requirements. Then Robbi was back and at my side. She grabbed my hand and dragged me to the van – Harry and Palmer ahead of us by five metres. There was an ecstasy of fumbling and we were away, rocking sideways in the back.

"Where to?" yelled Dave.

Robbi looked at me. "Ludo?"

I looked at her and sighed. She was right, of course, but I dialled his number reluctantly. I had brought trouble to enough friends without including the Clanroydens. It was answered after two rings. "This has to be John Hannay. Of all my acquaintances and friends, there is only one who would be calling at ten thirty at night. What's the problem, John?"

I told him.

"Well hurry up and get round here, my boy. There's some kind of thrash going on at one of those ghastly far right Think Tanks just down the way so I doubt you'll be noticed."

Dave was on the phone instructing Spinetti to lose the Mercedes and keep the bodyguards under wraps. Traffic was light, even on the Embankment, and we were in Lord North Street in ten minutes. I directed Dave into it from Smith Square and, parked on the pavement with the sliding side door open, we slipped into Ludo's front door without a single celebrating far–right–Think–Tanker noting our arrival. Dave parked the van in Smith

Square as we carried Mei Ch'en past the imperturbable Lockhart and into the drawing room. I introduced Harry and Palmer. Clanroyden was in bubbling high spirits. "Ah, Harry Livesey, the scoundrel of the group no doubt. I knew your uncle George and he was certainly a scoundrel so I hope you are doing your best to maintain the family tradition. Your name is Palmer? Excellent, excellent. You must be in need of refreshment. Lockhart? Lockhart? Where is the man? Good Lord and who are you, if I dare ask?"

Lockhart had entered bearing a tray with a decanter and seven glasses followed by Dave who came to attention.

"No don't tell me. I know who you are. Grab a glass and follow me."

Dave was led away to inspect regimental photos. Robbi pushed me into a chair and Lockhart held out a glass of single malt. Mei Ch'en stirred. I went to stand up and was pushed down again. "Better tape her, Harry." She threw him a roll of gaffer tape. Harry taped quickly. Clanroyden came back in followed by an amused Dave. He walked across to where Harry was finishing off and took over, frisking her for bugs. Nothing. He checked her fur coat and held up a small homing device hidden in the lining. Ludo watched.

"Mr Lord, I am reliably informed that Mr Medina keeps a suite at Claridges? I would suggest that rather nice fur coat is left there for safety."

Dave nodded approval, glanced at me and left. I thought for a moment, found my phone and dialled the army psychiatrist.

"I thought I told you to get some sleep."

"I did. I'm awake now though and I want to play."

He sighed. "I should never have allowed bloody Livesey to talk me into this. What's the problem now?"

"We have Medina's daughter."

"Where? Unwilling or willing?"

"Five minutes' walk from your office. Unwilling and sedated."

"How did you know I'd be here?"

"You think I don't recognise a kindred spirit?"

He snorted and I gave him the address. He thought it would take him ten minutes to arrange an army ambulance. Ludo took over whisky pouring duties from Lockhart. By twenty past eleven the army ambulance was departing as Angela returned from a night at the ballet and sailed into the drawing room. I started to stand up only to be pushed back down hard. She looked at me for a long time.

"Ludo, darling, I have no idea what you will say to the neighbours about this little escapade. Roberta, dear, lovely to see you and all of you too... John, you look dreadful. Has he been misbehaving, Roberta?" She turned to Palmer and laid her hand on his arm. "Hannays have no idea when to stop, you know. His grandfather had more bullet holes in him than a pin cushion by the time he was in his fifties."

Palmer's class hackles began to go down.

CHAPTER FORTY

I woke to the sound of Robbi singing. I felt bad enough already – heavy witted, furry tongued. I shouldn't have had the third whisky. I showered, shaved, dressed slowly and sat on the bed waiting for the dressing to finish. "Robbi. Six fifteen."

By 06:45hrs we were sitting at the oh–so–familiar desks watching the screens to see what had happened overnight. Sterling had risen another twenty points, but it was fragile. I walked across to talk to Don Bartrum, but in reality, today was simple. We start with a bang, buy the shit out of anything and then spring the trap.

The Boss came onto the Floor just before eight, sprinkling yet more fairy dust. I raised a hand to her. "Don't forget to make the two journalists sign an NDA."

"I'll try, but you know journos."

"They'll do it for you, Em."

She smiled slightly and gripped Robbi's shoulder. "Take care of him, Miss Beautiful. He still looks like shit."

I still felt like shit. Robbi pulled her chair alongside mine and took my pulse. I tried to shake her off. "John, they all know you're ill."

"Not now."

The bell rang. It was eight o'clock. I started to concentrate. For half an hour it went our way, but half an hour is only one sixteenth of the trading day and we were the ones who weren't clinically insane. I watched the monitor of Medina's trading floor in Palmer's office. It wasn't natural. He was down $20 billion and it was as if they were writing a shopping list.

The Boss was behind me. "James from the Financial Times and Rebecca from the Economist are here."

I nodded slowly without turning my head. Yet again I had managed to manoeuvre myself into a place where all my possible futures had dropped away leaving me with just the one. I sat for a second, feeling the ghosts of my family crowding round me. How many threads had I dropped? How many of the ungodly had I missed? How many would survive this coup to strike again? How many would seek revenge? I thought again of the promise of my grandfather's friends and whether James Artinswell had been wanting to help or to hurt all those months ago – too late to find out now, far too late – all my mistakes were now so very obvious. The Boss spoke softly. Her voice echoed in my head, half heard, lost as I was in my vision.

"John? Robbi, talk to him."

Now I could see my father clearly and my grandfather, arm round his shoulders, both faces watching me, full of pride. Not that I deserved their admiration now any more than when I had failed them as an eight-year-old boy. I shook my head to clear it and leave my haunted past behind. I took the breath and then the next one. I listened to my racing heart. It skipped a beat, stopped and started again. My vision faded. I picked up my phone, dialled, and spoke. "Dave, do it."

It took exponentially more effort than the last time, but I managed to stand up. I waved Robbi away. Self–obsessed bastard that I am I had made the decision that I was doing this on my own even if it was the very last thing I ever did. I beckoned the two journalists over to my desk and pointed at the screens on the wall above me. Palmer flicked a switch on his small mixing desk and the Bloomberg screen flickered, pixelated and was replaced on all the floor's screens by a high wide–angle shot. I pointed to it. "That's Medina Trading's Floor."

As we watched, a courier walked into reception and produced twenty identical packages from out of his bag. Robbi passed two of the same packages to James and Rebecca. On the monitor I could see the flustered receptionist sign for the packages. The courier left. A second one entered a moment later, very tall and very broad shouldered. He held one small package. This time the receptionist simply pointed at Medina's office. The courier knocked, placed the package on Medina's desk and left. God, was my heart going to give out now? I breathed. Palmer placed the special mobile on my desk. I picked it up and nodded at him. I heard it ring in my ear and we watched as Medina glanced at a mobile on his desk, picked it up and answered.

"Where are you?"

I took one last breath. "Hello, Dominick."

"ffitch?"

"No, Dominick, this isn't Julian ffitch although we were at school together."

"Who the hell…?"

"You know who this is, Dominick. I am the man whose grandfather your grandfather tried and failed to kill. I am the man whose father and mother your father killed. I am the man your father raped and you tortured and thought you had killed."

We watched. I waited. I counted five. "Dominick... acushla."

On the monitor we saw him jerk as I spoke those last words. He whispered. "Hannay."

I looked at Alan standing to one side and raised my eyebrows. He nodded. That was probably as near to a confession as we would ever get.

"You haven't opened your parcel, Dominick. Open it now."

He stared at the desk and then at the package and dazedly tore off the paper. Inside was a small video camera.

"Press play."

He glared at the mobile phone, turned it off and hurled it across his office. Palmer placed another phone into my hand. He had already dialled the number. We watched the monitor. The only sound behind me was the rustling of the paper as the two journalists turned over the papers in their hands. We saw Medina reach for his private phone still fiddling with the camera. He pressed the hands–free button on his desk phone.

"You just press the little button marked 'play'."

He shied like a half–broken pony and then the video started. Spinetti switched some of the monitors to show the same shots the camera was playing. Two bodies lay in hospital beds, side by side. A nurse checked the drips and took the pulse of the body on the right of screen. The camera shook and wobbled as the operator moved in for a hand–held close up of the face. It was ffitch. The camera pulled back and panned left to reveal the face of the body in the next bed, sleeping peacefully under sedation. It was Mei Ch'en. Medina was crouched over his desk. He licked his lips. "What do you want?"

"What do *I* want? I want old fashioned, eye–for–an–eye, tooth–for–a–tooth vengeance on you for all you have done to my family and to me. That's what I want… but that isn't what's going to happen." I nodded at Palmer again and he pressed the send button on the fax machine on the desk beside him. "One doesn't often get faxes these days, does one Dominick, but look, here's one arriving. The same document has been delivered to every person on your trading floor this morning. The fax is a copy and a translation of the birth certificate of Mei Ch'en… naming you as her father." I turned to the Army doctor behind me and raised my eyebrows. He studied the image of Medina on the screen and nodded. So now I bluffed. "Unfortunately – for you, you understand, not for me – we were able to persuade your erstwhile colleagues at the Chinese embassy to confirm that you knew she was your daughter. They did this in exchange for the location of Marius Haraldsen's horde of gold in southern China, which is why you haven't had the help you were expecting from Beijing during your failed attempt to destroy Sterling during the G20 meeting this week."

"I don't know what you're talking about. You're mad."

"It's a little too late to try that tack, Dominick, especially as ffitch has been singing his little heart out."

He laughed at that. He was regaining confidence. He needed a kick.

"He isn't the only one of your victims who is singing. Harry Livesey is sitting beside me. Say hello, Harry."

Harry leaned forward and cleared his throat nervously. "Er, hello, Harry."

"Harry witnessed many, let us call them intimacies, between your daughter and yourself, Dominick. You know I'm not quite sure you realise just how seriously people take this kind of thing. Doesn't look so good does it, Dominick?"

He flinched.

"Now I'm going to tell you what is going to happen. Two of my colleagues have been at your office for half an hour this morning, so I'm afraid you won't be receiving any help from your hired thugs. And, Dominick, two journalists from highly respected national papers have been witnesses to this entire exchange. Oh, again, last time, Dominick. Had you realised that we are watching you? You are looking round now for a camera. You are poised to run. Don't run, Dominick, there is much my colleagues need to learn from you. It isn't every day that they get to examine such an extreme case of Narcissistic Personality Disorder."

He ran.

"Paul!"

Paul's shot took Medina in the lower back and he cartwheeled across his office landing upside down against the glass wall, his legs sprawled above him. Dave, no longer in courier disguise, was by his side in seconds. I heard Paul's calm voice on my earpiece.

"I didn't hit anything vital, but he'll lose a lot of blood. Not a bad shot. Over five hundred yards with a downward angle of thirty–eight degrees. Twenty–eight kph cross wind too."

My heart was not good. Even I would admit this. It was pounding and missing like an over rich mixture in a carburettor. I turned to talk to the journalists as Mathers spoke.

"John?"

I looked at him. He was trying hard to look as unemotional as me. "What, Rupert?"

"Sterling's up four hundred points. Everyone's buying. We've won."

The Floor went silent in anticipation, but I wasn't savouring the moment. I was too ill to care. There were, however, appearances still to be maintained. I looked round at all their expectant faces. It had better be a good one.

"Not too bad then. But it got a bit sloppy this morning. I noticed a couple of trades you missed Jocasta… and Maxie, you call that leveraging?"

Balls of paper began to shower down on me thrown from all sides. I raised my arms, hands palm upwards.

"What? What?"

And then they were cheering and cheering and Sebastian came in with the whole of the top floor and he had actual tears in his eyes. The Boss was hugging Robbi who was looking at me over her shoulder and sobbing.

"Rupert, Giles, give me a hand."

They pulled me to my feet. I looked straight at the journalists. "What happened here was nothing to do with me. This is Emma Fitzgerald's Floor and Emma Fitzgerald's victory. My name will never be mentioned

348

and there are two gentlemen standing very close to you who will take great pleasure in slapping a DA–Notice on anything you try and print to which they take exception." I looked round the Floor again. They seemed to be expecting more. "Th–th–th–that's all folks."

The buzzing in my ears became a howl. The howl became a scream. Beneath my screaming head my heart was bursting. I turned towards her. But even as I turned, the world rocked, dimmed, faded and the earth was without form and void; and darkness was upon the face of the deep.

I had a dream, which was not all a dream…
The world was void,
The populous and the powerful – was a lump,
Seasonless, herbless, treeless, manless, lifeless –
A lump of death – a chaos of hard clay.
The rivers, lakes, and ocean all stood still,
And nothing stirred within their silent depths;
(From Darkness by Lord Byron)

THE END

Printed in Great Britain
by Amazon

74421728R00213